DODGEBOMB

Outside the Wire in the Second Iraq War

Darin Pepple

To Bushmaster Troop

ACKNOWLEDGEMENTS

My heartfelt thanks to Michelle Moriarty for her love, encouragement, and unconditional support as I completed this book. With her on my side, I can conquer the world.

Tremendous gratitude to my friend, teammate, and classmate, Renée Farrar for being my editor and publishing consultant. She is firsthand proof of what a brilliant editor can do to convert an amateurish book into a readable, compelling story. Next, I'd like to thank one of my oldest friends, Jeremy Klinger, for taking the original lackluster book cover and turning it into something first-rate. My thanks to Jake Hilton, an unknown marketing genius, who created the website and advertising campaign to get the word out. And lastly, special thanks to so many Army friends: Larry Baca, Steve Kim, Mel Levey, Bryan Dipalermo, and Blaine Decker for their insights, critiques, and corrections along the way.

Center stage in these accolades has to be the men of Bushmaster Troop. I owe a debt of gratitude to every last one of them. It was an honor to serve alongside them. I'm grateful for our Iraq tour together, which was a defining moment in my life. Additional thanks to all the other scouts, FISTers, mortars, Mustangs, Dog-Faced Soldiers, Redlegs, loggies, Black Knights, and other Army comrades that are too numerous to name. Lastly, a shout out to my West Point classmates, the Class of 2007, brothers and sisters and great Americans all that helped shape me and continue to keep America safe. Go Ducks! Go Army Fencing! Beat Navy!

A SILVER TOYOTA PICKUP TRUCK pulled up on a hill overlooking the American Forward Operating Base and three Arabs in traditional, white, man-dresses got out. They hastily assembled a rocket launcher, nothing more than four rickety, hollowed-out cylinders, each loaded with a 100-pound firecracker, and lit the fuse. They leapt back into the truck, racing away as the boosters ignited and careened their fiery warheads at the base. The rockets, glimmering like shooting stars, arced up jaggedly across the sky. Three overshot their target but one flew on, straight and true. It angled low above the FOB, floated, and then nosedived straight down onto a porta-shitter, exploding plastic, feces, and a man everywhere.

ACT I

CHAPTER ONE

(FOB Talon, Iraq)

IT WAS THE HEAT and the smell. They were inescapable. People would look at pictures of this backward, foreign land and go, "That's not so bad," as if it were a vacation getaway, an exotic dry wine country. But it was bad. This place was the reeking armpit of the world. Here, the environment dripped with hostility. The leeching temperatures and dirty atmosphere saturated a person and clung to his very being. Was that smoke or diesel fumes in the air? Burning garbage or choking dust? To a new arrival this foul place flashed foreboding, like reliving a bad dream, and it made him question why he'd volunteered to come here in the first place.

That was Iraq in 2008. Somewhere close to Baghdad during The Surge in the war. Here he was. Forward Operating Base Talon. 2nd Lieutenant Eddie Fitzgerald, U.S. Cavalry, U.S. Army, had been dropped here last night by a Chinook helicopter after flying across the world in a Boeing 747; Georgia, Germany, Kuwait, and now here. And he still wasn't there yet.

All he knew of the FOB and this country so far consisted of a blacked out two-story brick barracks with sandbags over the windows. He remembered being herded in the pitch-dark across a field of crunching gravel to his room, pulling out his sleeping bag on a metal bunk bed and soiled mattress, and trying to crash for a few hours. Oddly enough, the single noteworthy thing in his room was an old, Soviet vehicle part discarded in the corner. He deliberately remembered turning off the lights and crawling into his bag, but that serene, restful moment ended as soon as it began.

Fitz was roused from his dark unconscious by a shrill electronic voice bleating, "INCOMING! INCOMING! INCOMING! — GET TO YOUR SHELTER!" Its cry seemed to emanate from the hallways and penetrate his skull. He spilled out of his bed and threw on his boots, no time to tie them properly. He grabbed his uniform shirt top and helmet and fell into the hall.

The pain-in-the-ass robotic voice insisted, "INCOMING! INCOMING! — Get to YOUR shelter!" He ran down the hall to the only room open and alight and stood in the entryway. Inside was a desk, radios, and three soldiers sitting on a couch, playing XBOX on a flat screen TV, their backs to him.

"What the hell are you doing, guys!?" He twitchingly squeaked, "We've got to get to the bunker!"

A protracted, awkward pause occurred as the three men turned around to gawk at the interruption. They were two specialists and one staff sergeant and in that agonizing moment he could see their faces comprehend who he was and what he was saying. Another millisecond went by and their faces twisted into side-splitting laughter.

"Get to the bunker!" they mimicked in a squeaky voice similar to his own. They'd all now forgotten the game and were rolling over themselves giggling.

A child's hatred of being ignored and belittled welled up in him, and Fitz stood up straight, addressing the SSG in a more commanding voice: "Sergeant — you guys do as I say, grab your gear, and take me out to the nearest indirect bunker."

The sergeant remained unfazed but had an older man's gleam in his eyes of playing by the proper rules. He stood up from the couch and walked smoothly over to the lieutenant. He reassuringly touched him on the arm and guided him back down the hall to Fitz's room. "Sir," he spoke softly, deferentially now, "We get rocketed all the time. The worst thing you can do when you get indirect is to run all over the place trying to find 'proper' shelter. You hunker down where you're at and if your number's up then it's up. And besides, you're in a brick barracks right now."

The logic of that and the sergeant's calming demeanor sapped Fitz's panic level. The SSG guided him back to his room as if he were a child raving of monsters under his bed. "Get some sleep, sir," he reassuringly cooed and Fitz closed his door and sat down on his bunk. The adrenaline still throbbed in his veins, but he was flushed red from his ridiculous antic. It hurt that they hadn't taken him more seriously. He was a lieutenant, dammit! He sat there for the longest time feeling helpless, angry, scared, but mostly stupid. The "incoming" klaxon had ceased and he strained his ears to hear anything outside the barracks. Any whistles and detonations. Any monsters. He finally took his boots off and turned out the lights.

He awoke at 0600, hearing someone else's alarm clock echoing from the hall. Fitzgerald repacked his bags, shaved, and wandered upstairs to get some instructions. The Headquarters and Headquarters Troop Commander, a distracted looking captain, told him he'd be convoyed out immediately to a COP or patrol base. Those were the Army terms for temporary fortified outpost. It sounded like a stockade surrounded by Indians.

Fitzgerald somehow consolidated his duffel, rucksack, assault pack, body armor, and helmet together and heaved them all outside the front door of the barracks. He squinted and looked around in the daylight for the first time. The sun was a blinding, omnipresent amber blaze. He donned his issued ballistic eye protection, otherwise known as military sunglasses, and peered around. All he could see were more clay brick barracks, numerous tall wheeled vehicles, squat fat water towers, and copper antennae everywhere. Everything appeared a drab, monochromatic tan, as if the heat had cooked off the other colors. Either the fierce sun or the dust limited his visibility, but he couldn't tell which. He had to crane his neck up to see a pale blue sky above the bronzed landscape. Crisscrossing away from the barracks were numerous roads with fire engine red stop signs marking their intersections. The signs were lettered with the comforting English STOP alongside an Arabic squiggle that curiously looked like three men rowing a boat.

The first drops of sweat formed on his forehead as he half carried half dragged his bags to the vehicles parked by the barracks. He noticed several soldiers readying the vehicles, every one with a Third Infantry Division patch velcroed on each sleeve. The square patch's diagonal black and gray rows resembled a scrambled television screen. Fitz looked at his empty right sleeve and frowned.

"C'mere, slick sleeve!"

Fitz turned to see a neatly kitted out staff sergeant, scowling at him behind dark eyepro.

"What'd you say, sergeant?" he shot back.

"I said, LT, come with me."

The surly sergeant ushered him to the back of one of the five MRAP (Mine Resistant Ambush Protected) vehicles in the patrol, and he threw his bags in and sat down inside. This was Fitz's first time in one of these new bombproof vehicles. They were the stubborn solution to increasingly high casualties in Humvees from roadside bomb blasts. However, their "increased survivability" meant soldiers might only be terribly wounded instead of dying, which to Army standards was significant progress.

He peered out at the soldiers from the back of the truck. They were crowded around their patrol leader as he gave his mission brief. The men's ash-gray, pixelated uniforms clashed against their rust hued surroundings. Peering closer, Fitz could see that their clothes were slightly stained. It was apparent that the more the soldiers deliberately washed their uniforms in the muddy water the earthier they looked. Despite this adaptation, Fitz still couldn't fathom why they'd been given gray uniforms in the first place.

As he quietly observed the men, Fitz pondered why he'd been told that truck drivers and transporters were the bottom rung of the Army.

Despite the boasting of the Rangers or whoever, he could tell that these dusty, tired men with sad, solemn faces had been hit a few times before.

2nd Lieutenant Fitzgerald should have been included in the patrol brief, but no one cared enough to grab him. He was baggage. The patrol leader, a 1st lieutenant with dirty glasses, briefed the men on the route and actions on different forms of enemy contact. Then, as an act of consecration, the men all huddled together and said a prayer.

And with that, the men all scrambled to their vehicles and closed their hatches and doors. Fitz was seated in one of the four inward facing seats in the back for passengers and the driver and TC jumped in up front in the cab. The gunner came up the ramp and hooked himself into his harness, his turret open to the sky. His legs dangled just in front of Fitz and he watched him fidget with his M240 machine gun. He scanned the inside of the MRAP, noting the radios and the back of the driver and vehicle commander's heads. With an electric whine, the rear ramp lifted and locked into position while Fitz buckled himself in. He heard the crews' muffled chatter and looked for a headset. He put one on and played with the knobs until he could hear the intercom.

"Sergeant Stannifer — are we taking Chicken Run out to Dolby?"

"Yep."

"Why are we taking that route? Didn't Angry Troop get hit there the other day?"

"Because it's the only cleared route to Dolby, the rest are black right now."

"Fuck me."

Fitz bubbled with anticipation and he savored it. His mind wrote off last night's indiscretion. He was finally here after West Point, Armor Officer Basic Course, and the obligatory "Don't Die Within 24 Hours of Getting to Iraq" one week course that Fort Stewart had required. All he knew was that he had orders to join 8th Squadron 6th Cavalry, 4th Brigade, 3rd Infantry Division, a cavalry squadron that had already been downrange for months, taking the fight to the jihadists. He felt so excited to be part of the avenging American wave of bombs, tanks, and men that would crush these thugs. Finally, something that mattered. Something worth dying for.

An ignorant anger welled within him and he embraced it. He'd often seen bigotry in others, but he'd been raised by parents who didn't believe they'd been persecuted by any race or creed. A decade ago he'd been indifferent to Arabs. Yet now, after the Towers fell and Americans had been killed, he wanted to hate them all.

The swaying vehicle jostled him back to reality. It reminded him of being tossed about in a small boat out at sea. The sun, streaming in through the window slits, shifted from one side of the compartment to another as the MRAP maneuvered. The driver generously braked and accelerated at each intersection, forcing Fitz to cling to his seatbelt. He hoped it wouldn't be like this the whole trip. Finally, after a few more rough stop-and-go's, the patrol halted at the main gate for a last check. The gunner charged his machine gun and Fitz fumbled to do the same with his M4. He was going outside the wire!

The MRAP lurched forward and Fitz re-checked his gear. He was ready for anything and he craned his neck to look out his porthole at this alien Arab world. It looked like unimpressive brown earth with garbage strewn about.

It didn't matter, Fitz knew at some point in the patrol they'd get hit. Maybe the vehicle ahead would get blown off the road or an ambush of small arms fire would start pinging off their vehicle's armor. He imagined himself sliding out of a stricken vehicle and popping off shots into a swirling dervish of hooded Al Qaeda's. How many medals would that be worth?

He lived out these fantasies to many glorious conclusions and sat in his seat, like a toddler strapped in for safety. The gunner's legs still dangled a foot away from his face. The radio occasionally squawked some landmark or route ahead. He looked forward and saw the helmeted backs of the driver and TC's head. Earphones on, intent on the road ahead. His mind drifted, and he started to feel the heat again. No one noticed when he fell asleep.

CHAPTER TWO

WITH SOME MORE ABRUPT JERKS the MRAP woke him up. "Contact?" he thought, as he shook off sleep. The crew was still there, no immediate cause for alarm. He twisted to see out the slit window and realized they were approaching a coffee brown fortress, with dirt-filled walls and razor wire strewn along the tops. From his restricted vantage, he could only see a 20-foot section of barricades, and he yearned to be able to see the whole picture. He slunk back in his seat.

The MRAP made a few more twists and then stopped. With an electronic whine the rear ramp lowered and the streaming sun pierced the vehicle inside.

"Get out and clear your weapon," the TC grumbled over the intercom and Fitz fumbled with his straps. He groggily descended the ramp steps and then huddled around an empty oil drum with three other soldiers. He watched the first one remove his ammunition magazine from his rifle, pocket it, then pull back the charging handle which ejected a round from the chamber onto the ground. The soldier picked up the round then put his carbine barrel into the metal barrel and pulled the trigger. A metal click indicated he'd done it right and he filed back to his vehicle. Fitz aped his actions completely and walked back to the truck.

Meeting him at the back of the MRAP was his TC, SSG Stannifer.

"Sir, come with me. I'll show you where you go."

Fitz looked around the inside of this desert fort for the first time and was unimpressed. The mocha-colored HESCO ramparts looked exactly as they had from the outside, stacked giant grocery bags of dirt. Pre-packaged concrete towers stood at every corner, a camo net draped over their gun ports to hide the silhouettes of the soldiers in them. Machine gun barrels stuck slyly out at menacing angles. Well inside the perimeter, three or four converted Iraqi farmhouses were ringed with secondary earthen and concrete walls, interior lines of defense. Each structure bristled with antennae and satellite dishes. And the rest of the open ground was littered with shipping containers and neat rows of Army vehicles. Shoddy wood additions and doors could be made out on the containers and stacked everywhere were pallets of plastic water bottles. Except for the farmhouses, the rest of the camp appeared to have been line-hauled in on trucks. Albeit, it must have taken several convoys of tractor trailers to get this amount of material here. It all looked like it could be torn down and hauled away if enough trucks and cranes were dedicated to the project.

SSG Stannifer led Lieutenant Fitzgerald to a building ensconced within a half-moon of drab gray T-Walls in the center of the COP. T-Walls were slabs of concrete four feet across and twelve feet tall. If looked at from the side, a T-Wall bulged at the bottom and formed an inverted T. If observed head on, they simply looked like a tall rectangle of concrete. These portable Stonehenge pillars were an engineer's cookie cutter way of making bullet and mortar proof fortifications quickly. They were in short supply so Fitz knew he was headed to somebody's headquarters.

Fitz walked past the last T-Wall in the perimeter and 8-6 CAV Squadron Headquarters popped into his view. It was a large tan farmhouse in the center of the COP, about the size of a well-to-do American suburban home. This must have been a wealthier man's house as it had two stories, multiple doors, and a drained pool with Turkish tile. Fitz wasn't an architect but it had a mix of Persian and Mediterranean influences that suited Iraq. Camo green and khaki sun screens and nets covered the wings haphazardly, their support poles jutting into the ground at angles not to regulation. Bolted on, green stringy, daddy long legs and stubby rod antennae jutted off the roof and windows. To complete the picture, spilling out from underneath the house emanated angry rap music and the clanging of barbells and weights. Good to see that some Army restructuring had turned this rich man's basement into a soldier's workout gym.

SSG Stannifer and Fitz moved up the front stairs, and a youthful-looking, Hispanic Lieutenant Colonel accompanied by NCOs in gear strolled out the door.

"Sir!?" Fitz said.

"Ah good, you're finally here lieutenant!" said the LTC.

LTC Oskar Manuel Gutierrez looked too clean in his uniform compared with the accompanying sergeants. He radiated confidence and bravado, while everyone else around him looked worn out. It oddly seemed as if he were draining these men by sheer proximity.

"Sergeant, take a look at his gear and tell me if he's good to join me on this patrol."

A heavy-set sergeant first class without a hat walked over and started groping Fitz's pouches on his body armor. He had a big, bald, sweaty, shaved head. Fitz was taken aback a little at his roughness, but obediently stood still as the SFC inspected him.

"Yes sir, he's got his med-pack right here, clearly marked. If he gets hit he can reach his tourniquet before he bleeds out."

"Giddy up then lieutenant. Let's go."

Wasting no time, the LTC put on a pair of thin green riding gloves and resumed his procession. Fitz followed. He remembered to walk to the left of an officer that was senior, and obediently kept pace. He wondered how brand new he must look.

"2nd Lieutenant Fitzgerald," the LTC turned to him as they walked, "I like to take all my new lieutenants on a patrol with me as soon as they get into country, show them what I see as a squadron commander, and the decisions I make that affect this whole AO. It'll help you when you're leading your platoon to operate under my guidance and understand our crusading efforts here."

"Yes sir!" He wasn't sure if that required a response or not. He looked into LTC Gutierrez's eyes to gauge if this could be a discussion and understood that it wasn't. They kept walking from the Squadron TOC towards a new cluster of four MRAPs and men.

The vehicles were smartly parked in two columns, two in front and two in back. Their ramps lay open, hanging down to the ground, while their unattended radios beeped from the dark compartments inside. All the crewmembers, a band of staff sergeants, specialists, and one buck sergeant, were assembled by the first vehicle. Kevlar helmets were off and they were smoking cigarettes casually. These men had long black sweat stains on the collars and edges of their armor. Their uniforms were faded and almost to a man each one's infrared black American flag on his shoulder was ripped from constantly putting their armor on and off.

"All right, Patrol Brief — listen up!" It was a different SSG. His nametape said Sajer.

"This afternoon's mission is to take the colonel to Sheik Assad's house to conduct a Key Leader Engagement. We'll proceed out the gate along Route Rupp to Route Flyers and then to Route Jackson all the way into Busayefi. I'm in truck one, Rivera is truck two, Downtree is three, and Byers is four. Medics in truck four and the colonel's in truck two. We'll pull into Sheik Assad's house like we did last week, first two trucks inside the gate and the other two outside pulling security. Remember your 5 and 25's when you get out and everyone needs to drink at least one bottle of water while we're on the mission. Not a RIP-IT, not a MOUNTAIN-DEW, ...A WATER."

He paused for a second and then looked into the crowd for the soldier paying the least attention.

"BECKER! Give me actions on contact if we hit an IED!"

A dirty specialist with a dumb look on his face stammered for a moment and then regurgitated an answer.

"If we get hit, we'll return fire only if we get PID, push through, and charlie mike it to the sheik's house. Oh and call up to higher and give a SITREP."

"And what if one of the trucks gets disabled?" Sajer said.

This contingency caused Becker to have more trouble. After a slight pause he said, "Well, I guess we'll return fire, try to self-recover, and if not call back to Mustang X-Ray for EOD and QRF."

Becker's answer seemed to satiate SSG Sajer, who clearly felt the colonel's eyes on them. Sajer looked over at LTC Gutierrez and said "Sir — you got anything else?"

LTC Gutierrez shook his head and waved his gloved hand like a queen dismissing her subjects.

"Okay — let's mount up!" And with no more fanfare, they shuffled to their trucks.

Fitz stood there dumb for a second until a different staff sergeant guided him to truck three and showed him exactly where to sit. He felt like a toddler in the back of Mom's minivan. He would have buckled him in too if Fitz hadn't done it himself. He had the same VIP view of a slit window and unaccompanied access to a new gunner's dangling legs. The lone difference in this MRAP was a white oblong cooler that the gunner used as a footrest. With a whine the ramp raised and he saw the SSG settle in up front in the TC seat. He put on his headset but this time it was broken. At least it blocked out the noise of the engine's drone.

The vehicle lurched and they were off again. Fitz was a pro now, already on his second patrol.

It took about ten minutes for the patrol to finally weave out of the HESCO walls of PB Dolby and onto the canal roads. The farming canals lined every road outside the patrol base and were overgrown with tall, biblical reeds. The reeds' spindly green stalks and long leaf blades masked the water from his view. The heat crept in on him again, and Fitz felt weak. AC blowing out a nearby vent cooled his face but not much else. The sweat beaded on his forearms and his armpits began to drip. The cool air, combined with sitting in a shady vehicle, started to make his eyelids droop again.

"Sir — do you want a RIP-IT or a water?" shouted the gunner at Fitz.

The soldier's loud voice jolted him awake. Fitzgerald felt like he'd only drifted off for ten seconds, but he felt refreshed. He must have slept for the rest of the drive. The specialist was out of his harness and sitting on the raised floor in the center of the back, gloves off, fishing through the open white cooler. More water than ice sloshed around as he grabbed a plastic water bottle out. The truck had stopped and, as if on cue, the ramp started to lower with its now familiar electric whine.

"Gimme a water," Fitz croaked as he regained his senses. Bright yellow light joined him in the compartment as the ramp finished its descent; it crumped when it hit the ground. He gratefully grabbed the wet water bottle and swigged some down. Out the back, a courtyard with white-washed, concrete block walls and a sickly lawn came into view. His truck's TC, SSG Downtree, had already dismounted and come towards the back. His expression said, "Move your ass," but he didn't say a word as Fitz exited the truck.

They saw the colonel already talking to some Arabs and walking into a large house with his entourage. The house's lawn was an obstacle course of flowerbeds, vegetable plots, and leaky, discarded hoses. The garden reeked slightly of manure.

SSG Downtree maneuvered him up a brick path to the front of the meeting house. It had an ample porch, large enough to entertain on. The house's style appeared Persian with Greek columns to Fitz's young eyes. Sun bleached columns extended up from the landing, supporting an overhanging terracotta roof. Dark painted triangles wrapped around the crowns of the columns like dragon's teeth. The walls were sky blue with bone white grating and trim. A jumble of patio lights, half the bulbs shattered, were strewn across the porch tiles, apparently forgotten. The front door was open and they ducked their heads as they entered.

They joined group introductions already in progress inside. Straight through the foyer was the main room of the house with blood orange sofa couches along the walls. Coffee tables were in the center and a variety of Persian rugs or colorful blankets covered the floor. A large, cubic TV leaned against the back wall and an assortment of neon pink and blue colored paintings of horses or idyllic temples with waterfalls adorned the others. Fitz was puzzled by these design choices. Where were there horses in Iraq?

The Arab men had stood up from the couches, the plump ones wore loose fitting robes and either white or checkered head wraps. The thin athletic ones wore skinny drab running suits or soccer jerseys, no headdresses for them. LTC Gute was working the room, moving down the line of standing Arabs, introduced to some by his interpreter, recognizing others. The greeting seemed to be "Saalom Mal-akum" and was passed back and forth. Some strongly shook his hand, others effeminately, one fat sheik even awkwardly kissed both his cheeks like a French woman.

"Better jump in there, sir. Get some man-love." SSG Downtree pointed Fitz to the beginning of the receiving line.

Ready for anything, he stepped in behind the other officers, and started his own awkward greetings.

"Saalom Mal-akum."

"Mal-akum Saalom."

After he'd met three Arabs he couldn't understand, it ceased being uncomfortable. He shook hands and received the same kisses from the fat sheik. However, the experience of the man's sweaty and bristly Saddam mustache rubbing his face was not a moment he'd like to repeat.

They all took their seats and the Arabs all praised "Allah Bukare!" Fitz sat by the colonel's "terp" so he could understand.

"Allah Bukare!" the terp said.

Immediately, every Arab produced cheap cigarettes and offered them out. LTC Gute waved off the offer and tried to immediately talk business. Fitz took a cigarette from the man next to him and nodded thanks. He usually only smoked when he was drunk, but it seemed wrong to refuse.

"Shoo-Krawn buddy," SSG Downtree said to a skinny Arab standing by him. He offered him one of his genuine Marlboro cigarettes back as an equal gesture.

LTC Gute's face momentarily displayed annoyance by all this humanity. He re-adjusted himself in his seat and the same fascinated, sincere mask was back. He turned to the sheik and started talking to him as if he was the most interesting man in the world.

Fitz couldn't follow most of their conversation because they referenced affairs from many earlier meetings. Hearing the LTC say something and then waiting for the interpreter to translate and then have the sheik do the reverse made it a tedious process. He did notice that there was no small talk or "how's your family" from the colonel.

"Sheik Assad," LTC Gute got straight to it. "As leader of the Busayefi Business Council, I'd like to conclude our agreement on utility repair. We've brought some contracts for you to sign, all reflecting our previous discussions."

The sheik grinned and slowly fingered a set of prayer beads in his hand. His teeth were filled with gold.

"I would like that very much, colonel," the sheik said through the interpreter. "However, we must resolve earlier issues before we can begin new endeavors."

He then proceeded to talk about grievances or supposed agreements from last time. Some tribe member had been promised this compensation by the previous unit. He had not received it; when would he get his money? Fitz couldn't believe anyone could say no to a colonel, but here he was.

Fitz eyed up Sheik Assad and wondered what tribal chair or significance he held. He appeared to Fitz as just another fat Arab in his white man-dress with the same benign expression as the others. The sole thing that he seemed to know was that LTC Gute wanted his cooperation and would pander to him.

The electric lights flickered and went out. The sheik yelled something to one of his slim Arabs and the man went outside. A minute later a generator coughed, started, and the lights came back on.

The temperature had grown sweltering outdoors, but remained milder inside the house. The Arabs lounged in their billowy gowns and the Americans looked absurd still wearing their body armor. At least they had removed their Kevlar helmets; Fitzgerald disliked wearing that itchy thing.

Fitz could distinguish SSG Downtree sitting right outside the meeting room in a plastic lawn chair. The chair buckled a little bit from the weight of his armor but still supported him. He wore the bored, indifferent expression of a mall cop — present, but not giving a damn. He'd removed his helmet too and sat in the shade eating sunflower seeds, cracking and spitting out the shells one by one, leaving a nice little pile for someone else to clean up. He kept his rifle leaning against his leg, barrel down on the tiled patio.

The meeting moved along and Fitz couldn't discern what was agreed upon. LTC Gute introduced Fitz at some point to the sheik and the Arabs all pretended deference to this new lamb from America. Before Fitz could utter a word, the colonel cut him off and resumed the conversation. After an hour of discussion, the sheik offered a goat for lunch. The idea floated tantalizingly for a second until LTC Gute refused. He had some vital meeting back at his headquarters that could not be delayed for anyone.

The men offered their goodbyes and then left. Departing was less formal, waves and head nods instead of kisses. They donned their helmets and walked back to the trucks. He noticed how the gunners had stayed in their turrets, guarding them and the sheik's house for the whole time. As they boarded their MRAPs, all sorts of Iraqi boys rushed and clamored for "CHACO-latta" or "Pepsi" around the soldiers before they waved them away. SSG Downtree angrily yelled "ROO!" at them, which prompted them to run to the next group of soldiers to beg. Apparently, they weren't American soldiers but elves here to give out treats. A couple soldiers threw water bottles or Jolly Ranchers to the throng. A hefty Iraqi child bullied the smaller ones and tore away their prizes for himself. Lean Arab guards shooed the kids off and then begged for water themselves as the convoy rolled away.

CHAPTER THREE

THE PATROL ARRIVED BACK at COP Dolby uneventfully, and Fitz was deposited back on the front steps of Squadron HQ. The MRAPs drove off to the fuel point in the COP interior to top off their tanks. The NCOs walking out in front of each truck, guiding their drivers. Fitz looked around for the LTC or any authority figure, but finding none, climbed the stairs and went in the doublewide front doors of the big headquarters building.

He entered a large foyer and was confronted with a continuing wide staircase three feet ahead leading to a second floor with banisters. Perpendicular to the door stood a gun rack with assorted M16s and M4s notched into the metal ruts, their barrels skyward. To his right down a single step lay a tiled, open room jam-packed with desks and computers, workstations separated with signs saying "S-1,", "Adjutant,", or "S-4 NCO." Even if he hadn't known what those S numbers meant, the status charts, coffee mugs, and file cabinets would have betrayed it as an administration and staff officer pit. To his left was an ante-chamber with computers labelled "Internet Café" and straight ahead down a hall arose more desks and closed doors labelled with further S numbered signs. The walls' original Persian architecture peeked out from behind the plywood dividers and hexagonal work lights canvasing each room. Stacked sandbags obscured all but the tops of windows and red and green Ethernet cables were wrapped along the tops and bottoms of every wall.

He stepped down into the staff officer pit and looked for any competent human being. There was an awkward looking 1st lieutenant plucking at keys in the "Adjutant" workstation, so Fitz chose him.

"Hey, man, I'm Eddie, Lieutenant Fitzgerald, I just got in. Who do I report to?"

The 1st lieutenant looked up as if he'd asked him the meaning of life and he paused from his work to gather all his cognitive abilities. His uniform nametape said "Spinner" and he looked like he had been here barely a week more than Fitz. He had the worst kind of military haircut, a small skullcap pocket of hair at the very peak of his head with the rest shaved away — a haircut that would fit a wrestler or a bouncer with a broken nose, not a skinny white kid doing paperwork.

"Oh yea…..um hi! You're Fitzgerald, right? Yea…. You should go talk to the XO. No…..wait…. I've got a tracker right here that says where incoming personnel are going…. Lemme get that."

Spinner started to rummage through a messy pile of papers and tan folders, a remnant of what must have been a coherent system some time ago. Fitz stood by politely and gratefully felt the rush of AC overhead. He felt heavy in his gear. An angry looking, sergeant first class looked up and around from the next workstation and instantly became horrified at what his lieutenant was doing. His gaze then drifted to Fitz and he dutifully stood up to address an officer.

"Sir, go see the XO. He controls where all the new officers go. And you can take your gear off, you're inside the TOC now."

The SFC's tone was agitated but also tired, like a parent guiding his idiot kid.

"Where's the XO's office?" Fitz honestly did not know.

"Over there to your left as you walk in the main door — says XO on it."

Fitz thanked the SFC sincerely; he'd have plenty more new guy questions before this day was through. 1st Lieutenant Spinner, oblivious, still kept searching for the paper matrix with incoming personnel. Fitz just let him be. He walked back to the foyer, removed his body armor and helmet, putting them into a square pile in a corner, and put his M4 into the rack. He walked over to a big door originally part of the house and rapped loudly three times.

"Yea? Come In!" boomed a Boston accent from inside.

Fitz entered the room and stood before a desk with a distracted looking man sitting behind it. On his chest was a faded yellow oak leaf that now resembled a tan stain. The man wore glasses and looked intelligent. Fitz saluted and popped off, "2nd Lieutenant Fitzgerald reporting, sir!"

All U.S. Army battalions or squadrons had two majors in them. One was the XO or Executive Officer and the other was the S-3 (the title of the shop that dealt with operations and planning). The XO ranked technically as the second in command of the unit, head coordinator of logistics, and consolidator of all those vital but boring functions that units need. The S-3 planned and ensured execution of all the operations and physical tasks of the unit, but wasn't constrained by the XO's realities of logistics (i.e. food, gasoline, ammunition). These two vital positions were supposed to be filled by smart competent men, however typically due to the war, one major usually proved incompetent and the other major had to cover down for him. If Human Resources Command failed miserably, both men were incompetent. No matter what, lieutenants like Fitz still had to obey all their orders.

"Edmund — or is it Ed or Eddie?" The major said as he stared at a finely colored matrix with crisp names and columns on a single sheet of paper. He was shorter man with steel-rimmed spectacles and touches of gray in his hair. The man appeared neither athletic nor frail, simply a middle-sized build. He bore the same constant weariness in him that Fitz had seen in the NCOs on patrol, except this man had a presence beyond his rank.

"I go by Eddie, sir."

"Nice to meet ya. I'm Major McAdams, I'm the Squadron Executive Officer." He made eye contact with Fitz as he spoke and then paused. "Where ya coming from?"

"West Point, sir."

"Nah — like which state? As you can tell I'm from Massachusetts, the motherland."

"Oh….. uh Pennsylvania," Fitz said.

"Ah Yuengling — I love that beer. Not Sam Adams but it'll do."

Fitz smirked and felt himself relaxing immediately. MAJ McAdams was the first person in Iraq that was talking to him like a person.

"Anywho Eddie, I know you West Point guys are alright. I'm gonna push you out tomorrow to Bushmaster Troop. We don't need any more lieutenants here at squadron. You're gonna go out there and help them out. They've been short a lieutenant for a while. Your commander is Captain Holt, he's a good man — listen to him. Any questions?"

"No, sir," Fitz had a thousand questions.

"OK good," MAJ McAdams said with a smirk. "Now get the hell outta my office!"

Fitz saluted and backed on out. He closed the door and thankfully found SSG Stannifer there waiting for him.

SSG Stannifer walked him over to the far side of the COP, towards the fuel point and completely away from the living containers. Everywhere there were pallets and pallets of cheap plastic water bottles with torn sheets of Mylar plastic shrouds over each one. The other pallets of supplies worth taking were consolidated in a big pile on a far T-Wall, under close watch. Stannifer escorted him to a row of dark green, medium-sized tents anchored into the dirt with ropes and stakes. The tents had dry earth caked on their sides from some inclement sandstorm or rainstorm recently. Although the shipping containers and wooden shanties seemed barely habitable, he would have rather slept in one of those than these tents.

"Sir, your bags are inside this one. There's only one other guy in the transient tent right now and he's on tower guard. Two tents over is the female one, just don't fucking go in there," he said.

"Chow is served at 1730 over there by the Mobile Kitchen Trailers, and showers are over by Squadron. Meet me in front of Squadron at 0700 tomorrow with all your bags for the convoy out to Murray. Understood, sir?"

Fitz looked at SSG Stannifer's tired face and realized despite the man's gruffness he was here to help.

"Nah, I'm good sergeant. Thanks."

Without another word Stannifer strode off, leaving Fitz alone to figure out the velcroed canvas door and get inside. He found his gear on the floor in the middle of the tent. His duffel and rucksack had been duly deposited next to a vacant cot away from the air conditioner. He could tell that the AC unit wasn't designed for this tent, apparently inserted later with jury-rigged plywood in the corner. He didn't think it was doing anything against the oppressive heat, but it dutifully chugged away at full blast. Despite his beauty rest on the MRAP earlier, as soon as he took off his armor he felt exhausted. Must be the time change. He removed his uniform top next and realized his tan t-shirt had discolored splotches of sweat on it. After that, he had about enough energy left to take off his boots. He placed them under the cot, made sure his rifle was at arm's length leaning on his ruck, and then he laid back flat on the Army bed. He wiggled his toes and passed out.

Fitzgerald woke up hours later to his windowless tent. His stomach had been his alarm, and he re-kitted up to find chow. He also realized after opening the flap that he didn't need his body armor or helmet for dinner. Just his patrol cap and weapon would suffice inside the wire.

He walked over to the line of soldiers queuing for grub and took his place at the end. He shifted the sling of his rifle, his mind still groggy from the nap. The sun had dropped noticeably from before and the oncoming night made Iraq prettier than what it was — the darkness shading the buildings and palms recasting them tropical and exotic. He heard a robust laugh and turned to see two men with pistols and not rifles approach the line — a tell of officers that outranked him. It was LTC Gutierrez and an unknown major. Fitz went to salute but then remembered they were in a combat zone. He greeted them with a simple "Gentlemen" and eyed them with an expectant pupil's gaze. The colonel's demeanor seemed unchanged from earlier and this new major bounced beside him, full of energy.

Fitz met the other squadron major and sized him up. He was middle-aged man, bigger but not fat. Younger he may have been an athlete but now he completely lacked physicality or even a retired boxer's buried lethality. He laughed heartily at the colonel's comments reflexively and seemed unburdened by stress. His Velcro nametape and U.S. Army's on his uniform were a little off center, just enough to be noticeable. Fitz read his name, Cauzrahavek, on his chest at an angle.

"2nd Lieutenant Fitzgerald!" purred LTC Gute, "What a perfect opportunity! Please join us for dinner."

This wasn't a request among equals. It had all the uncomfortable stiff formality of an eight-year-old being dropped off at a great aunt's house for the weekend. But they were all standing there anyway. Hopefully, he'd get more answers on Bushmaster Troop and what their sector looked like. He unquestioningly complied with yet another choice made for him today.

He filed through the line with them and was pleased to get a broiled steak and a lobster tail. A small ear of corn, caramel pudding snack pack, butter, and BBQ sauce completed the main course nicely. If this was daily chow then Iraq could not be that trying. Fitz set his tray down, collected two paper cups of orange Kool-Aid, and then sat down in front of the two men. He shifted his rifle to rest against his leg as he sat. He waited patiently for them to start and then began devouring his food.

As he started feasting, LTC Gute focused his gaze on Fitz and began speaking at him.

"The XO's informed me that you'll be going down to Bushmaster Troop, as part of my guidance."

Fitz gurgled acknowledgement through a mouthful of steak fat. He wiped his mouth and reminded himself that he should be setting good first impressions.

"It's a shame you aren't certified yet as a platoon leader, but we'll have to send you out."

Fitz blinked uncomprehendingly at the colonel, not getting his meaning.

"I know you've graduated your commissioning source and Armor Basic Course to get here, but you haven't passed the 8-6 CAV Squadron Lieutenant Certification to get approved by *ME* to take a platoon."

Fitz stopped eating, obviously concerned by this, and MAJ Cauzrahavek stumbled into help.

"Fitzgerald, you see the squadron has developed an in-depth checklist—"

"Vetting," corrected the colonel.

"Vetting," the major corrected himself, "for required skills a lieutenant must master before he can take a platoon into combat." The major's jolly disposition sugarcoated the words.

"Like tank formations or reconnaissance techniques that they taught us at OBC?" Careful, Fitz cautioned himself, don't be a smartass.

"Well, yes, but more things like understanding an XO's logistics or an S-2's intelligence brief."

"And completing all the Fort Stewart mandated Family Readiness, Individual Resiliency, and installation services awareness," LTC Gute piped in.

"Oh-kay… sir," Fitz said.

The colonel took the lead again and droned on, "I've developed this squadron vetting process and it's received high praise from the Commanding General. Don't worry, you'll be at a disadvantage getting a platoon right away and not going to staff but we'll get you certified eventually. We'll get you to staff as soon as possible. Maybe we can even do it in Kuwait on the way back!"

Fitzgerald returned to his steak and muttered compliance. This was his first day in Iraq and this LTC was his boss. He must have looked confused and unenthused because LTC Gute eyeballed him mechanically. To cement his decree he continued on, as if briefing an audience on the merits of his plan.

"For your career, 2nd Lieutenant, you will need all those skills. You only get so much out of *combat*, you'll need all my mentoring to be able to survive in a staff in garrison. Now that's a hard job! When I was a junior captain working in the G-3 in First Armor in Germany, my boss developed a similar program. It's because of his development that I'm in command here today."

Fitz was no Schwarzkopf, but he couldn't see the use in what this lieutenant colonel was preaching. But it happened to be a one-sided conversation and he was junior. He wrote it off in his head as something he'd understand eventually. He really did want to believe that these men had his best interest in mind.

LTC Gute shifted the conversation to family and Fitz enjoyed taking the moment to remember and describe his tribe. However, it became clear that the colonel lost interest, when he realized Fitz was a first-generation West Pointer, and didn't have his father or uncles in command somewhere. Mercifully, a runner from the TOC interrupted to remind the senior officers of the 1830 Battle Update Brief (BUB). The impending meeting forced the two field grade officers to leave. Fitz respectfully saw them off and then contentedly resumed eating, alone. He was drained from the day and ready to get somewhere in Iraq where he could have less awkward conversation.

He stood up and headed toward the trash cans. As he threw away his garbage, he noticed other soldiers grabbing muffins and pop-tarts and putting them in their cargo pockets. He followed suit, tomorrow would be another long day.

CHAPTER
FOUR

FITZ WOKE UP AT 0600 in his transient tent and shaved without running water. Those luxuries were at FOBs; COPs had bottled water for everything. He set his hygiene bag on the hood of someone's Humvee and poured out half of a water bottle. Fitz then cut the plastic top off with his Gerber knife so that he could use it as a basin. He was thankful he'd packed a compact mirror and he lathered up with his mini travel shaving gel. He scraped off the little hair he'd grown in the past day and finished using his Army issue brown towel to clean up his face and neck. The air felt cool and crisp on his face before the Arab sun was up and the inevitable sweating began.

He managed to catch breakfast at the MKT, some French toast sticks, powdered eggs, and coffee. Then, he man-handled his bags to the front of Squadron HQ. It took him two trips. He noticed the same cast of characters as yesterday, NCOs and specialists, lining up and prepping the MRAPs for the convoy. He recognized Sergeants Downtree and Stannifer, but neither men did more than simply acknowledge his presence. He grabbed an ice-chilled water from the MKT and sat down on his bags. Fitz was learning.

Eventually, SSG Downtree came over and scooped up his duffel bag.

"Looks like I got you again, sir," he winked, in a better mood than yesterday.

They both lumbered over to the back of the third MRAP and tossed his luggage aboard.

There was no patrol brief this time, the colonel wasn't here.

Fitz knew the drill, he jumped familiarly into the MRAP's back side seat and buckled himself in. He made sure he put on a working headset this time and re-adjusted his gloves and eyepro. The gunner, SPC Williams, came up the back ramp with his gunner's harness already on.

"MORNING, SIR!" he bellowed over the truck's engine. "YOU ALL SET?"

"HOOAH!" Fitz shouted back with an enthusiastic double thumbs up.

SPC Williams turned around and held the back door switch to raise the truck's ramp. Fitzgerald mentally recorded where the switch was as the ramp closed with a whine and then a heavy metal thump. Williams, crouched over, walked forward to his hatch, picked up his helmet that had an unopened Red Bull can in it, and climbed up and into the turret. The pulsating thrum and vibration of the MRAP's monster engine was comforting. Fitzgerald felt like a road warrior.

SSG Downtree came around the front and saddled into the TC seat. Fitzgerald still hadn't met the driver. All he saw was the back of his helmet and hands on the wheel. They did a quick radio check, "Truck four this is three" and then they were rolling. Fitzgerald thought it odd that they didn't have more elaborate call signs, but then thought better of it. Especially if they usually had a field grade riding along with them.

Fitz waited until their truck drove outside the HESCO barriers before he pulled out an ammo clip and inserted it into his M4's magazine well. He pulled back the charging handle and let it ride forward, sliding a round into the breech. All that he had to do was take it off SAFE and pull the trigger.

The patrol left the COP Dolby walls and towers behind and started to slink up the connector road to the first route. Fitz could see the thick ferns in the parallel irrigation canals and realized how easily a man could hide in them. Or someone could hide a dead body. Or a barrel of home-made explosives. They took a right turn, and then headed down a rural road onto a wide flat plain.

All across the plain, an olive green patchwork of crops straddled the land. There was visibly much more vegetation and irrigated farmland than he had expected. Small clusters of palms, some with trunks, some without, dotted the foreground. Tilled rich clumpy earth stretched away from the roadside, along with the occasional farmhouse or structure. Many houses at first look appeared ruins, but at second glance showed goats or children playing around them. Most were of shoddy thin bricks or cinderblocks, humble structures of gray or beige cubes; however, a few larger houses with grander architecture stood out from the landscape.

The route was an unimpressive, flat, dirt, country road hemmed in by snaking irrigation ditches on each side. The ferns and reeds sprung out a few feet from the canals but must have been four to six feet tall in total; the waterways as wide as a truck. The vegetation would be cleared away in certain sections, allowing a person to see flowing water or a rusty, gushing pipe.

The real trademark of this pastoral Iraqi countryside was the trash strewn everywhere. Fitz didn't know if there had ever been utilities or garbage men under Saddam but obviously there was nothing now. Rusted metal frames, used car tires, dog carcasses, and shredded plastic wrappers decorated the sides of the road. Countless empty, baby blue water bottles and silver metal cans jutted out from the caked dust and grime on the lane's fringe. Whatever idealized Fertile Crescent this had once been was now tainted with the oil stain of modernity.

The patrol rumbled on. Twenty minutes turned into an hour. SSG Downtree, Williams, and the driver talked on the intercom to stay alert. Williams couldn't stop talking about the latest *Grand Theft Auto* game for Playstation: the realistic gameplay, the interactive city map, the prostitutes a player could cyber bang. Fitzgerald didn't know how a video game could trump the reality of Iraq. Wasn't manning a gun turret during a combat patrol enough? SSG Downtree didn't think so and let him talk.

They passed through a collection of farmhouses on a road intersection. Criss-crossing above the roads were low hanging electrical lines, some connected to poles, others entirely suspended from the houses, all a tangled yarn ball of constant patchwork and additions. The MRAPs were so tall that the gunners had to use their rifles to unhook the turrets or else they'd snap the wires.

A couple bored, skinny, Arab men stood watch at a checkpoint by the farmhouses. The checkpoint consisted of a few road cones, an Iraqi flag, and a sleeping mat in the shade. They both wore dusty, black, Adidas tracksuits with white lines running up the sleeves and had AK-47's slung over their shoulders. The TCs waved from their windows and the gunners threw them a couple waters, but nobody stopped. Even if they'd wanted to, they didn't have a terp along for this mission. The Iraqi men solemnly looked back.

It was slow moving along the rural roads as the sun kept rising higher. The patrol broke out from the constricting route and started moving across a paved throughway, alongside a wide, engineered canal. The concrete sloped down in a V and the trench must have been three MRAPs wide. The muddy flowing water hand-railed the road out into the countryside. A checkpoint was called up on the radio, and Fitz contentedly stared out ahead through the truck's windshield.

The explosion came unannounced. There was a brief, brilliant flash and then a dust cloud engulfed the truck ahead of them. Everything slowed, as Fitz gaped at it. Then he heard the CRUMP and felt the concussive force slap him as the dirt plume rushed over their MRAP. His mind blanked, and he felt heat lick his exposed face, throat, and arms.

"CONTACT FRONT!!" Williams shrieked into his intercom and started firing his 240 ahead at his one o'clock. Fitz's ears rang and he felt a slight decompression. His ears popped. Spent hot brass started rattling down Williams' legs and the step onto the floor at Fitzgerald's feet. The truck shuddered to a stop.

"CEASE FIRE, CEASE FIRE! — WHAT THE FUCK ARE YOU FIRING AT?!?" SSG Downtree bellowed and then turned to hit Williams in the legs. Williams stopped after another few seconds of burst.

"YOU DON'T FIRE UNLESS YOU GET POSITIVE ID OR I TELL YOU TO FUCKING FIRE! WHAT ARE YOU KILLING? PALM TREES?!"

The radio squawked through the headset, *"Two — this is Four. What's your status, over??"* It was SSG Stannifer.

Fitz's ears were still ringing and he smelt burning plastic in the air. He wriggled his arms and legs to make sure everything still worked. He anxiously looked around and picked up his rifle that he'd dropped onto the floor. Williams swiveled his turret nervously, trying to find a target, but nothing was out there. The expended brass lay all over the boat-shaped metal hull, a couple errant casings decorated the empty chair next to him. Truck Two still hadn't responded.

A truck engine growled loudly behind them and the radio chattered, *"One, Three, this is Four, stay put, I'm pulling up alongside Two and helping them out."*

"WILLIAMS! TURN AROUND TO YOUR SIX — YOU GOT REAR SECURITY NOW!!"

As Williams' legs rotated, he saw SSG Stannifer's truck move up ahead on the driver's side. Their ramp was already half lowered as the vehicle pulled up. Before it had rolled to a stop, a medic leapt out and raced to the stricken MRAP. From behind, the truck looked like a slain metal elephant on its haunches, its head lying limply in the dirt.

He heard the steel latch and front passenger door pop and realized SSG Downtree had just dismounted too.

"To hell with this," Fitz muttered and unfastened his seatbelt. He was tired of being baggage. He moved to the ramp and flipped the switch he'd seen Williams operate before. It began to lower with a clank and an electric motor's whine.

"SIR! — What the hell are you doing?! Stay in the tru——"

But he didn't care. Fitz bolted down the ramp stairs and then button hooked left around the side to go help SSG Downtree. He squinted as the bright, natural light overwhelmed him for a second. He focused on SSG Downtree kneeling ahead alongside Truck Two and ran up to him. Another electric whine signaled that Truck Three was raising the ramp behind him.

Fitz crouched down too and rested his arm, holding his rifle on the other knee. He was already breathing heavily and felt sweat on the nape of his neck. He paused, caught his breath, and looked outward for anything hostile. SSG Downtree sensed his presence and tensed. His neck and shoulder muscles tightened up and he turned and glanced at Fitz. He sighed, but didn't say a word.

Fitz peered out ahead and spotted a dense, dark palm grove. His vision couldn't penetrate beyond the outlying trees. On its fringe, the yellowed tree palms, rough trunks, and clusters of dates flexed in the light breeze. The batches of dates, resembling baby gold pears with purple tips, drooped down from the treetops like massive blistered beehives. Fitz scanned the grove again for human movement. But he could see only hostile dates and leering trees.

He turned back and looked at Truck Two for the first time since he'd dismounted. Again he thought of an elephant carcass with its head smashed and drooped forward. The MRAP's front cab had absorbed most of the blast, one tire twisted forward at a ninety-degree angle like an ear.

From what he could see, the TC was dead, the driver was bleeding, and the gunner was dazed. Fitz thought he must do SOMETHING, he had to help SOMEHOW, but SSG Downtree impatiently pulled him down when he attempted to rise.

"Doc's got it," he said with a finality. "We pull security."

The medic had pulled the now limp, catatonic driver out of his hatch and ripped off the man's armor. He produced angle tipped scissors and cut the uniform top open neatly in a straight line down his torso, like he was giving his shirt open heart surgery. The stricken soldier looked so vulnerable in only his undershirt and pants, his face a corpselike pale. The medic worked smoothly and efficiently. He kept certain blotted patches of tan shirt or gray pants in place to help clot the wounds while peeling away the rest. He laid out bandages and gauze next to the man, neatly sliced the green packages open, and slapped them over the oozing wounds, like a bricklayer with a trough. A few errant streams of blood squirted out from the driver's belly and splotched onto the medic's hands. Uncontained rivulets of blood dribbled down his chest, reaching the ground in small red spots. The protruding little globules quickly flattened out to crimson stains. The parched earth beneath them sucking down the fluid thirstily.

The rear MRAP had pulled up ahead for security, and SSG Stannifer had opened his front, TC door. He perched halfway out the door with his M4 cradled in his lap and radio hand-mic to his ear. He stared back at the medic and the downed man, as he calmly called out the lines of a MEDEVAC, the radio call for a helicopter to airlift the wounded to immediate medical care and surgery.

"LINE ONE: MIKE BRAVO FOWER NINER SEVEN TWO, SIX EIGHT SIX TREE.

LINE TWO: PHOENIX FOWER, SINGLE CHANNEL, CYPHER TEXT, SIX FIFE TREE ZERO ZERO..."

SSG Stannifer continued, but Fitz focused back outward towards their phantom enemy. The driver groaned groggily. Fitz must have missed the medic spike the stricken man with morphine. The world whirled around Fitz as he clutched his rifle.

Twenty minutes later he heard the familiar drone of helicopter rotors. He scanned the sky fruitlessly until he saw two Black Hawks barreling in. SSG Stannifer had designated the adjacent field as the Landing Zone and laid out a VS-17 signaling panel, a reflective orange and pink cloth rectangle, in the center. One bird angled down while the other veered off and circled overhead. SSG Stannifer, the medic, and two other men rushed the wounded driver on a spine board to the sliding side door of the Black Hawk as it descended. It hovered effortlessly a foot above the ground as its crew chief reached out for the man. Fitz snapped his head forward, as the rotor wash and heat rushed past his face. He heard the roar and felt the grit scatter over him. A higher pitch howl indicated the bird was lifting away, and after ten seconds it faded to a WHUMP WHUMP WHUMP WHUMP diminishing into the distance.

The remaining soldiers stood back up and re-traced their steps back to their MRAPs. Fitz wearily paused with SSG Downtree by the front of their truck and gazed at him.

"Alright then sergeant.....so onto Murray?"

"No LT, now we wait for EOD."

The afternoon heat soared as SSG Downtree escorted Fitz back to their truck. Downtree closely watched him get in, ensuring he didn't go astray again. The ramp raised with a mechanical whirr and clanged shut like a jail cell door. Fitz found his familiar spot.

Fitz stewed in his seat. It took a while for his adrenaline to peter out. None of the crew wanted to speak to him since he'd run off, if they'd ever wanted to talk to him in the first place. His body began to broil in this armored paddy wagon. He fussed with his collar and undid his vest straps. Where was EOD? Checking his watch was meaningless unless they had an ETA.

He slid over to the AC vent and loosened his Velcro shirt cuffs. The fabric unsnapped crisply as he adjusted them. The icy air billowed directly into his shirt cavity and cooled his core a few degrees lower. Fitz brooded and felt the perspiration slowly form in the small of his back, wriggle down the contours of his spine, and drip off his ass crack. Again and again and again. His uniform sponged it up and instantly dried when he shifted positions. "How much longer now?" was all he could think.

Several hours later the Explosive Ordinance Disposal team arrived in their four Marine Corps MRAPs. These MRAPs were boxier than the MAXXPRO version that they had, but still were good at getting blown up.

The EOD in their sector were Navy men, instead of the usual Army route clearance, but it didn't matter. They combed the road ahead with mine sticks and remote controlled robots. An onlooking NCO with a PlayStation controller maneuvered little tracked RC toys with arms and cameras. After fifteen minutes their lead petty officer approached SSG Stannifer with some burnt wires and metal splinters. He'd discovered it had been a pressure plate IED, a bomb detonated by something heavy rolling over it and completing the circuit. No trigger man, no complex ambush, an American killed by a light switch.

"First vehicle just missed it or didn't make solid contact. Second one hit it straight on," the petty officer declared matter of factly.

Better the second one than the third thought Fitz darkly.

A wrecker and another patrol from Dolby had arrived to secure the recovery. They would deal with Truck Two and the TC's body still inside it. SSG Stannifer and the petty officer each took pictures of the destroyed vehicle on a digital camera at a respectful distance. Neither man was ready to photograph the dead sergeant or to pull him out of the sticky red metal. The Navy man put on latex gloves and collected embers and fragments from the road, sealing them neatly in plastic bags.

Eventually, mercifully, EOD packed up and escorted them to PB Murray. It comforted Fitz to know they were continuing, but he was too numb and exhausted for coherent thought. The withering heat and retreating adrenaline had drained him of anything more than sitting in the MRAP. The whole crew was silent for the remaining half-hour trip to the patrol base. The seven vehicles arrived unmolested.

CHAPTER FIVE

THEIR PATROL APPROACHED PB MURRAY in the evening's long shadows. Fitz didn't know who Murray had been, but he bet his parents were proud of him. The small base stood obstinately removed from the outskirts of an Iraqi town along the Tigris River. A dirt and then gravel road leisurely connected it to the main traffic artery. Where the town met the PB's driveway, an Iraqi soldier squatted in the obligatory Iraqi Army (IA) checkpoint. The soldier's little post would have been a better lemonade stand, a wooden booth for one with a single sheet of plywood overhead as cover. Dusty, empty fields separated Murray from the village, the open space covered with machine guns kept encroachers at arm's length. The trucks slowly drove through the fields past a few parked civilian cars and one of Uday Hussein's summerhouses that was caved in by a laser-guided bomb.

At the outer perimeter, the fields turned into a lawn of gravel. Parked in neat rows were tan vehicles: one trackless Abrams Tank, a score of Bradleys, and numerous trucks and Humvees. Bradleys were armored personnel carriers that looked like light tanks. They had caterpillar tracks, a turret, and a lethal main gun, but weren't technically classified as tanks. Just like how tomatoes are fruits and not vegetables.

They drew near the inner cordon and it resembled Dolby's walls. T-Walls intermixed with HESCO. Rising above the ramparts were multistory, concrete watchtowers with camo netting drooped over their tops, machine gun barrels peeking out. Razor wire ran along the top of the interior ring's wall. In the vulnerable corners and angles, scores of sentinel cameras and devices on tripods beeped, clicked, and slowly rotated.

A sentry let them through the main gate, and the NCOs dismounted to ground guide the vehicles in. The gravel crunched as the trucks crawled forward. There were even less formalities here. Gunners swiveled their turrets towards the T-Walls and cleared their 240's. Fitzgerald pointed his barrel toward the truck's floor, ejected his magazine, and popped the round out of his M4's breach. Releasing it had scratched off a little of the green paint on the round's tip.

After a few hundred meters they stopped at the Bushmaster Troop Command Post and dropped ramp. Fitz walked down the back steps of the MRAP and surveyed the building. It loomed large before him, a two-story blockhouse that dominated the base and the surrounding town. He craned his neck up to see it all, a towering beige brick manor with a saw-toothed top. Every window had been heavily sandbagged and fitted with wooden loopholes and box air conditioners that jutted out. The roof was concealed from view by a parapet crowned with numerous antennae and a corner machine gun nest shrouded with a camo net.

Underneath the shadow of the blockhouse, crowded against the perimeter wall, rested a long, wooden shed with an aluminum roof. Surrounding the CP were numerous humming generators. The smaller ones resembled metal boxes welded onto wheeled carts, while the two primary ones were gigantic khaki cubes deposited over tarps and circled by sandbags. Extension cords and massive power cables connected the generators to the house. It seemed as if some engineer had unthinkingly dropped off generators until the house had enough power.

Flanking the side of the house stretched a gravel lot filled with U.S. Humvees parked end to end. Each vehicle had a swiveling turret with a gunner's shield, the machine gun taken out and locked up when not on patrol. Appropriately, a few palm trees sprouted up between the vehicles.

Beyond that lay rows of shipping containers and off to Fitz's far left were Iraqi Army soldiers milling around more Humvees. He could tell that they were IA Humvees because of their outdated Desert Storm, chocolate chip camo patterns that made little sense for actually concealing anything. The vehicle models were older and looked poorly maintained. Fitz didn't want to talk to any Iraqi right now.

Before he could finish taking in his new surroundings, Fitz realized he had to piss like crazy. Drinking water bottles and energy drinks all day, while being cooped up in an armored vehicle was not a good combination. He frantically looked around anywhere for a latrine or porta-john and was relieved to see the soldiers from his patrol all purposefully going behind a nearby mound with ferns, their body language denoting urination and relief. He half sprinted to the spot and after the two men in front cleared out he realized the bathroom happened to be three PVC pipes driven straight down into the sand. The bare pipes stood two to three feet out of the mound, at perfect genitals level. Each four-inch-wide Mario Brother's portal was a urinal to piss in. At this point he'd go anywhere. Fitz lifted his armor groin flap, unbuttoned his fly, and whizzed joyfully. As he drained himself into the tube and reveled in the relief, he noticed that some very scraggly red ferns grew out of this dirt mound. The whole area reeked of urine.

Fitzgerald returned to SSG Downtree's MRAP and found that Williams had already pulled his duffels and ruck out the back. He half carried, half dragged them to the front of the CP, content now that they wouldn't be lost or ratfucked by some Iraqi.

Finally, at his destination, Fitz squatted down on his bags and removed his helmet. He buried his face in his palms and granted himself a moment. His brain wouldn't stop replaying the IED attack. Dead or wounded, those guys weren't coming back. No one would ever tell him what happened to them. More replacements like him would have to be sent here to take their place. He closed his eyes and tried to reset his mind, but he couldn't unsee the bleeding driver or the dead TC. He took a long breath and stood up before anyone noticed him.

Fitz took another second to double check his uniform, and then opened the Command Post door. He paused in the archway to gaze around. He could see the Bushmaster CP was another high-ceilinged living room turned radio room, with a winding chamber further down to his right. Thin sheet wood cuffed the bottom four feet of the walls, flanking long tables for computers and double stacked green radios. Above that rose the original Arab stucco and brick walls, the ceiling curving ten feet upwards to a cobwebbed light fixture. An American flag, various white dry erase boards, paper status trackers, and a Minnesota Vikings cheerleader calendar decorated the walls. From her outfit, Fitz could tell that the monthly girl was staunchly supporting the troops. On the exterior wall to his left hung a flat screen television playing the Armed Forces Network. Centered, facing the television, was a plush amber couch with elaborate gold rope tassels. Desk chairs, plastic chairs, and benches lined the tables, half of them filled with soldiers. The men had removed their uniform tops, dressed down to their tan undershirts for comfort in the heat.

Another room of people to meet. With grim determination, Fitz walked over to a big burly staff sergeant sitting by a computer. The man had been curiously eyeing him as soon as he walked in, obviously snagging any excuse to stop word processing. He looked like an irreverent brute pawing the keyboard.

Approaching him, Fitz realized that the guy wasn't merely big, but huge. He loomed over the desk, a massive ogre with a shaved head and a string of barbed wire tattooed on his bicep. The six foot mass of thuggish muscle's eyes beamed irreverently; he looked like he didn't take most of society's rules seriously. But it was a playful gaze, not an arrogant one.

"Hey, Sergeant.....I'm Lieutenant Fitzgerald. I'm here to join Bushmaster Troop."

"Oh really?" The big man chuckled. "When's the rest of you showing up?"

Fitz couldn't help but laugh. True, he wasn't close to this bear of a SSG, but he didn't think he was a skinny twerp.

"Aw I'm just messing with ya, sir. I'm Sergeant Corefelt." The man stood up and grinned like a jack-o-lantern. He extended his hand and crushed Fitz's in a death vice handshake.

"First sergeant told me about you. You're gonna be my new LT, which is good because I got a lot of paperwork for you to do."

"Oh really?" said Fitz. "Well before I start all that, I should really see Captain Holt."

"Pssssssssh — Captain Holt's at some meeting. Have you eaten yet? You can come back here after chow and start on all your ossiffer work. And besides, you look like you could use a meal." He winked with that last statement, relaxing Fitz more.

"Fine," Fitzgerald relented with a smile. He couldn't help but like this guy despite his comments. He dropped and bundled his gear in a corner while SSG Corefelt put on his own uniform top. Fitz fished his patrol cap out of his cargo pocket and they exited the CP together.

"You first, sir," Corefelt said with an exaggerated wave of both hands. He looked like the silliest vagabond, his body too big for the sunglasses and uniform the Army had given him.

Fitz gracefully went through the door first but let Corefelt lead him to chow. They waded out into the gravel parking lot and Fitz noticed the MRAPs he'd arrived on were neatly parked along the edge. The edges of the motorpool were shallow with gravel but if a person waded through the center the rocks were deep and slowed him down. There were also three columns of Humvees, all facing toward the exit road, bumper to bumper, three or four vehicles deep. The two men crunched through to a main street of wooden pallets, lined on either side by shipping container houses.

The shipping containers were all red or blue, twenty-foot, corrugated steel rectangles, their shorter square sides opening out to the walkway. Their loading doors were braced back to reveal wooden half walls and door frames built into them. Some were elaborate with crafted doors and water bottle pulleys, others merely a few squares of wood. All seemed to work just fine.

Every twenty feet there'd be a sand-colored sunshade roped overtop the path, the shades' corners anchored to the tops of the living containers. Sunshades were exactly that, tan camo nets that helped reduce temperatures by about ten degrees. Ten-foot tall plastic support poles with a flat circular pedestal top propped up the shades. Wide berths of open sky offset them down the line.

Half the soldiers of Bushmaster Troop sat along the pallet pathway. Most had their uniform tops removed like inside the CP, the majority sporting tan t-shirts, but others wearing a dark green version. Some were eating, others were cleaning weapons, all nonchalant and content after another long day. Each seemed to have their own designated camping folding chair, stool, or lawn chair — there being an exact number of chairs for only them.

Corefelt stopped a couple times for greetings or brief exchanges. He introduced Fitz to a sergeant first class who didn't seem to care to meet a new guy. Most of the men also didn't, some looked up with minor curiosity, but their meal or work quickly regained their concentration as Fitz and Corefelt strolled through. No one saluted, that wasn't done downrange.

Halfway through Main Street, SSG Corefelt deliberately introduced Fitz to 1st Lieutenant Phil Lee, lounging in a folding chair, cleaning his M9 pistol. Fitz and Lee made eye contact like two dogs in a park, instantly oblivious to the rest of the world.

Lee was an athletic, coal-black haired Korean with intense eyes. He stood shorter than Fitz but his upper body had a muscular V shape.

"Hey — I'm Eddie." Greetings again.

"I'm Phil, First Platoon. So you're the new Blue One?"

Fitz realized he must be referring to the platoon names. "I guess, I haven't met Captain Holt yet."

"Well you are. White's PL's name is Maloney. XO's Nitmer, FSO's Peppel. If you need anything, this is where I sleep." Lee gestured to his shipping container that looked virtually identical to all the others. Fitz tried to count how many it was from a table, the sole recognizable landmark.

"Thanks, Phil." Fitz emphasized his name to make himself remember. They nodded and he moved along with Corefelt. Lee eyed him closely as he walked away.

The containers and path ended, as they looped around a dust-soaked green tent, a few giant wood spindles, and an immobilized Humvee to a line of soldiers outside another mobile field kitchen. The field kitchen resembled a vacation trailer camper with extendable ends and roof, except on either side was a walkable grating for hungry men to file through. There were two lines, unlike Dolby, and Fitz grabbed a thick paper tray and got in line alongside the SSG. His stomach rumbled in anticipation and he couldn't wait to try Murray's cuisine.

"Orange pasta again? Seriously!?" he heard a soldier in front exclaim.

Fitz edged his way up the steps under the overhanging fabric and saw his intended meal. Big cauldrons and vats boiled in the center and the vittles were lumped in deep metal pans. He tasted disappointment, as he saw the orange noodles and instant scalloped potatoes scooped onto his tray. Creamy congealed lumps of protein. At least it was hot.

"It's mostly this during the week, they usually make chicken strips or hamburgers on Friday."

He grabbed some bread and pop tarts after they exited the trailer. Even the orange cup of Kool-Aid looked watered down. He was definitely away from the flagpole out here.

Corefelt and Fitz hurried back to the pallet main street and grabbed a spot on a bench between two containers. The gap had been turned into an outdoor rec room, with a dusty couch and wooden crates as tables. Fitz aligned his tray on the bench, straddling the plank with his legs. He steadied his M4 against the metal folds in the container wall and commenced wolfing down his dinner. With the sun setting, it seemed ten degrees cooler and downright comfortable outside.

Sitting nearby around a box were four soldiers playing cards. Corefelt paused from his meal to introduce them to Fitz.

"Sir — here's Serrano, Stenracker, Northland, and DeVaughn. They're in my, I mean our platoon," he said with a smirk.

The soldiers muttered greetings. Stenracker turned his head around and waved, before turning right back to their game.

"Hey guys," Fitz said between mouthfuls. He returned to his scalloped potatoes.

Northland threw a spade down on the makeshift table and announced, "Nobody makes me bleed my own blood!"

DeVaughn tossed out a spade too and countered, "If you can dodge a wrench you can dodge a ball!"

Stenracker laid out a heart. "We're going streaking!"

"Dude! Wrong movie!" Northland said. They all glared at Stenracker.

"That's not fair. That movie doesn't have that many quotes!"

"Duh. That's why this is a hard game," DeVaughn said matter of factly.

Serrano put down a higher spade and scooped up the four cards. The four started another round.

Fitz finished his chow and bullshitted with Corefelt, until a runner from the CP said Captain Holt and the first sergeant were back. Fitz threw away his trash and hurried back to meet them.

Back at the CP he waited contentedly on the plush couch watching the Armed Forces Network. With the exception of a SSG manning the radio, he was left all alone to watch television. It didn't matter what was on, it just felt comforting to do something that he used to consider normal. TV, and TV with more than one channel, had become a luxury.

The phone rang. It bleated electronically and before he could move the SSG answered it.

"Bushmaster CP, this is Staff Sergeant Stalls, how may I help you, sir or ma'am?"

The SSG paused and listened for a couple moments. "Ah huh, ah huh. Well I don't know. Let me check." His voice was high and nasally. He turned and yelled back to the other room.

"Top! Squadron's on the phone again, some RFI about the number of patrols we did today?"

A visibly livid man strode from the back and yanked the receiver from Stalls.

"What do you want??!" he spat into it.

He had a backwoods country look to him, medium build, high and tight haircut, thick hickory brown mustache, and scornful clear eyepro with eyeglass inserts in them. The man had stripped down to his tan t-shirt like everyone else, but Fitz didn't need to see his rank to know he was the first sergeant, the "Top" enlisted man in the troop.

The man listened for a minute, stewing impatiently. He let whom-ever say his piece, before speaking sarcastically back.

"Ohkayyyy, lemme check."

He threw down the phone and stood next to it for thirty seconds. Then, without missing a beat, he picked it back up.

"Oh I dunno, Four, three, six, and zero." He slammed the receiver down and walked right back to the other room.

Fitz decided he would meet the first sergeant later. He continued to wait another ten minutes until Captain Holt walked in the door. Fitz stood to meet him.

Captain Douglas Holt strode in, an unassuming cavalryman with a smirk on his face. He didn't seem as hurried as other officers, but his eyes were hard and piercing.

"Sir, I'm Lieutenant Fitzger—"

"I know, sit back down."

Captain Holt motioned for him to sit and he sat right down next to him on the couch. He wore the Vietnam era boonie cap instead of the baseball hat patrol cap that everyone else sported. He took that and his clear eye protection off and folded them together into the couch cushion. Fitz pulled out a green memo notepad to professionally signal that he wasn't an idiot and knew how to pay attention.

"So I'll need you to take over for third platoon, Blue Platoon. We haven't had a lieutenant there for a month."

"The tank platoon?"

"Nah it's a recon platoon — they should be tankers but with this operation being so messy we haven't switched platoons with the armor company. Don't worry, they're scouts."

"What happened to the last guy?" Fitz assumed the worst. Especially after today.

"Don't worry, he was just garbage. We eighty-sixed him back to squadron," Holt said with a twinkle.

As Fitz racked his brain for more intelligent questions, Captain Holt faced about and yelled to the back room. "Top! You got anything for the new LT?!"

The mustached first sergeant appeared around the corner, scowling and grinning at the same time. "Yea. Welcome LT. Don't get fucking killed." And with that he popped back out of view.

They continued talking. Captain Holt laid out his expectations in a direct, nonchalant manner. Fitz liked this mode of talk much better than the earlier ones.

"Here's my command philosophy: every cavalryman in this troop has his job to do. Do your part so that others don't have to do it for you. If you get confused, use these three rules to guide you. One: take care of your team, squad, platoon, troop. Two: make rational decisions not emotional decisions. And three: once you're out of Bushmaster, you're out."

"What's that last one mean?" Fitz inquired.

"Oh, you'll see in a year or so. Until then, enjoy it," Holt said with a knowing smile.

ACT II

CHAPTER SIX

(One Month Later — Outskirts of Zambraynia, Iraq)

Fitz cleared his head with a cigarette he'd bummed from a soldier. He heard the POP POP POP of far off, sporadic gunfire.

Everything had gone to shit in the past few days. Another troop in the squadron, Courage Troop, had been tasked with clearing a nearby village called Zambraynia and they'd gotten royally fucked up. The whole Area of Operations was laced with IEDs and they'd sustained five casualties, a lot of amputations. LTC Gute thought Courage Troop should take a knee and he called in Bushmaster to finish the assault.

They'd occupied Courage Troop's old position along Route Bug. Lee's platoon was set south of the road and Fitz's had been arrayed to the north. White Platoon had swung up farther north of Fitz's platoon while Captain Holt came up behind with HQ and the mortars. Route Bug had been so heavily laced with IEDs and booby traps that it would take a week to clear it. An engineer platoon was some miles behind down the road, inching up to them.

And now Bushmaster Troop was ordered to clear the way to Zambraynia and then clear that, too. Fitz's Blue Platoon, like every line platoon, had three Humvees, three Bradleys, a forward observer, and a medic attached to each, overall about twenty men. Headquarters Platoon had a few more men, but their role was supporting the line platoons. So Captain Holt had his Bradley and the mortars behind them in case anything got weird.

Fitz led his platoon on foot, trailed by his Brads pulling overwatch. He squinted in the sun and saw Lee to his left doing the same with his guys across the road in the other fields. Lee's lead was re-assuring and their platoons alternately hopped forward and then stopped to cover the other. It was now Blue's turn to cover Red and Fitz and his guys were enjoying the moment's rest as Lee's guys maneuvered.

The familiar silhouettes of his men in his peripherals made him feel less alone. Although each man had to wear the exact same gear, each soldier wore his kit just a little differently or had a distinguishing body feature. They'd spent so much time together now that they couldn't help but recognize each other in even the faintest light. SSG Corefelt had also dismounted and walked with the guys on the far right — he'd said "...if his LT was walking then so was he."

They were advancing through Arabian bocage: tilled soil farm fields separated by thick hedges of branches and brush. The borders were hemmed with lush thickets — date trees, palm fronds, and ferns sprouting out of the irrigation channels. From the air it looked like a quilted patchwork of flat cocoa brown with olive borders; they crept through it grid by grid. It was easier to clear this land than to go down that IED road, but there was still a chance that an Al Qaeda in Iraq fighter had buried a little mine to pop a foot off. It was best to avoid the "natural lines of drift": the easiest natural paths through the dirt troughs. Those were deadly rookie mistakes.

One platoon would clear a grid, crossing through the open ground until they were stopped by the next farm's hedgerow. They'd settle up right behind it, poke their crew served weapons through the palms, and establish a clear field of fire to cover the adjacent platoon's leapfrog. Blue had just moved and was set as support by fire. Red started to advance through theirs now.

Red's next parcel had a sandstone farmhouse on the far side of its plot. Beyond it stood a two-story, gray building lying cattycorner down the road in Red Platoon's path. Fitz was gently reminded of the Bradleys behind him from their steady, clacking caterpillar treads. He watched as Lee and his men slowly picked their way to the farmhouse. He inhaled his borrowed cigarette's smoke and felt the slight rush of nicotine course through him.

Lee's men cleared the sandstone farmhouse without incident as Fitz observed them. One or two soldiers in gray, pixelated fatigues kept walking in and out of the house. There must have been something to see within it.

Fitz couldn't contain his curiosity and called Lee on his MBITER radio on his vest.

"Red One this is Blue One."

A slight pause.

"Blue One, this is Red One, go ahead." Lee's speech was deliberate and piercing, even over the radio.

"Whattaya got over there that's so interesting?"

"Oh…. We got a torso of some guy over here. He must have been shot by an Apache and then drug himself into the house to die…. Smells great." Fitz heard cackling laughter right before Lee unkeyed the mike.

After a couple second pause to break up the transmission, Lee came back on the net.

"We're gonna pause here for chow for twenty mikes. Recommend you do the same."

"You're hungry after seeing that?"

"I'm always hungry."

"WILCO Red One, lemme know when you're prepared to move again."

"Roger — will do."

Growing hunger pangs made Lee's guidance too good to resist. Fitz was nearly about to call over Corefelt when a rapid chatter of AK fire spurted out of the gray building beyond Lee's cleared farmhouse. They all sprawled for cover, Lee and Red Platoon dove behind the house and its adjacent berms. Fitz could see the little dust puffs of rounds hitting ground all around them.

There were two muzzle flashes coming from the gray house's second story. Nothing larger than a Kalashnikov, anything fiercer would have had a meatier sound. It had surprised Red Platoon but Blue was so far back they had time to breathe, think, and respond. Had Bushmaster disturbed AQI naptime?

"Blue One this is Two, can I engage?"

It was SGT Breyer on the radio behind him in his Bradley. Red had already started pelting the gray building with their machine guns and M4's, gaining fire superiority. The bricks fissured and belched dust as each round impacted and ricocheted off the building face. One of Red Platoon's soldiers popped up and fired his M203 grenade launcher into the upper story window. For some reason Red's Brads hadn't opened up yet.

"Yea — just don't hit Red. FREE TO ENGAGE."

Breyer's 25mm chaingun loosed a single sensing round forward to confirm the target and then started belching salvos of three. The building started to evaporate into dust plumes and toppling brick in seconds. One corner of the far wall stubbornly refused to cave but the rest collapsed in on itself like eggshells and fine china. A shattering clatter seemed to confirm that they had unquestionably broken it. Red Platoon's Brads had opened up just as Breyer started. The mechanical clanging and whirring of the Bradley's gun feeder ejecting weapon brass down the side of the vehicle jarred Fitz to act.

"CEASE FIRE, CEASE FIRE, you definitely got them."

A swirling impenetrable dust cloud lingered over the ripped open house. It didn't want to disperse and clung to it for theatrical effect. Nothing moved but the churning sediment.

The engagement became the excuse to stop and consolidate for the evening. Fitz and Lee each sent up SITREPs to CPT Holt, and he told them to sit tight. IA and local militia would be moved up to them for tomorrow's push and more importantly — hot chow was on the way. They'd been eating Meals Ready to Eat for the past few days and any alternative to them would be greatly appreciated.

Red Platoon used the torso farmhouse as the anchor for their position, but Blue remained exposed in a farm field. SSG Corefelt turned a Humvee and a Bradley around so they'd have 360 degree security. The six vehicles formed a defensive circle like covered wagons. The gunners in the turrets stayed alert, but it was a moment for the remainder of the platoon to rest. They sat in the back of the Bradleys, took off their helmets, and smoked cigarettes. As the shadows lengthened, Fitz felt spent.

Corefelt clambered into the back of the Bradley and sat across from Fitz. The seat cushion groaned as he plopped heavily onto it. His body was too big for the space left him on the seat, too tall for the cramped crew compartment. He took off his helmet, whistled, and laughed.

"I dunno what THOSE guys were thinking, but that wasn't a very good plan."

He giggled like a kid and flashed his jack-o-lantern smile. Fitz didn't respond.

"They teach you how to make plans like that at ossifer school?" he baited Fitz.

That comment broke through to Fitz. He'd been so strung out during the past 48 hours that the absurdity of Corefelt got the best of him. He started chuckling and then the dam burst. He put his head against the metal bulkhead and laughed deeply, losing himself for a moment. He wiped away tears.

"You're so stupid."

Hearing the laughter, SGT Breyer opened up the turret shield door and joined them. He sat on the turret floor and dangled his legs out into the rear troop compartment where Fitz and Corefelt sat. He took off his Combat Vehicle Crewman helmet (CVC) and put a large wad of dip into his lip.

Breyer made eye contact with both of them and said, "If you don't chew Big Red then fuck you." He spat into a Mountain Dew bottle.

"Don't you put that evil on me, Ricky Bobby!" Fitz threw back.

Corefelt joined in. "I'll come at you like a spider monkey!"

They continued, talking and joking about nothing particularly important.

An engine droned far behind them, and Fitz saw a high back Humvee on the horizon, plowing straight through palm hedges and dirt plots toward them. The driver was off-roading and trying to keep it in their platoon's vehicle tracks as much as possible. When the driver hit a high mound the engine revved and surged.

"That's gotta be Top," said Corefelt.

They watched the Humvee slowly get closer for the next ten minutes, until it pulled up into their protective circle. It stopped with a jerk and First Sergeant Tapwell leapt out, scowling with a lit cigarette. He turned and barked at PVT Northland who was sitting down in the other Bradley.

"Hey! Pussynuts! Give me a hand with this!"

Corefelt and Fitz climbed out the back of the Bradley and ambled over to the rear of the high back Humvee. Top Tapwell peeled back the canvas skin flaps and dropped the truckbed's door. The two seater's truck bed was stacked with olive green mermite food containers, jugs of coffee, water, and what looked like a clear trash bag filled with muffins and loaves of bread. Within seconds half the platoon had appeared to lend a hand.

"I only need a couple guys," Tapwell snapped. "The rest of you men back off — what if a round lands in the middle of us?"

Top Tapwell shooed Fitz, Corefelt, and most of the guys back to their vehicles and proceeded to open up the mermite containers and pull out paper cups, trays, and plastic utensils. Mermites were perishable food cooked in the rear and transported forward. He made Northland and his driver, Foster, lather their hands in sanitizer gel and then put on plastic gloves. The two privates climbed behind the containers in the truck bed and sat on their knees to serve the chow. Satisfied it was set up properly, Top poured himself a cup of coffee from the mocha-colored jug and beckoned to the first vehicle.

"Alright, come get it. By two's and threes."

Blue Platoon men took turns going to the back of Top's truck. They'd file by Foster and Northland who would scoop steaming piles of Yakisoba or something beef and noodles onto their trays, then they'd grab a couple slices of bread, muffins, and a leaky cup of Kool-Aid or coffee and steal back to their vehicle dens.

"Make sure you get trays for the gunners!" Breyer yelled.

As the soldiers scurried back and forth, Top made his way over to Corefelt and Fitz's Bradley. He leaned against the bustle box on the back and partially stood on the lowered ramp.

"How's it going out here, LT?"

Tapwell's tone surprised Fitz. It was the first time Tapwell hadn't yelled at him. He glanced over at Corefelt, who showed no emotion. SSG Corefelt visibly restrained himself whenever Top appeared, like he didn't want to get bit.

"Good, Top. We're taking our time…. Trying to be as safe as possible. How's the rest of Bushmaster faring?"

"We're holding our own. Especially after Courage led us into this mess." Tapwell spat on the ground. He looked away and took a drag from his cigarette.

"Thanks for bringing chow."

The comment irked Tapwell. "Well, you men have earned it… Fuckin' squadron will send ya out to this shit and then say *it's not saaaafe* enough to bring you hot chow. Those clowns will spend all day telling you how not to do something but won't lift a finger to ever help!"

Corefelt snorted and laughed and then quickly composed himself again. "How far did you drive to get here?" he asked.

"Not that far. Captain Holt will be up here by dark."

Tapwell paused for a moment, sipped his coffee, and finished his cigarette. He turned back to Corefelt.

"You know you're gonna have to deal with this shit when you're a first sergeant. You get the soldiers their chow *no matter what.*"

"I know Top, we talked about this….. I ain't no stripe-wearer."

"Yea…yea. You gonna be ready for the Board next month?"

"I was studying, Top. Before we had to deal with this."

They waited a few minutes for the last soldiers to get their share. After Breyer and the Bradley crew had switched out, they stood up to get their dinner.

"You guys be quick and then I gotta run over to Red Platoon," Tapwell said.

After they grabbed their trays, Foster packed up shop quickly and started the Humvee's engine. Top opened his passenger door and then paused for a second. He looked back at Fitz.

"You're doin alright LT. Just don't do anything stupid."

The oncoming night brought the relief of more than two hours of sleep, so they had curbed their caffeine and nicotine intake before dark. They'd been moving pretty furiously the last couple days and a real meal coupled with orders to sit until morning was an unexpected gift. It'd be uncomfortable sleep. Reclining in body armor in a cramped vehicle's boxy seat wasn't relaxing. But when a soldier was this fatigued putting his head on an MRE box and zonking out felt divine.

Of course they all couldn't rack out at once. Six vehicles meant six gunners scanning and alert. NCOs made soldiers field clean weapons to at least dust off the powder that had accumulated. Night vision goggles were prepped. Guard shifts and radio watch were set. And either the platoon leader or platoon sergeant needed to be awake, so Fitz and Corefelt took turns.

Sometime after sunset, Fitz sprawled out in the front passenger seat of his Humvee. Corefelt had demanded that he take the first shift, always trying to prove he could outdo the LT. Fitz let him have it. He took his helmet off and loosened his boots, keeping the door ajar to collect a stray breeze. It was still insufferably hot.

The radio chattered softly with its bedtime stories. Comfortably beeping and providing the white noise of static and muffled voices. Fitz's mind drifted and switched off.

Fitz woke with a start. The radio screeched insistently. He reached down to confirm his M4 was there and then checked his wristwatch. Almost 2300. Somebody wouldn't stop jabbering loudly on the troop net.

"Serrano, wha.. what's going on... on the net?" Fitz said.

SPC Serrano had climbed in behind Fitz and was now up in the gunner's turret. His legs dangled behind Fitz's head.

...

"I dunno, sir. White Platoon just started five minutes ago," Serrano always spoke very softly. He slowly unfastened the radio hand-mic and cord that stretched up to the gun turret and handed it back down to Fitz.

Fitz carefully grabbed the mike from his hand and leaned forward to listen. He shook off sleep as he heard static. The Arabian night appeared impenetrable as he gazed out the Humvee's windshield.

"WHITE ONE THIS IS BLACK FIVE, RESEND GRID FOR MEDEVAC, OVER!"

Someone keyed the mike to respond, but the response was distant and muffled. Blue Platoon must have been too far away from them.

"WHITE ONE — WHO WAS IN TWO-THREE?"

Nothing could be heard when the radio keyed again.

"WHERE IS WHITE FOUR?"

Something was terribly wrong. Fitzgerald pulled out his notebook and referenced White Platoon's internal net. He swung over to the bottom radio and turned the knob to switch nets. He dialed in White's over Blue's and punched the STO key to store it.

After an agonizing pause, White Platoon's bedlam reverberated into his truck.

"...DOC's STILL IN THE MRAP!"

"That truck's on fire — TELL WHITE FOUR TO GET AWAY FROM THERE!"

Serrano peered down from his perch and stared at Fitz. They both locked gazes for a moment, horrified.

"WE'VE GOTTA HELP HIM!"

"He's already dead."

"No No NO — I DON'T CARE IF DOC's STILL IN THERE!"

"WHITE ONE THIS IS BLACK FIVE, DUST OFF, ETA ONE-FIVE MIKES!"

"...GODDAMMIT!"

Then the cries ceased abruptly. Only intermittent silence and static escaped from the radio. Too much of it. Later, he heard Black Five, LT Nitmer, on the net, but couldn't focus on the words. Fitz shivered and felt cold for the first time since he had arrived in Iraq. He was grateful when Corefelt came to get him at midnight. He was wide awake.

CHAPTER
SEVEN

IN THE MORNING Captain Holt showed up with an Iraqi Army and Sons of Iraq militia convoy. His Bradley drove in the front of the procession like a mother duck leading her babies. It was still early, around 0600ish, and the sun hadn't started to bake yet. Holt and the Iraqi's arrival assuaged last night's horror. The platoon knew that White had taken casualties, but didn't know the details. They'd deal with that loss when this fight was done.

The IA had arrived in a desert camouflage splotched camouflage Humvee for their junior officers, called Mulazim, and a five-ton Soviet truck for their soldiers, referred to as Jundi. They didn't seem to have any sergeants here so their lieutenants mechanically yelled at the conscripts to disembark the truck. The Iraqi Army soldiers leapt down looking confused and very young. They all wore their chocolate chip desert fatigues with a hodgepodge of vests, pouches, ammo belts, and gloves. Some sported helmets, others red berets, others slouch caps. A shrewd observer could tell they wore their accessories to mimic Americans, because U.S. soldiers were the professional, bigger brothers, but the IA gear made no sense. Some would have two pairs of sunglasses on their heads, and others multiple walkie-talkies that obviously didn't work — as if a fashion designer had dressed each one to look like they were "military." The majority had AK-47s but a few had wooden stock old M16s. Their commander was nowhere in sight.

Behind them, the Sons of Iraq had rolled up in two white Toyota trucks, each truck bed filled with a dozen smiling Arabs waving AK-47s. They either wore dirty running suits or a soccer shirt matched with stained pants. All wore brown leather sandals on hairy feet. To prevent friendly fire, some supply sergeant had given them orange and pink road construction safety vests to wear overtop their shirts, which inadvertently made them conspicuous targets.

The amateur SOIs looked ridiculous as they piled out of their trucks like Keystone Cops. The IA were a little more quiet and professional, but using the word "professional" was a stretch. Fitz laughed but was cheered by their numbers. It meant a lot that the Sunnis had shown up.

The Sons of Iraq movement had started a couple of years ago, when the disenfranchised Sunni minority had realized that the American occupiers were less awful than Al Qaeda in Iraq. This was an unexpected shift because the crusader Christian Americans had shot and bombed their way into Mesopotamia, while AQI consisted of fellow Muslims. For a while the Sunni were completely fine with the AQI trying to blow up Americans. But the AQI were brutal thugs to the Sunni: imposing strict Sharia Law, degrading their women, closing schools, creating torture houses, and all the while being hypocrite Muslims themselves.

Fed up, the Sunni tribes wanted to be free of these AQI gangsters who justified their intimidation with religion, so they turned to the infidel Americans. Both sides made peace and the Americans moved Army and Marine units out into towns to protect them. More importantly, since there'd been no jobs since Saddam, the U.S. paid every military age Sunni man a living wage and provided them with weapons to protect themselves. And if the Americans were going to pay tribal leaders higher-management wages and allow them to fund reconstruction contracts through their local cronies, then even better.

Captain Holt dismounted the Brad and three tall, bronze Arabs parted from the crowd. They were the SOI leaders. They casually joined

Holt as if the four of them were drinking buddies. Their easy familiarity was noticeable. Fitz approached them and they strode out to greet him. Holt introduced them as Jaleel, Ali, and Abbad. Three brothers. These three wore clean maroon running suits and didn't bother with the clumsy orange construction vests. Each had a bright flicker in his eyes, like he'd been waiting for this moment. Jaleel grinned, Ali spoke, and Abbad held back.

Jaleel, their leader, had a thin, elongated, tan body and a wispy mustache on his upper lip. His sly facial expression made it appear like he was scheming and laughing at the same time. Ali, the spokesperson for the trio, wore a neat, secular beard, was chatty, and appeared considerably less devious. Abbad, the quiet one, also sported a respectably sized beard, and had a reserved, kind look to him. Fitz noticed an immediate friendliness from the brothers instead of the normal xenophobic distance other Arabs gave him. He just knew in his gut that these three would be reliable.

Ali acted as the group's interpreter.

"Hello Feetz-gharald! Excellent to meet you!"

"Great to meet you too." What else could he say?

"You follow us and we'll show you the way into Zambraynia."

Fitz tried to feign enthusiasm but he was pretty drained of niceties by now. He felt mostly numbness or anger these days. He smiled and nodded.

CPT Holt smirked like he was bringing backcountry cousins to a poetry reading. He was enjoying Fitz's response.

The brothers turned to each other and chattered in Arabic. Captain Holt turned around to Fitz and looked straight at him. He pointed to the closest Humvee hood with his Nomex-gloved hand and beckoned for Fitz to follow. Holt made a point to get out of earshot of the brothers.

"It's a little more complicated than that."

The two officers strode over to a nearby Humvee. Captain Holt pulled a map out of a plastic bag from one of his vest pouches. He carefully unfolded it and laid it on the vehicle hood. It was a cut up section from a standard 1:50,000 U.S. Army map of the area. Zambraynia was circled in grease pen and military graphics of squares and diamonds were arrayed all around the town. He started his brief.

"Here's the situation, Eddie. Enemy's still the same, a company-sized AQI cell is dug in within the vicinity of Zambraynia. We're in their disruption zone right now. Mostly pressure plates, crush wire, and even some entire house rigged IEDs. Watch for occasional snipers and triggermen, but you shouldn't see the bulk of them until you hit the town. Their most likely course of action is to try to attrit us like Courage Troop as we clear the area. Dunno if they'll fight when we hit the town or bug out."

Fitz regarded Captain Holt, but he didn't look up from the map. Holt fingered the square with a slash denoting Blue Platoon and continued.

"Mission is to clear the town of Zambraynia of AQI. You and Red Platoon are going to continue advancing on the town, straight down this avenue of approach. Continue to use the road as your boundary and assume it's laced with IEDs. White Platoon is still to your left. I'll continue moving up behind you with Headquarters."

Holt paused and inhaled slowly. His gaze never left the map, it seemed he could see the terrain sprouting from the contour lines.

"All of this you already know. What's changed is now we have the SOIs and the IA to screen ahead of us — so hopefully they'll run into anything before you or Lee does. You should reach the town by tonight, depending on how fast you go. Your Limit of Advance is the end of Zambraynia along route Ambush. The order of march is SOIs, IA, and then you."

"As you reach Zambraynia's perimeter, these canals will retard your vehicle's approach. If you can't find a point to ford them, be prepared to act as a Support By Fire for Red Platoon's advance. Again, under no circumstances use the main road into town. DO NOT USE ROUTE BUG. It is daisy-chained with explosives."

Fitz took this all in. Just like that, huh?

Holt continued. "How you doing on water, fuel, ammo — all the classes of supply?"

"Green on class I and V. Amber on fuel, sir." Fitz said.

"Ok, Top will bring up some fuel cans tonight for you. That should hold you."

Fitz must have betrayed some emotion, because Captain Holt now regarded him closely.

"Don't worry LT — I'm right behind you with the FSO and the mortars. You run into any trouble and we'll call in an Apache or use the mortars. Just don't rush into anything."

Captain Holt's smooth confidence appeased Fitz's mind. Fitzgerald paused to think as Holt took a slurping drink of water from his camel back straw. This was finally it. Whatever this combat experience was, he'd get it over the next few kilometers. He hoped he wouldn't let Captain Holt down.

They were interrupted by a soldier.

"Sir!" It was CPT Holt's driver. "Mustang Three is on the radio again. He needs a situation report."

Holt deliberately paused for a second. A long moment where the peripherals around the map came back into Fitz's view and he could hear the SOIs chattering nearby again. Holt waved off the soldier's impertinence. He looked at Fitz with a spark in his eyes, swiveled back to his driver, then said, "Yea. I'll get to that guy later."

The soldier turned and left. Another pause. Captain Holt reached into his pocket and produced a cardboard tin of Copenhagen, long-cut, smokeless tobacco. He snapped the burgundy and black can against his fingers, THWACK THWACK THWACK, jerking the loose dip together. He popped the top and deposited a healthy tobacco wad in his front lip. He licked the brown flecks off his lips and spat a dark sludge onto the earth by his boots.

"Alright. You know what to do. Get your guys going."

"Roger that, sir!"

And with that, Fitz ran off with his purpose.

"SPREAD OUT!"

An hour had passed and they were walking towards Zambraynia. Corporal Gonzalez was yelling at everyone to keep their distance from one another.

"Three to FIVE METERS between EVERYONE! That's three M16 lengths. EVERYONE SPREAD OUT!!"

The Americans obeyed. The Iraqis ignored him or didn't understand. The Iraqis walked in little clusters together, but at least they went first.

Fitz paused and peered ahead. The sun was out now and he could feel the first dribbles of sweat slithering down his back.

They walked for a long time. The SOIs out front, IA Jundi in some semblance of a line, dismounted Americans, and then the Brads and trucks loudly in tow. The Brads would hop more than creep, getting in a good spot to overwatch until the infantry had outdistanced them. A roaring General Motors engine revving and a belch of smoke always signaled they were bounding again.

Fitz's radio crackled. He watched his steps and he picked his way through a farmer's field. He rested his M4 against his vest, muzzle downward as he stepped. His ammo pouches transferred some of the M4's weight away from his arms. The protective lid for his ACOG telescopic sight was on, as was his safety. They only took a second to flip.

Ali and Jaleel were walking back and forth between the echelons. They gravitated towards him after a bit. The brothers were grinning. Their AK-47s with foldable stocks fit snugly under their arms.

"Hello Feetz-gharald," said Ali.

"Oh hey, Ali."

"Where en Amerika are you from?"

Jaleel kept grinning and eyeing Fitz.

"I'm from Pennsylvania." Fitz's mind whispered OPSEC (Operational Security), but he told his brain to shut up.

"PENCIL-vania?" Ali slowly mouthed the place to try to understand it.

"Mmhmm — that's right."

"Is that close to Oh-HI-O? Captain Holt is from Oh-hi-o."

"Right next to it, Ali. Very close." Fitz half leapt over a drainage ditch. The three of them continued to creep forward through the crops.

"O-kay! You must be part of Holt's tribe then." Ali turned his head to Jaleel. "I *told* you they were from the same tribe!" They bantered back and forth in Arabic for a bit.

"We are from the Jabouri tribe. ALL of us," Ali grinned proudly.

Fitz didn't know how to respond to that. He assumed that mattered. After a couple more steps he had a retort.

"Are the IA also Jabouri?"

"OH no no No NO!" laughed Ali. "They're all Shia from Baghdad."

"…They're almost Dulaimi," Jaleel piped in for the first time.

Ali chuckled. Jaleel smirked. Fitz blinked.

"What's Dulaimi?" asked Fitz.

"Oh…..they're this stupid, STOO-PID tribe that live near us. They always do bad things."

Ali offered him a smoke. Fitz took it, lit it, and they continued walking. A few ramshackle farmhouses were coming up as the same unvarying terrain stretched on ahead. A large palm grove was off to the left more in White Platoon's sector. The sweet tobacco smoke combined with the heat and sucked the moisture out of him.

"I have a joke," proffered Jaleel.

Fitz said nothing and nodded.

"This dumb Dulaimi is in the desert riding his camel. And he wants to have sex with it, BUT he is very short," Jaleel said. His English was very good.

"Probably has a small…" and Ali gestured with his finger to demonstrate.

Jaleel and Ali giggled. Jaleel waved his hand at Ali so he could continue.

"So this Dulaimi needs a box to stand on so he can have sex with his camel." Jaleel gestured to show the dynamics but they got it. They all got it.

"But every time he gets up behind his camel and stands on the box, the camel takes a few steps forward. So he keeps moving across the desert this way. He gets up behind his camel, the camel walks forward. He keeps doing this until he comes across this beautiful woman. She is trapped by a lion. He kills the lion and she says, 'Thank you thank you — what can I do to repay you for freeing me?'"

"And this Dulaimi says," he paused for effect, "Will you hold my camel so I can have sex with it?"

The two brothers chuckled hysterically. Fitz smiled and forced a little laugh. He got this game.

He searched his mind for all the dumb, racist jokes he could find and started telling them. A Dulaimi walks into a bar. A Dulami, an Iranian, and a Jabouri are walking on the beach and they find a genie in a lamp. How many Dulaimi does it take to screw in a lightbulb? The brothers ate up these jokes as they advanced.

The skulking pace continued. The sun got higher. Fitz felt the moisture started to collect in his back, pits, and recesses. His uniform fabric become saltier, damper, and started to cling to him. Fitz finished the water bottle he'd crammed in his cargo pocket. He'd have to fetch another from one of the trucks soon.

The brothers strode off, and he continued on by himself. He took off his gloves and rolled up his shirt cuffs. He hoped his sleeves might catch some breeze that way. Perhaps a kilometer ahead, a two-story house jutted out of the palms. It was brick, but had some wooden paneling that made it look fancy. Fitz figured it would look right at home next to Spanish architecture in a California suburb.

As they approached it the SOIs started jabbering and gesturing at it. They were obviously keeping it at a distance. The house's dark windows peered back at them.

As the house came into perspective, its details grew finer. Ornate, crescent, glass windows decorated the front door and its border. Gold cursive edging laced the door and every window. It was remarkable to think that with all the concrete block farmhouses, no one had squatted in this abandoned mansion. An inviting, tile-laced path led to the front door and the structure tempted them as a cool place to rest.

Fitz pulled out his radio and called a halt. The Arabs sat down on their haunches and smoked cigarettes. The Americans crouched down on one knee and smoked cigarettes. Everyone faced the house.

"Sergeant Corefelt!!" Fitz bellowed over to him a few hundred meters away.

"Let's get a detail together — check out that house."

"You coming along too? ….Sir?" Corefelt taunted back.

"Shut up. You know I am. Just grab some guys."

Corefelt grinned and gathered Stenracker, Serrano, and Northland. Northland's M249, a short barreled machine gun, would be ideal for anything squirrely in that house. Northland was irate that he had to do anything extra.

Fitz started to make his way over to Corefelt, watching his path. He'd also have to assemble some Arabs to clear the house.

Ali ran up to him in a flurry, flailing his arms. He didn't think Arabs knew how to run. Good — he wouldn't have to go get them.

"That house is mu zayn! VERY bad. Don't go," he said.

"Moo-zien?" Fitz butchered it.

"Sure. It is bomb. Will BLOW UP and kill EVERYBODY!"

"I get that." Fitz's eyes grew wide. Corefelt heard everything Ali said and froze.

Shit.

Fitz keyed his radio mike.

"BREAK BREAK BREAK — All elements this is Blue One. Avoid that house up ahead by the palms."

He unkeyed and then keyed the mike again.

"BE ADVISED, the SOIs designate it as a HBIED. Don't get within four hundred meters of it."

"Blue One — this is Black Six." Holt didn't wait for Fitz to acknowledge.

"Get an eight digit grid on that house and send it over to White and Red. Squadron, too. Give it a wide berth and keep moving."

"Six this is One, WILCO."

"Good. Six out."

Ali looked at Fitz again. Their eyes locked.

"Mu Zayn House."

"Yea…Moo-Zien. Thanks, Ali."

A delayed surge of adrenaline prickled the hairs on Fitz's neck. He needed to think out here. That was close.

The Mu Zayn House seemed to laugh at them, like a firecracker that beckoned to be played with.

CHAPTER EIGHT

THEY MADE SLOW HEADWAY for the rest of the day, but it was still progress. The Mu Zayn House faded away behind them as they continued to pick their way through farmers' fields, cinder block shanty houses, and irrigation ditches. They radioed up to higher other suspicious dwellings and tripwires, marked them with engineer tape, and approached Zambraynia cautiously.

Blue up the center. Red slightly ahead on the right. White beyond the palms on the left. Black floating behind in reserve. Somewhere up ahead AQI.

A few more kilometers or clicks ahead, the SOIs found three plastic half drums full of Home-Made Explosives. Luckily, they weren't rigged to blow — just lazily tucked under some shrubs by an irrigation ditch. No blasting cap, no initiator, but still disconcerting enough to make a soldier question how close he should get.

Each man's personal safety wasn't some academic question here. Every soldier made a hasty assessment, said fuck it, and hoped he hadn't missed something. Fitz walked up to the HME tubs after the SOIs had trampled over them. The containers were thick white plastic ovals, filled with a chunky peanut butter colored explosive paste, kept in the shade for storage. Whoever's farm this was would have to answer to the Iraqi authorities for these — if they could be found. Fitzgerald pulled his digital camera out of a grenade pouch, snapped some pictures, and moved on.

The day went by and the platoon consumed gallons of water and gas. Cans and packs of tobacco were emptied. The Iraqis were supposed to have their own supplies, but instead mooched off their U.S. partners. If an IA was going to step on a bomb before him, Fitzgerald couldn't deny him a cold bottle of clean water. Besides, they would get a resupply; there was always more, they were Americans.

Mercifully, the sun descended quickly from straight above to the horizon. Its lower angle dropped the temperature and made the shadows stretch. They'd take long and short halts, but they kept going. No hot chow, no bivouac for the evening, they kept trudging along to the objective.

The daylight began to slip under the horizon and Fitz called a short halt to prepare Night Vision Goggles and swap out dark for clear eye protection. Some simply put their sunglasses away and didn't bother with another binding plastic burden. The soldiers attached little folding metal arms to their helmets first, then their NVGs. The NVGs or NODs had different variants, some with two eye pieces like binoculars, the newer ones with just one. They clicked and snapped the brackets into place, but still angled the devices vertically, not using them just now. The men looked like armored beetles with antennae jutting out of their foreheads.

They kept walking. SOIs were still up front even if they had no night vision. The soldiers ignored the pink sunset for some time until all the light had fled. Fitz swung his NVGs down over his left eye and switched on the eyepiece. The artificial zombie-green glow beamed his vision ahead, but lacked normal depth perception. Fitz adjusted the monocle's sharpness and his mind adjusted his visual perception. It ignored his right eye, which stared into darkness as he became a green-eyed cyclops.

He felt disconnected from the ground, but still they kept advancing. The SOIs ahead prowled quietly through the farm fields. Fitz tripped a couple of times and cursed himself silently for not being stealthy. The road between Blue and Red Platoon was an easy feature to handrail, and he infrequently paused to check his map. When he did, he'd take a knee, swing up his NVG eyepiece, lay his folded map on the dirt, and check his position with a red lens flashlight and his GPS. He'd draw a tiny tick with his pencil, collect his gear, and then hustle forward each time.

Fitz's body armor weighed down on him, and his shoulders ached. He readjusted his vest and felt the cool night breeze caress and cool his sweaty skin. He felt more caught up in the momentum, than in control of his platoon and his mind shut down non-essential parts for the night. Fitz pressed the emerald lamplight for his wristwatch again and again, seeing the black digital numbers tick away the night.

21:26

21:30

21:33

21:44

He could still discern the vehicle engines behind him. They could not be sneaking up on anyone.

21:51

22:01

Fitz felt he won a game by making it to the hour.

22:09

An infrared illumination round hovered in the sky way off to his left. IR illum were parachute flares shot skyward by howitzers. The artillery shells would break apart midair and the flares would slowly float to the ground. The IR ones created light uniquely visible to people with NVGs. Devilishly smart. White Platoon must have seen something.

"Wake up. Pay attention," whispered Corefelt on the radio.

22:14

22:15

High above, only a crescent moon hung in the sky and even it kept fleeing from them. Each time it vanished behind the clouds, the inky night grew blacker. Despite his NVGs, Fitz felt he was always about to walk into something. He could see the backs of Stenracker, Corefelt, and a few other guys spread out ahead. The reflective cat eyes on the rear of their Kevlar helmet bands glimmered at him as they paced ahead. The

IA and SOIs were still up front, but had collapsed closer back to the platoon. They seemed as if they could sense Zambraynia approaching.

22:23

22:30

That was a lucky check.

22:34

22:42

22:45

On his map he approximated the town to be about a kilometer away.

22:53

Peering forward through his unearthly green vision, Fitz thought he could make out buildings ahead. Specifically, a two-story white building when he fidgeted with his NVG's sharpness nob.

"Everybody hold up."

Fitz paused and inhaled.

"Blue Two this is Blue One. What can you identify ahead with your ISU?"

He heard a Bradley engine's long whine behind him. Breyer could see better and farther with his night sight than Fitz could.

"One is this is Two. Thermals show multiple buildings ahead and a few dismounts moving around."

"Two, One. Acknowledge all."

Fitz rested on a knee and took a swig of water. The rest of the platoon had already done so. SSG Corefelt ambled back to Fitz and sat down on the ground next to him.

"Whattaya think, sir?"

"I guess we're here. Let's start by getting the Iraqis online and th-"

POP! *Pop! Pop! Pop!*

They were interrupted by far-off gunshots. Warning shots. Everything else was still. Corefelt delicately raised himself to a crouch and peered around cautiously.

"One this is Two. Somethin' changed. Lots more movement in the town now."

"All Blue Platoon elements hold up. Blue One send me your frontline trace." It was Holt.

Fitz whipped out his map and fat fingered his grid. Corefelt protectively put his back to his LT and started methodically scanning in a circle.

"Black Six this is Blue One. My frontline trace is Mike Bravo Fife Zero Six Fife — Seven Zero Fower Fower."

"Roger that Blue One. Hold your position for now….. Conduct an area reconnaissance of Objective Zambraynia. Recon guidance is stealthy and deliberate. Engage the enemy only if engaged."

The radio mike keyed again.

"Be prepared to attack Objective Zambraynia in four hours. Black Six OUT!"

Fitz spent the next few hours preparing his men and equipment for a fight. Killing others without dying as well took significant effort.

Fitz couldn't do too much to probe into Zambraynia without kicking the hornet's nest. He pulled back the SOIs and IA to within his platoon so he could control them. If not, they'd wander into Zambraynia, start shooting, or who knows what. The Arabs were content with his orders and most flopped over and snoozed on clumps of dirt or sleeping mats they'd brought.

The NCOs had priorities of work that they did without their lieutenant's direction. SSG Corefelt ensured the platoon restocked ammo, water, batteries, and did a field cleaning of some of the bigger crew served weapons. No one wanted to disassemble a machine gun in the dark in an Iraqi dirt patch with jihadists about, but these weapons had been used over the past days. Wiping the carbon gunk off a bolt or brushing away accumulated brown dust might prevent a jam or a misfire.

Meanwhile, Breyer's Bradley turret pivoted slowly and canvassed the town with its night sight. He used his thermals to draw a sector sketch of the buildings and his laser range finder to confirm distances. Knowing exact distances greatly enhances the lethality of direct and indirect fires. This and other observations was about the best anyone could do with a "Look but don't touch" night reconnaissance.

At midnight, the SOI brothers, IA Mulazim, and Fitz were summoned back to Captain Holt's Bradley for a war council. They clustered around the lowered, back ramp, and Holt gave the same brief he'd given Fitz a day before, albeit less detailed. They'd attack in the early morning and Holt stressed where the Arabs should be during the engagement. He wanted them involved, but didn't want them in the way or committing fratricide. The message resonated clearly for Fitz: guide your little brothers, make sure they don't get killed or shoot us.

Fitzgerald was too tired for conversation. He bummed cigarettes from Ali and Abbad and stood there for solidarity. The Arabs were fascinated by helicopters and kept asking when the helicopters would arrive. Magical American dragons that would smite their enemies effortlessly. Captain Holt humored them.

"Army Close Combat Attack helicopters will be on call throughout this whole fight," briefed Holt. "The FSO, LT Peppel, and I will control them."

"Apaches?" Ali asked eagerly.

"Yes — Apaches. And maybe some Kiowa's or Little Birds. We've requested those air assets, they'll be here."

This assurance made all the Arabs chatter and smile. Bedouins love to fight, when they know they're going to win. The uncertainty of a fair fight makes them reconsider.

They bubbled and buzzed, visibly relieved after the helicopter comments. The rest of CPT Holt's speech was a pep rally to bolster more confidence. Holt finished and the council's members dispersed for other conversations. Fitz saw the opportunity for a side bar and approached CPT Holt.

"Sir — you gave me four hours until this kicks off. Why not earlier? They know we're here."

Holt looked at him with a sly smile. They paced away from the Bradley to ensure they were out of earshot.

"Of course they know we're here, but they want to attrit us like Courage Troop. Wound or kill a few guys. They don't care if they lose twenty foreign fighters doing it. That's why they haven't bugged out already. That would be a victory for them."

"Then why not earlier? Why wait till 0300?"

"Because that's sleepy time, LT. Look how tired you are. 0200-0300 is the perfect time to hit them while they're catching a quick nap before sunrise. That's when they think we're coming. That's what I told our Arab friends here."

"Oh…" guffed Fitz. Through his fatigue, that bead of clarity made simple, smart sense.

"Get back to your guys and keep observing the objective. Send me a report at 0250 and, based on that, I'll give you the go ahead."

"Yes, sir," Fitz said.

"That's good tho Eddie — keep thinking. That's what officers are supposed to do."

Holt was right. Fitz's mind ached and protested at being kept awake. He had gotten some coffee and bummed a dip of Copenhagen, but it seemed that almost everyone else had bedded down for the night. The one exception was Corefelt, who roamed around like a tranquilized bear, keeping a quarter of the platoon up for security. The SOIs and IA snored loudly on their mats. The Bradley turrets pivoted slowly to prove that someone was still awake, but Fitz knew the other two crewmembers were catching Z's. Especially the drivers.

He played the watch game again and paced around until 0230. Then, freed by an arbitrary digit, he walked over to the back of Breyer's Bradley. He pried open the rear crew door, the lever giving with a muffled clank, and crept inside the metal monster. He shambled through the oval porthole and crouched inside the dark crew compartment. Dim blue lights from tiny bulbs winked at him, and Breyer's gunner roused from his improvised bed on the crew seat. The gunner, Arnold, had racked out on a seat cushion with a camouflage blanket and his helmet as a pillow. Seeing Fitz and no danger, he flopped his head back down and resumed snoring energetically.

The whole compartment smelled like man odor: unwashed, unfumigated, stank in a can. Completely inside the Bradley now, Fitzgerald could feel its pulsating hum. The turret, a metal cylinder within this steel box, whined and hummed, white light emanated from behind its corrugated skin. He scuttled up to the turret and pounded on the turret shield door.

"Is that you LT?"

"Yep."

"Ok...Hold on."

Fitz watched as Breyer rotated the turret back to the 12 o'clock position. The machine whirred, and the white inner light danced, as the metal wall rotated. The inner and outer aluminum skins had to align to allow anyone to crawl from the back to the turret.

Breyer lined it up neatly and then unlatched the shield door. He slid it open with a WOOOSH. Fitz squinted in the brightness and looked up at Breyer. The dials inside the turret twinkled with more white, green, and red lights. Breyer peered down from a step and his commander's seat. His CVC was off and he wore a felt PT cap over his bald head. His big ears made him look like Dopey from the Seven Dwarves.

"Hey," said Fitz. "Seen anything?"

Breyer took a second to spit tobacco into a cut up Mountain Dew bottle. His bottom teeth were brown with the lump of tobacco saddled in it.

"No, sir. A technical truck drove away about two hours ago from the town. Besides that I haven't seen nothing."

"Fantastic," Fitz said flatly. Captain Holt was right, it was sleepy time for jihadists.

He exhaled deeply and collected his thoughts. Breyer eyed him wearily.

Alright. Let's begin.

"Sergeant, hand me the troop net there." Fitz pointed to the two, radio, voice mikes clipped inside the turret wall right above his head.

Each was connected to a radio at the 6 o'clock of the Bradley turret. One for the platoon net, the other for troop.

Breyer carefully unclipped it and handed it down. Its long, curled cord stretched with the distance.

Fitz keyed the mike and waited the long moment for the net to beep.

"Black Six this is Blue One. Black Six this is Blue One…"

The net was mute for a groggy instant. Arnold snored merrily along.

"One this is Six. Go ahead."

"Six, negative contact in my sector for the past two hours….. looks very tranquil."

"Good. Get your guys set. Be prepared to attack in two-zero mikes."

"Wilco."

"Alright LT, show me what you got. Six out."

CHAPTER NINE

BLUE PLATOON CAUGHT AL QAEDA NAPPING.

At 0305 Fitz gave the order, and his Brads started spewing High Explosive rounds into enemy positions on both sides of the canal. The twenty-five millimeter HE churned up the figures in the gunner's sights. In unison with them, the dismounted troops opened up with their small arms. The IA and SOIs fired wildly with their AK's up in the air and sprayed bullets around and over anything towards their front. The air filled with whistling ruby and glowing green tracers, straight and curved streams of angry hornets careening forward into enemy dirt mounds. Some rounds ricocheted at sharp angles with a shrill whine. The cacophony was exhilarating, as it reverberated across the landscape. Reality seemed to shudder from it.

The Brads ceased their thirty second fusillade, and Corefelt and the NCOs kicked and shouted at the Arabs to move up. The Al Qaeda scouts hadn't had a second to react, and now their bodies were peppered with metal slugs. The IA and SOI Jundi gleefully surged forward into the nearby holes to rob the corpses. Fitz could make out a black-clad figure sprawled over torn-apart sandbags on the other side of the canal. The long, limp body hung out and almost touched the water. Part of the jihadist's head wasn't there anymore.

Small arms fire furiously spurted at Blue Platoon from the buildings in Zambraynia and Fitz ordered the Brads up to the canal line. Their engines roared as they clanked forward, careful not to crush the infantry scattered before them. The men took to the ground or hunched behind the Bradleys for safety. Although the first few minutes had been successful this fight was just starting. Normal and IR flares popped in the sky and torrents of tracers were exchanged on the peripherals. Red Platoon also began advancing, which the AQI didn't like much, either. More and more chatter and noise flooded the radio, and Fitz had to focus his mind to sift through what was relevant and what was not.

"Blue One this is Black Six. Sitrep, over."

Fitz hunkered down by a mound fifty meters from the canal now. He struggled to hear Holt's transmission clearly over Breyer's Brad shooting behind him.

"Six this is One, have moved up to the canal and are now engaging the enemy. Receiving a lot of small arms fire from town."

"Acknowledge, One. Maintain fire superiority and send hostile, crew served weapons grids to the mortars net. Keep it up!"

Bullets pinged off the adjacent Bradley. The turret's air intake shrieked as it tried to cool its overheated main gun. Fitz's heart and mind were racing. It seemed impossible that he'd been exhausted only moments earlier.

He paused and listened to the crescendo of small arms fire. The snap, crackle, and pop background noise held steady, but as soon as either side tried to move the rushing crackling would increase at a frenetic rate. Seconds before a Bradley would start spiting its larger rounds across the canal, its cannon's feeder would emit a shrill, metallic whine. With a hog's squeal it would spin and feed more rounds into its hungry maw. And then the rounds would fire. Donk. *Donk, Donk, Donk.* The much larger, beer-bottle-sized rounds rushed overhead and crashed into buildings in the semi-darkness.

As the Bradley spat another stream of glowing, white metal, Fitz shifted positions. He bounded over to another mound that Corefelt and Northland were coiled up behind. Corefelt had grabbed Northland's machine gun and was banging the side of it with his bare hands. Fitz wriggled closer behind the embankment and caught his breath.

"Dammit man — when was the last time you cleaned this thing!?!" Corefelt berated Northland.

"Just yesterday, sergeant."

"YESTERDAY! What the FUCK were you doing last night?! You've got grime all over the bolt here — no wonder it jammed!"

With a bash Corefelt ejected a bent round out of the weapon's breech. "SEE!" He held it up to Northland even though no one could see anything in the faint light.

"Sorry, sergeant," muttered Northland. It was astonishing that one man could scold another in the middle of a firefight.

Corefelt tore off his glove and wiped down the bolt and the top of the feed tray with it. He did the same with the cover and then stuffed the dirty glove into his back pocket.

"Alright — now try it."

Northland reattached a drum of ammo and rocked back the charging handle on the side of his gun. He propped it up over the berm and pulled the trigger. CLICK. The machine gun didn't comply.

"It's on safe, dumbass."

"Oh yea," Northland laughed. He pushed in the safety and was rewarded with the weapon's bark. He gleefully started spraying bullets in the enemy's direction.

"HOOAH! There you go Northland! Fuck 'em up!" Fitz yelled out in encouragement.

Northland's screw up momentarily forgotten, Corefelt and Fitz watched him add his gun's voice to the symphony. As Northland would traverse left or right he'd chop up reeds with his M249 like a lawnmower. The flying plant particles pelted their heads and caked them with green splatter. Fitz paused to wipe it off his face. Corefelt smiled proudly at the LT and shrugged his shoulders. All was forgiven.

Fitz touched his wristwatch's lamplight and it read 4:38. How had that much time passed? He looked around and made an assessment: Blue Platoon was stuck. They'd walloped the AQI forward positions, but this canal to his front would stop any vehicle from fording it. Its bank walls were steep and he couldn't tell if its water happened to be shallow or deep. Captain Holt was right, they'd have to sit here as Support By Fire until one of the other platoons flanked or daylight revealed new intelligence.

It dawned on Fitz that this whole time he hadn't fired his M4. Well, if they were SBF he might as well make the most of it. He waited for Northland to start reloading, before he angled himself up a little higher and popped off his first rounds in combat.

The sun took its damn sweet time rising that morning. Even without their NVGs, there'd been ample illumination all night from flares, tracers, and moonlight. But now it was an offsetting twilight between night and dawn. Fitz didn't know if he should keep his NVGs on or use the natural light.

Time flew or crawled by, depending on the moment. Fitz lost track of time, during short exchanges of gunfire or periods on the radio. Fitz's adrenaline piqued every time he shot or was shot at. He wild-eyed, fucking LOVED it. One radio report he'd sent up from Breyer's Bradley must have taken twenty minutes. His memory reduced it to a few quick images of him scribbling in his notebook and cradling the radio mic between his neck and shoulder. Other moments were insufferably slow. When the shooting would slow to a lull, time limped by. Lying behind a berm, it seemed that he had stared at the putrid canal and adjoining Zambraynia farmhouses for hours. His mouth was parched, and he could feel the loose soil that had gotten into his gloves. The night fighting had been a blur, but now he was stuck near the canal in its clingy, morning dew.

A faint gurgle from the canal below made him snap back to his front. He scanned the steep sediment and down to where the black water bended out of his sight. Was that bubbles he saw further down the way? The reeds poking out from the murk swayed slightly with the breeze. Who knew how much Saddam-era, rancid trash and mutated river creatures swam in this filth? He'd prefer to stay out of it.

Dangerous sounds brought his attention back from the canal. The hissing pops of small arms fire were enough to remind him to stay low. A shrill whistle rang overhead and a muffled explosion sprang from somewhere behind him. It sounded like an inflated trash bag being popped, accompanied by a tremor that cascaded from its origin. There was a pause and then another sharp whistle and crump, only this time creeping back closer to him and some of the platoon behind the berms. FUCK! These bastards were directing mortar fire on his position.

He keyed his radio mike:

"Two this is One. We're receiving indirect fire. Identify any plausible observation points in these outlying farmhouses and light them up!"

"Roger that, One!"

Breyer's mike transmitted for a second or two longer and a *"Shake and Bake!"* came out onto the airwaves.

The hog's squeal behind them returned and Breyer's Bradley's familiar "Donk...Donk, Donk, Donk" muzzle sounds reverberated across the landscape. Fitz marveled for a second as the highest masonry of the village crackled and fell away in puffs.

Another closer crump and jarring tremor rocked Fitz and he heard a sharp cry fifty feet away. Two IA Jundi had just been bullseyed by a mortar round. Shit. This observer wasn't neutralized.

Somehow one of the Iraqis had survived the impact. He wailed like a wounded animal. A pitiful, anguished cry for help. Gonzalez the medic started bounding over to their fighting position, berm by berm.

Three more shrill whistles sounded in rapid succession and the poor Iraqi was blanketed with crackling explosions and a plume of brown dust. Fitz winced and grinded his teeth, as the concussive force made his ears ring. The Jundi didn't make any more sounds.

Fitz wiped grime from his eyes and peered ahead into the town. Where was this guy? It still wasn't bright enough for him to put on his ballistic sunglasses. Nothing occurred to him as he scanned the flat farmhouses and rooftops. A lot of mangled antennae and electrical wires. No scurrying or movement. No movie cliché church steeple, hiding some German sniper.

He looked over to his right side where Northland was bunkered down behind another dirt pile.

"Northland — you see where this FO is?"

"What, sir?"

"DO YOU SEE where this observer is?" Fitz shouted.

"NO!....sir," Northland added with a giggle.

Another mortar's shriek interrupted whatever Northland was saying next and exploded behind them. This time Fitz heard metal fragments cutting through the air, and he burrowed into the ground to try and avoid them. His helmet brim ploughed through the dirt, tossing some onto his face. He spat the dirt out of his mouth.

Northland, squatting, hadn't dove for cover like Fitz. Instead, he paused oddly and dropped his weapon. He looked down at it and appeared to be searching for words. He turned to look at Fitz and then sagged forward, falling flat on his face.

He rolled onto his side and screamed. Then started writhing, clutching his left arm with his right. He kicked his legs wildly, as if to fend off his tormentor. He stopped screaming to gasp for breath, and then started wailing again.

If the Jundi's fate was any indication, a second mortar round had Northland's name on it. Fitz could not let that happen. He clipped his M4 to his vest and sprinted over to Northland.

"LT — I'M BLEEDING..."

"I know buddy, I got you," he said.

Fitzgerald scooped up Northland and threw him onto his back in a fireman's carry. Thank goodness Northland weighed less than 100lbs. There's no way he could carry one of the bigger boys like Corefelt.

Fitz turned around to get Northland to safety. His lungs burned as he sprinted away from the berms and back toward the Bradleys. Northland's weight pushed hard into his back and made his legs want to buckle. Every other step Fitz took, one of Northland's plates would grind against Fitz's shoulders and make him wince in pain. He looked ahead and saw how far away the Bradleys and safety were. Fitz started to panic, he was not moving fast enough, and they were not getting away.

"COVER!" shouted Corefelt and everyone started firing into the village, so that Fitz had a chance to get Northland out of danger. The line of Bradleys behind them followed suit and sprayed the outlying buildings with fire. Hopefully, that would keep the observer's head down.

The shrill sound of incoming mortars triggered Fitz's adrenaline, and he dove forward as far as he could. Northland toppled off of him, limbs flying, and they both tumbled onto flat dirt that offered no protection. The explosions crumped nearby, but were mercifully off target. Fitz wheezed and felt Corefelt grab the back loop of his vest, lifting him up. Gonzalez started dragging Northland, and all four of them stumbled the last hundred feet to the Bradleys.

The four of them collapsed behind Breyer's Bradley. They huffed and wheezed raggedly; Corefelt popped off his Kevlar and stood up, still trying to catch his breath. His big, bald, shaved head was drenched with perspiration. He bent over, leaned on his knees, and started hacking up his lungs.

"Sir," Corefelt's breath was ragged and his sentences were gasps, "it's a good thing…. you don't weigh….much."

"Shut up sergeant," He ripped off his helmet and gloves, and tossed them aside. He couldn't breathe with all that itchy, restrictive gear on. He rolled over onto his back and tried to regulate himself. The air felt cool on his uncovered head.

Someone propped Northland up against the Bradley's tracks. Gonzalez was already working on him.

Fitz took stock of the situation, still catching his breath. Corefelt sat down next to the LT, with his back resting against the Bradley's armored hulk. Northland cried and whimpered pitifully.

Gonzalez was more concerned about Northland's wails than the severity of his wounds.

"Private. PRIVATE! Shut up! You're going to be fine. You're crying like a little bitch."

"Doc — how bad is it?!"

"You got nicked by that shrapnel. Could've been a lot worse."

Gonzalez had removed Northland's armor and ACU top, and sheared away his tan t-shirt. He'd doused Northland's whole shoulder with brown iodine and then wrapped a pressure dressing over the wound. He used additional bandaging to secure the covering in place and neatly tucked the dressing knots under the bandages. Gonzalez finished it off with artistic flair, pulling out a black sharpie and writing the date time group.

"Do I get morphine?" Northland moaned.

"Nope. Little bitches don't get morphine."

To accentuate that Gonzalez wrote "NO MORPHINE" onto Northland's bandage.

Seeing Northland safe, calmed the two men down. Fitz felt secure, even if the battle continued to rage around them. He scooped up his gear and moved to the rear of the Bradley. He banged on the combat door and then turned the heavy handle to open it. It swung open with gravity. Of course it wasn't locked.

He ducked inside and closed the hatch behind him. He had to give it some ass to pull the solid door shut and latch it at the same time. The turret shield door slid open behind him.

"Is that you LT?" yelled Breyer.

"Yea, it's me." Fitz yelled back.

Fitzgerald flung his Kevlar and gloves onto a troop seat and shimmied over to the turret door.

"Any traffic on the net?"

"Roger, sir," Breyer said. "Squadron's been pretty active for a while. I think the colonel's coming out to us. They may have gotten hit."

"Wonderful. Maybe he'll bring up some ammo along with his Personal Security Detachment warriors."

"If you ain't first, you're last." Breyer shrugged. "You want to listen anyway?"

"Yea — give me the hand-mic."

Breyer handed down the mike and Fitz took the corner of the troop seat closest to the turret. He rested the earpiece against the side of his face as the curled cord straightened out to reach him. He listened. At first it was empty static.

"Two this is Four. We got the wounded and are CASEVACing them back to Dolby along Route Bug."

Morons. Why were they on Bug?

"Roger that. We're going to link up with EOD and continue to push up to Bushmaster."

Fitz sighed. "Breyer — did you hear how all that happened?"

"Nah, sir. I only switched over from the troop net ten minutes ago. They were hot-rodding up Route Bug to get close to us and I guess hit something. Couple guys wounded. Hopefully not bad."

Fitz sighed again.

"Ok — can you switch it over to the fires net?" Fitz asked.

"Sure." Then a pause. "Which one's that?"

"Try 52800."

"Got it." Breyer punched it in the radio and hit STO.

The radio chirped and then belched static.

"Longbow Six this is Red One. I have eyes on the village and will talk you onto enemy targets."

. . .

"I copy you Red One. Continue."

"Targets are the large buildings about one thousand meters from my location. Receiving numerous small arms fire from the two story house with a deck. Target will be marked by tracers."

Damn. Lee sounded lethal over the radio.

"Disregard marking target, Red One. I see it."

Fitz wished he could see which enemy were being targeted. Maybe that mortar spotter was included.

We'll be conducting a strafing run over you Southeast to Northwest."

. . .

"Inbound now."

Fitzgerald heard an approaching roar of turbine engines and the menacing beat of their rotor blades. The rush of the rotor wash was deafening as it passed over him. Everything rattled. As he braced to bear it the sound began fading, fading, and then was gone.

A couple moments elapsed, and then Lee got back onto the net.

"Longbow, good guns, good guns. Come back around for re-attack."

"Negative, Red One. We're headed off station to refuel. You're on your own for now. Longbow Six out."

CHAPTER
TEN

THE FULL MORNING LIGHT confirmed that Bushmaster Troop was bogged down. They had held the initiative, but now couldn't find a spot to ford the canal. And that resilient AQI spotter wasn't dead. Or he'd been replaced by his equally skilled friend. Every time somebody moved, a few mortar rounds got lobbed at them. The day grew brighter and hotter, as the sun rose high.

At eight in the morning, Fitzgerald could sense everyone's frustration. Bushmaster had bloodied these jihadists real good, but couldn't get inside the village. And the jihadists that were left were smart enough to hold on to their positions and hope that the Americans would make mistakes.

It became a waiting game, and Americans don't like waiting. Captain Holt came on the net and told Lee to push again with Red Platoon. Red was in the best position to do something, because the Zambraynia canals tapered off to the east.

Fitzgerald had headed back to a berm where Corefelt and Gonzalez had set up. Northland had been declared "Walking Wounded" and was making his way to the Casualty Collection Point in the rear. Fitz surveyed his guys' positions overlooking the canal and confirmed their fields of fire. He checked the battery charge on his MBITER handheld radio. He tuned into Red's net now so he could coordinate fires and movement. They listened and waited for Red to begin.

Fitz heard the revving of a General Motor's engine and gave the order to fire.

Two of Lee's Brads, Red Two and Red Three, started bounding north towards the town, while the rest of Red and Blue gave covering firing. Their fire was thick enough to keep down any significant rebuttal but the mortars predictably started falling as soon as the Brads began moving. Each mortar came in the same: a low whistle, a crunch, and then the ground convulsed.

It appeared that these mortar rounds were lower caliber (61mm and 81mm,) which meant only a direct hit could really hurt a Bradley, but it was enough to rattle the crews. They didn't want to be stationary for too long.

Fitz couldn't see much of their progress, but he heard about it shortly.

"Red One, this is Two."

"Two, One, Send it."

"We're stuck. I don't think we threw a track, but I think we ran over and pulled some concertina wire with us — my driver says he can see it out of his hatch. Wrapped around the drive sprocket."

Fuck. Red Two's crew was not about to get out of their armored hull to fix it anytime soon. More whistling steel crashed in around the stopped Bradley. This advance wasn't working. Corefelt yelled at the platoon to reduce their fire.

"DON'T GO BLACK ON AMMO YOU IDIOTS!"

"Red One this is Black Six, I'm coming up behind Blue, hold what you got."

"Roger that, Six."

Through all the noise Fitz could detect a nearby diesel engine charging up behind him. It was Holt's Bradley. He watched it crest over the uneven landscape behind them as it came closer, its hull bobbing up and down over the ruts. It stopped a few hundred meters behind Fitz at Breyer's Bradley and a few soldiers popped out the back rapidly. It pivoted quickly and then started churning over to Red's position.

A couple minutes later Breyer called Corefelt on the platoon net.

"Blue Four this is Two, can you get One back to my Brad?"

Fitzgerald looked over at Corefelt. Corefelt couldn't help but smirk and play coy despite everything else going on.

"And why would he want to do something like that?"

"The Squadron Two is back here and needs to talk to him."

Another look from Corefelt.

"How the hell did he get up here?"

"I dunno. Just relay it."

"Yea, yea. He heard ya. Acknowledge."

Corefelt couldn't help himself. "Oh sir, the Squadron Two requests your presence back in Sergeant Breyer's Bradley."

Gonzalez cracked a laugh.

Fitz shot Corefelt a death glare. Now he had to deal with the S-2's untimely request and Corefelt's wisecracks. In a combat zone no less.

"Thanks sergeant, you're the best."

Despite the jokes, the squadron intelligence officer didn't have a reputation for wasting people's time. From what Fitzgerald had heard of him, he was a former Bushmaster LT that had been moved up to squadron once he made captain. And the fact that a staff guy had managed to make it all the way out here during this fight meant that he had some balls.

"Alright — I'm going to go see what he wants."

"Yes, sir... oh and one more thing."

Corefelt leaned closer with a clownish grin. Fitzgerald braced for it.

"What, sergeant?" he snapped.

"Change your radio back to the platoon net. I'm tired of taking messages for you."

Fitzgerald growled and rolled his eyes. He took a second to pull himself up into a runner's stance and then did a crouching sprint back to Breyer's Bradley.

In a huff and a blur Fitz zigzagged his way over to the back of Breyer's Brad. He paused to catch his breath, and then banged on the ramp to announce his presence. The combat door swung open, and he found Captain Leery in the back peering over a map. Leery was a smaller guy with a big cranium and shrewd eyes. He'd taken off his helmet to reveal a shaved, sweaty head. His hair follicles revealed that male pattern baldness loomed on the not-so-distant horizon. Sitting next to him fidgeted some 19-year-old specialist with big boxy glasses and freckles. The kid had on an older ballistic vest and nervously gripped a full length M16A2 instead of the shorter M4. Definitely an intel analyst along for the ride.

"Sir — what can I do for you?" Fitz asked.

Captain Leery waited for a second to make eye contact.

"Hey LT. Thanks for obliging me. I rode up here with Captain Holt to try and get some intelligence on this AQI element you're fighting. He said you had collected some bodies of their fighters from last night."

"Yes sir, we overran some of their OPs first thing. They may be ratfucked by the Iraqis by now tho."

"That's alright — can you take me to them?"

Fitz took a long moment to contemplate that ask. It was an ask, because although Captain Leery outranked him, Fitzgerald answered to Captain Holt, his direct boss in the chain of command. He wasn't required to do anything here. But from what he knew, Captain Leery didn't make stupid requests. Maybe this could help.

"OK, sir. I'll take you out there. Just give me a second."

Fitz slid past Leery and the specialist and banged on the turret shield door. He could hear the radio chirp and chatter, alongside the gun fan. He yelled above the noise.

"BREYER! WHAT'S HAPPENNING? WHAT'S CAPTAIN HOLT DOING?"

Breyer hollered back through the thin metal door and the noise. The gun fan sounded like a restroom hand dryer going at full blast.

"SIR! HE'S HEADED OVER TO HELP RED PLATOON."

"OK! KEEP ME INFORMED! I'M TAKING CAPTAIN LEERY WITH ME!"

"ROGER SIR!"

With that, Fitz and Leery leapt out the back into the mud. The S-2 Specialist began to follow until Leery held up his hand.

"Stay here until I get back, Lerner," Leery said.

Fitz couldn't tell if it was disappointment or relief that washed over the specialist's face. He didn't care. He slammed the combat door shut and latched it.

Fitz tried to use as much of the vehicles and natural cover as he could, as he and Leery bounded over to the captured OP site. It was amazing how much the terrain changed from nighttime to daylight. Long distances were now short, large berms were now anthills. They didn't bother with trying to synchronize their movements. It was just two guys dashing from spot to spot trying to not get killed.

Constant since dawn, the crackle and buzz of small arms fire followed Fitzgerald wherever he went. It felt like a swarm of angry wasps were chasing him, always buzzing just a few feet behind him. Periodically a ricochet or the increased chatter of rounds would make him dive for cover, but he had to keep moving. Keep moving or else he'd get stung.

They'd filtered through most of Blue Platoon and now were running through IA and SOI positions. He swore there'd been more Arabs here last night. They waved and made themselves obvious as friendlies, so they didn't get fratricided. The Iraqis weren't firing too much, but he couldn't be too careful. Some were eating, more were crouching with cigarettes, and every Arab looked at him with an expectant gaze as he ran past. He conceded that having the Iraqis here with them was better than nothing.

Fitzgerald paused them behind a bush and scanned all the nearby positions. He saw Ali behind a mound with a couple SOIs, and he motioned for him to join them.

"Ali! I need your help!" he shouted over.

Ali grinned and waved back to them. "I come Feetz-gharald!"

Ali tossed his cigarette, grabbed his compact AK-47, and sprinted over to join the two Americans.

"Hello my friends!" he said as he baseball slid into their position. Here was one guy, who could be a combat multiplier.

"Ali, this is Captain Leery."

"Yes. We have met before at Dolby."

Captain Leery looked at Fitz and nodded that they had.

"Sure, OK, great," he said hurriedly. "Can you help us locate that big position with Al Qaeda we took during the night? The one with the sandbags on our side of the canal?"

"Of course, sadeeki. This way," Ali said.

Fitzgerald was reassured by Ali's presence. There were mortar craters and ripped up growth everywhere that he didn't recognize. Ali took them along a circuitous path north towards the canal. Fitz knew if he could walk along the edge of the canal he'd find it, but he'd also expose himself. He was impressed with Ali's navigational skills.

As they crept through other fighting positions, they found the two IA that had been directly hit with mortars. Fitz saw their facedown forms splattered with blood and soil. He felt sorry for these dead comrades, but didn't have time to linger.

After a few more minutes, they crept up on the liberated AQI position. They cautiously approached, wary until they could see that no living being inhabited it. Their destination dropped down into a great, earthy gash adorned with ripped and scattered burlap sandbags. Clumps of wet, grainy dirt ringed the foxhole, making little heaps that resembled sandcastles. The three slid into it and scoped it out. The hole was dug three feet down with the loose dirt deposited on the sides to make it deeper. It felt noticeably cooler in the hole compared to the surface. The spot would have been a welcomed respite, if not for the dead.

The immediate, sweet stink of corpses betrayed that they weren't alone. It reminded Fitz of a fresh, fungal rot. The AQI bodies were lumped in the corner of the trench, grotesque mangled piles of meat with scraps of clothing still attached. Footprints everywhere indicated that they'd already been moved and robbed.

Wasting no time, Captain Leery moved over to the bodies and forcibly pried the top one from the pile. It oozed off the others and slid to the side, releasing a putrid smell and a cloud of black flies. The stack was a jelly sandwich of sinew and excrement. He turned his head to the side and gagged.

"LT," he paused to cough. "Go through that one while I check these."

Fitz started to move and then stopped. He didn't work for this guy.

"Nah — I'm not going to do that, sir."

Leery glared at him and then went back to his undertaking.

Fitzgerald and Ali reclined against the trench wall and shared a cigarette. They welcomed the smoke to help mask the smell. Fitzgerald turned the volume up on his MBITER so he could hear any developments. Captain Holt and Red Platoon were on the move again. He could hear the gunfire ratcheting up to the east.

"Red One this is Two."

"Two, One, go ahead."

"We're exposed out here. They're starting to bring out higher caliber weapons against us — THOMPSON! RPG TEAM ONE O'CLOCK! GET EM! GET EM!!"

The radio net pinged again and Fitz knew Thompson had gotten them.

"One, this is Two, how copy over?"

"Good shot Red Two! Black Six and I are moving up to you from the southeast. You see us?"

...

"Roger."

"Alright, hang on. Red One out."

Fitz needed to wrap up this errand and get back to his guys. Not hang out with SOIs and Captain Leery halfway between Blue and White Platoon.

"Sir — you done yet?" Fitz asked impatiently.

"It would go faster if you helped LT."

Leery continued going through the pockets of the corpses. He wasn't finding much, but he scrupulously scribbled long notes on his writing pad.

The radio pinged and then crackled incoherently.

"Say Again??"

"Dushka! TWELVE O'CLOCK!!"

A DShK or Dushka was a Russian heavy machine gun. Similar to an American 50 caliber. Not what they wanted to have in play against them. Fitz could hear its meatier tone start to reverberate from Red's direction.

"Sir! We gotta wrap this up!" Fitz was starting to get anxious.

"LT, I'll be done when I'm done," Leery paused, irritated. Then to appease Fitzgerald, he muttered, "We'll head back soon."

Captain Leery sat on his haunches and stared intently at each corpse, categorizing them. He stuck his pen into the corner of his mouth and gnawed on it in deep thought.

"Ali," he finally said, "Did any of these guys have radios or comms on them that your guys picked up?"

"Oh yes — like this one?" Ali said.

Ali fumbled with the bandolier on his chest and opened up a pouch. He took out a handheld Motorola and showed it to Leery. He rotated the top dial to the "On" position and its interface displayed a channel number.

"We heard Al Qaeda talking earlier, but they stopped."

Leery looked at him dumbfounded like he'd just found a winning LOTTO ticket.

Abruptly then the crescendo of fire escalated and the U.S. radio net went crazy. He heard a rumble and then a brown plume of dust wafted up from the far side of the village. Fitzgerald was missing the whole show.

"BLACK SIX — ARE YOU OK???"

There was a long, unsettling pause.

"...We're fine.... We threw a track. We're immobilized." Holt sounded more annoyed than hurt.

"Alright sir, we've got to head back now!" Fitz insisted.

Ali looked concerned that Captain Holt could be injured.

"No LT — this is important." Leery turned back to Ali, his gears turning. "Ali — get them talking. Ask them if they need ammo or something."

Fitzgerald, frustrated, had switched back to Blue's Platoon net.

"Blue Two, this is One. Send SITREP, over!"

"Roger One. Red's getting engaged and Black Six just got stuck. We don't have eyes on from our position."

"Copy Two."

"Do you want us to move to the other side of Bug and support?"

"Negative. Maintain position and support by fire."

"Roger One, over."

"One out."

Fitzgerald felt helpless and frustrated. Ali started jabbering over the Motorola net.

"What'd you say?" inquired Leery.

"I asked them if they could see your tanks. And what the tanks were doing," Ali said.

They listened to empty air for a moment and then a hissing, Arabic whisper started talking at length. Ali rotated the volume dial to max so that they could hear it. It was guttural long strings without pauses. Fitz and Leery gawked at Ali and waited for him to translate.

"He says he can see two tanks and both are broken. One had moved up to help the other and it got hit by a RPG. It's...uh wheels are broken and it can't move."

"How far away is he?" Leery asked.

Ali spoke a quick message into the radio and then got a response in the same hushed voiced.

"He says thirty paces away. Up from the river."

Thirty paces! What was that? 50 or 70 meters? How could their spotters be so close without being seen and killed? Were the AQI in a trench or a bunker?

And then it dawned on Fitz and Leery at the same time. They were in the canal! Their spotters were swimming around in that gunk. No wonder they couldn't find them!

Different hushed voices relayed more intelligence to Ali. He was not acknowledging these additional spotters, just letting them talk.

"Ali," said Leery, "write all this down, write everything they tell you down!" Leery handed him his notebook and pen. He turned to Fitz. "We've got to call this in!"

Fitz fumbled for his radio. He keyed the mike.

"Blue Two, this is One!"

"One, Two, go ahead."

"We've found an AQI radio and are listening to their traffic. Codename 'Ali' is translating for us.... Their spotters are in the canals. I SAY AGAIN, AQI SPOTTERS ARE IN THE CANALS! Say again back to me."

"ACKNOWLEDGE ONE. HOSTILE SPOTTERS IN THE CANAL."

"Affirmative! Call up Black One Fife and call in rotary wing attack on the canals!"

"WILCO ONE. CALLING IN ROTARY WING ATTACK ON CANALS."

"Good copy! Blue One out!"

They let Ali copy down the AQI conversations for another five minutes. Even if this was a turn in their favor it didn't feel like it. AQI and Bushmaster were still spraying rounds at one another across the canal. Fitz, Leery, and Ali packed up their gear and hightailed it back to Blue Platoon. They tried their best to not get shot.

CHAPTER ELEVEN

FITZ, LEERY, AND ALI weaved their way back to the relative safety of Blue Platoon's Bradleys. Captain Leery and Ali splintered off to report their findings, and Fitz couldn't be happier to be rid of them. No matter what was happening, he needed to be with his guys, not running down squadron errands, no matter how critical.

Fitz ran up to the berm that Corefelt and Gonzalez were behind and dove down next to them. Corefelt had just finished firing his rifle. The sergeant ejected his empty magazine, carefully tucked it into an ammo pouch, and then pulled out a full one. He examined it, blew the grit off the top rounds, and then smacked it into his M4's magazine well. He pulled the charging handle back and then acknowledged Fitz.

"Well, well, well, nice of you to join us sir," Corefelt said.

This guy. It never ends.

"Thanks sergeant," Fitz said. "We can't all hide behind berms during this. Some of us gotta lead."

"Yea well some of us gotta fight."

Fitz rolled his eyes at Corefelt. To change the conversation, he squirmed up to the top of the berm and popped off a few rounds at nothing in particular. After he finished firing, he slid back down the mound to Corefelt.

"We found an AQI radio, and Ali translated what they were saying. It seems they have spotters in the canal calling in fire on us."

"WHAT?!" Corefelt shouted. He couldn't hear above the gunfire.

"THEY HAVE SPOTTERS IN THE CANAL!" Fitz shouted.

"OH, YEA?" Corefelt moved closer and stopped shouting. "I heard that. No wonder they keep dropping mortars on us."

"Did Breyer call it in?" Fitz asked.

"Roger — Breyer's good about those type of things."

That intel being sent up was positive, but things still weren't looking good. Blue continued burning through ammo, taking casualties, and those immobilized Brads were attracting fire from the other side. Something needed to change — right now.

Fitz keyed his hand-mic, *"All Blue elements, this is Blue One, send me an ammo status, in sequence."*

...

"One, Two, I'm amber right now."

...

"One, Three, I'm red. Need resupply."

Corefelt looked at Fitz. "Sir — I've got three mags left. I figure most of the guys are about the same or worse."

That was honestly better than what Fitz had anticipated. But it would be unsustainable for much longer. He'd have to rely on his better assets: his radio and brain.

He switched over to Black Platoon's net. He'd have to call the XO and beg for ammunition.

"Black Fife, this is Blue One."

"One, Five, go ahead."

"Request Class Five resupply, some of my squads are going red on ammo."

"FIVE FIVE SIX, SEVEN SIX TWO, or TWO FIVE MIKE MIKE?"

"All of it."

"Acknowledge One, I'll try to push something to you soon."

Fitz needed to know more than that.

"Specify ETA until resupply?"

...

There was a pause and then Fitz could hear the tone in the XO's voice change.

"One, I'll get you what I can soon enough. Red needs it more than you do right now."

"Roger that Five! Appreciate the HELP," Fitzgerald said. He got that Nitmer was second in command but c'mon guy, they were both lieutenants.

"FIVE OUT!"

Fitzgerald paused for a moment to let that friendly interaction sink in. Maybe the FSO would be better. He keyed his hand-mic again.

"Black One Fife — what's the status on getting those rotary wing assets?"

…

He waited and then repeated his plea. Was anybody hearing him?

"BLACK ONE FIVE, ETA OF AIR ASSETS, OVER"

"Blue One, One Fife, WORKING ON IT."

"Roger One Five, BLUE ONE OUT!"

These jackasses. Fuck Nitmer, fuck Peppel, and fuck Headquarters. Were they ever going to get off their asses and do anything?

Despite Fitz wanting to dwell on this, the small arms fire started up again. It rumbled like a brewing storm, and his soldiers responded by firing, as well. Corefelt wriggled up to the top of the berm and started popping off shots. Gonzalez had grabbed Northland's M249 and had set up in a break between their berm and the next. He curled his finger around the trigger and massaged steady bursts out of it. He definitely seemed to be a more active medic than others.

Fitzgerald crawled up next to Corefelt and saw that he was firing at muzzle flashes coming from a cinder block farmhouse across the canal. He guessed the range to be about three hundred meters away. Fitzgerald peered through his sight, leveled the red reticle on the window, exhaled, and pulled the trigger. He jerked it a few more times. Corefelt ducked back down behind cover, and Fitzgerald realized he should follow suit. He rolled over and slid down to the bottom of the berm. Loose soil poured over his vest, caking his backside brown with dirt.

He heard the whistle and crump of mortars again but they were over by Red Platoon. The AQI were trying to isolate and hurt Red Two and Black Six as much as they could. All Blue could do was keep firing. Fitzgerald scrambled back to the top of the berm and laid flat in the prone. He sighted the same farmhouse from before and sent aimed shots into each of its empty windows. He rolled and then slithered back down the mound again to Corefelt. Abruptly, beyond the canal came the heavier growl of a Dushka coming into play. Its sound was intimidating and the hair on Fitz's neck warned him to stay low.

"Three this is Two," his radio chirped and then crackled.

"…Roger."

"Do you see him? He's right in that alley between the two houses."

CHUNK CHUNK CHUNK CHUNK CHUNK…

Fitz could hear the Dushka's large rounds scything through the air above, and then the smack, plop, and splatter as it plowed up earth all around them. He and Corefelt tried to burrow down farther into the side of their protective mound. He grimaced as he saw dirt clods and grass roots flying by overhead, raining soil all over them. Thankfully, the Dushka's crew seemed more focused on spraying their position rather than zeroing in on anyone. One round would hit the top of their berm and then the next would continue down the line. As the gunfire swung left to hit other positions, Gonzalez took the opportunity to pull back to join them.

"See the muzzle flash?" Fitz's radio assured him that Breyer was still there.

CHUNK CHUNK CHUNK…

"I got 'im"

Fitz heard the familiar warming up WHIRRRR from a Brad and then the steady DONK, DONK DONK DONK from its barrel. A couple of crumps and then the Dushka's bark abruptly stopped.

"Watch it! A couple of dismounts came back and righted it!"

Gotta love Soviet hardware: they'd killed the Dushka's crew but the gun was fine. Another crew just ran up to it, re-adjusted it on its tripod, and were back in business.

CHUNK CHUNK CHUNK CHUNK...

This time the Dushka team was aiming at something. Probably Blue Two or Three.

DONK DONK DONK DONK DONK DONK DONK DONK ...

"Gotcha bitch!"

The Dushka and Bradley chaingun both stopped. Blue Three's engine and gunfan shrieked loudly to cool itself down.

"Blue Two this is Three, I'm black on ammo."

Relieved, Fitz sank back against the berm and pulled out his water bottle. The heat was unbearable. He drank deeply from the clear plastic bottle and poured some on his face. The warm water washed away the grime and soothed his parched face. He handed it to Corefelt, who greedily gulped the remainder and then tossed it aside. Fitz exhaled and listened. He could hear the steady gunfire but there was something else. Something droning in and getting louder by the second...

Fitzgerald looked up and saw a Little Bird helicopter hot-rodding across the sky. A couple of seconds later, his wingman came right after, barely four or five hundred meters off the ground. They were trim attack helicopters with nothing more than glass teardrop cockpits and rails on the side for ordnance. He could see both the pilots as they careened by, the sun at their backs. It was one of the most magnificent sights Fitzgerald had ever seen.

The pilots lined up on the canals and started strafing them with their machine guns and rockets. The canal water geysered up in white fountainheads, and the reeds were shredded and slashed. The rockets careened down lazily and exploded deep into the reeds, churning and tossing the stems into the sky. Smoke and atomized plant debris filled the air.

The Little Birds kept racing down the canal lines, peppering the waterways with rounds, golden brass from their guns raining down onto the earth. The shells clinked like coins, as they fell from the floating helicopters. *Clink, clink, clink, clink, clink.* Fitz marveled at the havoc. The canal water sloshed violently back and forth after each rocket's concussion. Flames danced over the reeds and brush while dark, foul smoke billowed up from the waterway.

"SIR! LOOK at that!" bellowed Gonzalez.

Fitz crawled over to Gonzalez and searched for what he was gesturing at.

"RIGHT there!" the medic pointed at something with his meaty finger.

A body floated down the canal, half covered in broken reeds. It was wearing a black wetsuit and it bobbed up and down in the turbulent water. No wonder they hadn't been able to see those guys with thermals.

The fires in the canal reeds kept spreading, the smoke obscured the sky in tall, thick plumes. The helicopters buzzed away as quickly as they had arrived, cartwheeling back and forth in victory.

White One came up on the net and reported that they had found a ford across the canal on the far side. The platoon that nobody had heard anything from all morning was across and in the enemy's ass. They rolled up the AQI flank and were punching into Zambraynia. The small arms fire dissipated as the remaining jihadists melted away.

CHAPTER TWELVE

DURING THE MORNING'S BATTLE, Major McAdam's had been a reassuring presence on the squadron net. He'd ensured that aviation and artillery assets were quickly pushed to Bushmaster, while synchronizing movement with adjacent units. As Squadron XO, he'd set the stage so that Captain Holt and his men could shine. But after a winning performance, the curtain had been drawn and he'd gone off the air. His absence signaled that it was time for Bushmaster to reform and reinforce its gains.

Fitz had gone back to the Casualty Collection Point to check on Northland, and he paused by the Bushmaster XO's Humvee to drink some water. Top Tapwell reclined in the driver's seat as Nitmer sat in the front passenger's. Top's lit cigarette lazily burned smoke tendrils up into the air. As Fitz rested against the side of their truck, the net started to insistently crackle again. The mike was turned all the way up and the sound penetrated out into the field.

"BUSHMASTER FIVE THIS IS MUSTANG X-RAY. SEND SITREP, OVER."

Fitz gazed wearily at them, his mind dull after being up for days. Nitmer and Top were drinking coffee in their seats and zoning out for the first time this morning.

"BUSHMASTER FIVE THIS IS MUSTANG THREE. SEND SITREP, OVER!!"

"Really??" Nitmer said as if waking up. "Nothing's changed since the last two I gave them."

Mustang Three was Major Causrahavek. They hadn't heard from him since the fighting began.

"BUSHMASTER FIVE THIS IS MUSTANG THREE. I NEED A SITREP AND FRONTLINE TRACE IMMEDIATELY!!" His voice sounded frantic and insistent.

Nitmer sighed and began to reach for the radio hand-mic, until Top stopped him. "Nah LT, I got it." He painfully put down his coffee and grabbed the mike, stretching the coiled cord out to him.

"This is BUSHMASTER SEVEN. NUTHIN'S CHANGED. We're exactly where we was an hour ago. When sumthin DOES change, WE'LL LET YOU KNOW." And then to punctuate it, he let go and the hand-mic recoiled back to the radio with a SMACK!

There was an awkward pause, and then Causrahavek started talking quickly again.

"...well WE NEED TIMELY REPORTS. MUSTANG SIX NEEDS THE LATEST INFO. CONTINUE TO UPDATE X-RAY REGULARLY. MUSTANG THREE OUT!"

Top took a drag from his cigarette and returned to his neglected cup of coffee. The silence was greatly appreciated.

Bushmaster Troop took a couple of hours to consolidate its position around Zambraynia. White Platoon was in the town and Black, Red, and Blue still on the southern outskirts. Everyone treaded lightly. They let the IA and SOIs poke around until EOD made it up to them. The town appeared mostly deserted, although an old man appeared to lay first claim for "war damages" on his property. The Americans tiredly told him to keep his distance and talk to the IA.

The canal fires had burnt out, but the ground still simmered. Glowing embers fell from wilting stalks and hissed when they touched the water. Smoke loitered around the water's edge, skirting the town with a noxious haze. The town had never been glamorous, but now virtually every building had gaping holes across them. Roofs were cleaved off and the walls lay pulverized in jumbled piles of broken bricks.

Captain Holt assembled all his lieutenants by Nitmer's Humvee to coordinate defense and have an After Action Review. Top walked over to join them. They were all grimy and sullen. Victorious and exhausted. The squadron commander's PSD had finally inched their way up to Bushmaster, and Holt expected the SCO would want to assess the situation.

The Bushmaster men enjoyed their moment with tobacco and cold coffee. Even the non-smokers took a long drag to catch a clean buzz. The men exchanged a few words and compliments about the engagement, but mostly they savored the quiet company.

The remaining three squadron PSD MRAPS appeared out of the horizon and lumbered toward their position. The PSD followed an EOD vehicle closely and drove in its wheel ruts. The convoy approached, until it was a few hundred meters away and then circled like wagons for protection. The MRAPs dropped their ramps and out spilled ten PSD men scrambling madly to secure the position. Top Tapwell regarded the performance and laughed. He took another drag from his cigarette and kept laughing.

"Thanks for the help!" he brayed.

"If ya ain't first, you're last," Fitz added.

LTC Gute and MAJ Causrahavek emerged from the back of an MRAP and surveyed the field. Colonel Gute assumed a commanding posture and strode dramatically towards the Humvee. Major Caus fumbled with a map case and yelled at a specialist carrying a backpack radio. They both scurried to keep up with the colonel.

"CAPTAIN HOLT! Get right over here right now and explain this!!" puffed LTC Gutierrez.

Holt grabbed his Kevlar helmet resting on the Humvee and trotted over to the lieutenant colonel. The two officers were in easy earshot of all the other men.

"Sir, it's over. The town is ours," he couldn't help but grin with satisfaction and relief.

"Yes. Fine," LTC Gute said impatiently. "But the attack was supposed to commence at noon by *my direction*."

Holt returned his look, unfazed. "Okaaay, sir."

"No really, *captain*, explain this."

Holt searched for his words like a man explaining where money comes from to his child. "Sir…It's too hot at noon for my men in their body armor to move around. We hit em' early when it was cool, and we caught them sleeping."

"I understand that, but the CG is supposed to be in the Squadron TOC in an hour to watch it on CPOF and then come out here to view specific airstrikes. It's part of his Marne Top Ten priorities to incorporate all our ABC digital systems into our warfighting! And now we have to cancel those airstrikes! We're going to get such a black eye from brigade and the Air Force for canceling those sorties without 72 hours' notice!!!"

"Well sir, what do you want me to do? Give it back?" Captain Holt tried, but couldn't suppress a smile at LTC Gute's failed micromanagement.

LTC Gute paused for a second as if considering it and then narrowed his eyes at Holt.

"Listen here, *captain*. How many years do you have in the Army?!"

"Ten, sir."

"Ahuh, well I have eighteen. There's no way you can make judgements well beyond your troop perspective with your lesser time in service! Only I, *the most experienced man in the squadron*, can make such a call! You've turned this operation into such an *embarrassment* for us."

"Sir, we took the town."

"YES, but you didn't take it *correctly*."

Captain Holt stood firm and stared back silently with his defiant eyes. He knew this was the colonel's first deployment.

LTC Gute fidgeted under Holt's gaze and then straightened up to his full height. "I'm waiting on an answer *captain*."

"I stand by MY decision, sir."

This set it off. LTC Gutierrez grew incandescent now, fuming that anyone would willingly deviate from his guidance. With this dressing down about to get even worse, Major Causrahavek finally caught on.

"Alright men, good job, GOOD JOB TODAY! Get back to your platoons!" He ushered Fitz and the other lieutenants away from the commanders, his big arms outstretched, shoo-ing them away from the scene as fast as he could. It was not quick enough as LTC Gute's shrill yells could be heard as they shuffled away.

Six hours later, Angry Troop came up to relieve them. Before Bushmaster could retire though, they had to orient Angry to the AO and sign over the two immobilized Brads to them. It'd be days before a wrecker or a recovery team could make it out here. However, despite being released, it broke the scout's hearts to leave their maimed, mechanical mounts behind. Fortunately, they'd see their steeds again, instead of having to put them down.

With that complete, Bushmaster Troop regrouped and prepared to head back to Murray for the first time in ten days. The promise of a shower, some sleep, and hot food was too seductive to refuse. The men piled into every remaining working vehicle and sped away.

ACT III

CHAPTER THIRTEEN

BUSHMASTER RODE BACK SLOWLY to PB Murray along Route Bug. The road was pockmarked with fresh craters and rubble from EOD's morning clearance. An early twilight beckoned and the setting sun cast the surrounding Iraqi fields in an orange shade. The plumes of smoke from Zambraynia billowed high behind them, as their column of vehicles motored away. Few could appreciate the view, as military vehicles aren't designed for their crews to admire the countryside. Most men just gazed out at Arabian fields through their small periscope, window, or slits. Only the gunners could look back.

The cavalrymen were exhausted, but wary. Exhilarated by victory but with no end in sight, they plodded on to their next objective. But, compared with where they'd been, it was intensely satisfying to ride home in a dry, safe vehicle with a padded seat. They could finally turn parts of their minds off. Some crews had rigged internal speakers to play tunes in their vehicles. Whether it was Sinatra, Tupac, or Britney Spears, if it was American, it sounded sublime.

Eventually, after dark, they rounded the last curves in the road into Murray. They could almost taste the hot chow and feel the wet showers. Their stomachs growled, and they realized how filthy they were.

However, there was still work to be done. Returning to base meant refueling trucks, downloading ammunition, unloading equipment, accounting for sensitive items, writing patrol briefs, parking vehicles in line, and cleaning weapons. No man would be released until those tasks were done.

The wait made the reward more gratifying. Their chores finished, the men slurped down their Hamburger Helper Pasta Spectacular and raided the blueberry muffins and Cinnamon Toast Crunch packets. They ambled back to their shipping container lodgings and kicked out the camel spiders. Some men collapsed immediately onto their wooden bunkbeds. The more ambitious put on their PT clothes and shower shoes. With headlamps glowing, they trekked slowly across the gravel over to the green, sodden shower tents. Their prize was icy water out of leaky showerheads, but being clean felt like being reborn. Refreshed, they returned to their corrugated metal homes to join their already snoring comrades.

It took a few days to return to "normal" or whatever Iraq-tolerable was. The Army had perfected taking away a basic human need, returning it, and then calling it a reward for a job well done. Make a man freezing cold for a day, and then give him a blanket. Let it rain on him for days, and then bring him indoors. Deny him bathing for a week and then give him a ten-minute shower. Maybe even hot water, if he's on a FOB. Have him eat rations out of sealed plastic bags for a week, and then cook him up steak and lobster. Make him shit in a hole or a plastic bag, and then give him a porcelain toilet. Above all, it made a person appreciate what he had, and understand that his comfort threshold could always go lower.

Regular mail was a prime example of those luxuries. Because this was Fitz's first tour he received numerous care packages and letters from home. Family and friends were still awed by the novelty of fighting overseas. Second and third tours did not receive the same attention.

Fitzgerald checked the mailroom the first day back and was pleased to find he had two care packages and four letters. He spirited his bounty back to his bunk, where he could safely open his loot unmolested. The care packages he received were crammed full with junk food. People back home naturally suspected delicacies and treats were in short supply, so they packed their payloads with candies, crackers, Slim Jims, canned items, and EZ cheese. TastyKakes and other pastries were the sweetest prizes. They also assumed the worst hygienically, so they sent soaps, deodorants, razors, and toothbrushes. In reality, the Army had been in Iraq for a while, so they weren't that hard up on those toiletries. Regardless, no item went unappreciated or unshared among the men.

Enclosed in the packages or by themselves were also inquisitive letters. Family or friends had taken a moment and penned updates and questions — constantly asking, "How are you and how is it over there?" "Is it hot?" "Did you shoot anyone?" "What are Arabs like?"

The letters all repeated the same obligatory phrase: "Thank you for your service." Fitz couldn't understand that line. It was a sentiment he only would expect an elderly grandmother to say. It seemed to mean, "Thanks for doing what I cannot." But almost anyone could help the war effort in some way or another. It struck him as a convenient, societal cop-out said by people shirking their civic duty. Imagine doing that back home during an emergency: "Help! There's a fire in the neighborhood, and we need everyone's assistance!" "Nah, I don't want to, but *thank you for your service.*"

Yet, Fitzgerald knew it was more complicated than that. A problem on the other side of the world is harder to face. Families and obligations complicate things. Not everyone is a disposable, military-aged person or wants to fight. Civic responsibility and American pride are in decline. But even if patriotism isn't cool anymore, how could people ignore 160,000 U.S. troops in Iraq? How could so many Americans be so removed? At least these people took a moment to express thanks, but selfishness wasn't solved by just sending shelf-stable treats overseas.

He turned his attention to a letter from Michelle, a girl he'd met at a friend's wedding a year ago. They'd gotten drunk and danced together all night. He'd gone back to his Army training and she'd gone back to college, but they'd kept in touch. She wrote humorous anecdotes and asked secretive questions. "Do you do a lot of Top Secret Intelligence work over there?" Fitzgerald missed her conversation and women in general. The female perspective was always a delightful 180 degrees away from his or the Army's. He smelled the perfume on her letter and yearned for a woman he didn't really know.

Fitzgerald folded up his letters and put them in one of the boxes with the food he wanted to keep for himself. He secreted it away carefully in a shelf by his bunk. He poured the rest of the treats into a different box, ensuring that some of his precious TastyKakes got included. He picked it up and headed off to find his soldiers. They were probably playing *Grand Theft Auto* or *Call of Duty*, and he could spend some time with them.

Over the next month, enemy activity dropped off considerably in their sector. AQI had slinked off to lick its wounds and intimidate easier AO's. Despite the improved conditions, Bushmaster kept up its vigorous patrol schedule to maintain its gains. They parked their Bradleys and switched over to Humvees and MRAPs, since they were deemed by squadron as having a "friendlier" posture. Three to four patrols a day. Long and short patrols. Wheeled and dismounted patrols. Combat patrols became presence patrols. The days began to blur together.

Presence patrols were like a cop walking his beat. Although senior commanders cringed at the term, it was a known requirement of counterinsurgency. After kicking out the bad guys, soldiers drove around and ensured the enemy stayed gone. They'd talk to locals and prove to them that they'd be there if AQI thugs tried to come back and kill them for cooperating. They'd check up on SOI checkpoints and see if they'd had any disturbances. Soldiers looked for signs of prosperity like bustling markets, children going to school, and women walking around freely. They'd observe signs of intimidation like deserted streets and fresh Arabic graffiti on walls.

The heat made their work difficult. Typical temperatures over the summer were 110 — 120 degrees. Add wearing heavy Kevlar armor, a helmet, long sleeves and pants, carrying a rifle and equipment, and operating in sealed bombproof vehicles with barely functioning AC units. The heat baked them and they had to stand there and take it. Sometimes, after a man became drenched with sweat, a cool breeze would blow, and his wet skin would burn as if it was on fire. The men were hardy and acclimatized, but the day-to-day grind took it out of them.

One morning, after receiving his daily orders from CPT Holt, Fitzgerald left the CP to brief Corefelt. Fitz spoke his mind.

"Man, sergeant. Sometimes the language Captain Holt and especially Colonel Gute use makes us sound like crusaders here," he said.

"The Templars were crusaders," Corefelt said back, stone cold seriously.

"Okay... yes they were. What's your point?"

"The Templars controlled the world when they were here in the crusades. Before they lost it all to the Illuminati."

"What? That really doesn't relate to anything."

"I'm just saying, sir..."

"Get in the truck," Fitz cut him off. "We're doing the same presence patrol as yesterday. We're counting new light poles and graffiti in town."

Fitz realized Corefelt was most likely saying anything to break the tedium. What could they do or say to make today memorable? Probably nothing. They'd all been here far too long.

On this forgettable day, Fitz's platoon had the task of driving to observe the progress of some Iraqi contractors restoring broken power lines in Busayefi. They grabbed what they could for breakfast, did a patrol brief, and then rolled out. Patrols were now almost fluid, unconscious efforts. The patrol varied its route, taking different roads than the last time, approaching the site by mid-morning. Fitz and

Corefelt got out to count how many new poles had been propped up and wired. They talked to the workers with their terp, Tom. The contractors were all cousins of Jaleel and Ali. Of course they were, that's how they got the job.

The platoon sat there and watched the work, baking in the sun. They observed numerous people walking down the street, conducting their daily business. Two Iraqi girls with headscarves passed, carrying baskets.

The platoon net chirped: *"Please be eighteen!"*

That jolted Fitz out of his heat-induced delirium. He couldn't help but laugh.

"I'm all amped up on Mountain Dew!"

"El Diablo. It's like Spanish for like a fighting chicken."

The flood gates had opened. The whole platoon joined in.

"Man, I gotta lay off the peyote."

"Help me Tom Cruise! Use your witchcraft on me to get the fire off me!"

"In the words of the late great Colonel Sanders: I'm too drunk to taste this chicken."

Fitz gave them five minutes and then cut it off: *"Alright knock it off. Let's move on to Checkpoint Eight."* He paused for a second and then added, *"Shake and Bake!"*

"SHAKE AND BAKE!" someone echoed over the radio.

They drove to Checkpoint Eight and lingered there for an hour, as well. If only to show everyone that they were there. Today maybe they'd stop by Jaleel or Ali's house, and tomorrow maybe they'd stop by to visit a sheik. Sometimes they'd hit up a local falafel stand, but they could never do that consistently. No telling what somebody might put in it.

The patrol schedule started to become predictable, measuring economic, civil, and governmental improvements each week. Fitzgerald would time their patrols by meals so that they could either be back by dinner or hit up Dolby for their better field kitchen. Above all, no one wanted to miss dinner — that was just poor planning.

CHAPTER FOURTEEN

THE THREE SOI BROTHERS, Jaleel, Ali, and Abbad, had been talking about having Captain Holt over for dinner since Zambraynia had been liberated. The brothers had visited Dolby and Murray countless times for business or dominoes, and they wanted to return the favor. After a few cancellations to ensure unpredictability, Captain Holt confirmed with Ali and tasked Fitz's platoon to escort him. On the day of, Blue Platoon did the standard mission prep, Fitzgerald gave the patrol brief, Captain Holt strolled out of the CP, and they rolled out at dusk.

They drove the few kilometers over to Ali's house in Busayefi under the setting sun. Ali's home was right off the main road in a line of suburban houses built alongside a single-lane road and a tangled knot of power lines. If not for the undeveloped land beyond the residences, this could have been a sleepy street in suburban America, but with much more trash and some disconcerting cracks in the pavement. Random dogs barked as sentries as they drove up. The platoon pulled up into his backyard and set up a semicircle perimeter around his house. Although trusting Ali's intentions, they maintained security at all times outside the wire. They just didn't know what else could be out there.

Ali's property stood out as a one story, flat roofed, yellowish-tan house with an exterior wall a few feet beyond the structure. The wall looked to be the same warm color as the house and was almost as neatly painted. From the top of the brick exterior wall sprouted a foot of elaborate iron trestle fencing and deck lights. The house had large, paneled windows with the shades drawn and a solid, ornate, wooden door. Ali's house, like each Iraqi house, had a robust, distinct door that gave the home a personality. Each one was unique, so much so that there should be a coffee table book for only Iraqi doors.

Taking away from the house's well-ordered image were box AC units slapped onto half of the windows. Each had its own wooden, support struts, and no two frameworks were alike. A spiderweb of jerry-rigged electrical wires descended from the tops of street poles to connections on the roof. Two satellite dishes bolted on top hinted at Western amenities perhaps unexpected by a passerby.

Ali's residence was a real structure, compared to the many cinder block homes and farmhouses most Iraqis had in the Baghdad periphery. The home's affluence spoke that the Jabouri brothers were doing okay in these unpredictable times.

Captain Holt, Fitz, Corefelt, Breyer, Gonzalez, DeVaughn, and Picasso the terp dismounted and approached, while the rest of the platoon stayed outside on watch. They slammed their heavily armored Humvee doors shut as they got out of the vehicles. The dinner party took their pistols in but kept their rifles in the trucks. Fitzgerald offered to rotate guys inside for chow but Serrano and the rest of the gunners didn't seem too interested.

Ali welcomed them with open arms as they approached his front door. Jaleel, Abbad, and two young male children were in the foyer to greet them. The female family members were not invited.

"Sadeeki! Hello my friends! How was the drive from MEEReey?"

They all greeted each other with emphatic gestures and warm embraces, the men being accustomed and relaxed comrades. They were kin now, who had cleared out Zambraynia together. The two boys were introduced as Ali and Abbad's sons. Fitz missed hearing their names and didn't ask for Ali to repeat them.

Captain Holt and Fitzgerald took off their body armor and helmets as a sign of trust. The NCO's and soldiers removed their helmets but kept their armor on. They cared more about their lives than dinner manners. Ali ushered them through the foyer after they'd grounded their gear inside the doorway.

They stepped into a modern kitchen with appliances and tablecloths over all the surfaces. The inviting smells of cooked, freshly slaughtered meat rose to welcome them. Laid out on the kitchen table was an ample spread of chicken, kebab, cut vegetables, flatbread, rice, dates, nuts, and baklava. In a small ice tub alongside the table were thin Pepsi cans and carbonated drinks with little pieces of fruit in them. Instead of ketchup or BBQ condiments there were similar Heinz squeeze bottles with yellow or horseradish colored sauces. Fitzgerald had tasted them before and remembered how delicious they had been.

Ali was the smiling, gracious host, "Eat. Eat! Help yourselves! Take some and then we go into the main room and watch TV." The Americans quickly complied. Fitzgerald politely waited a moment for the NCOs to start and then jumped into the feeding frenzy.

Fitz grabbed a plate of chicken, some flatbread, and a heap of green vegetables. He squeezed a generous glop of the yellow sauce onto the side of his plate and snatched a Pepsi. Balancing all this in his hands, he maneuvered past everyone and secured a spot on a couch in the TV room. There were two ample cushioned couches to choose from, one crush orange and the other lime green, both facing a large television set. The plush sofas' tassels and pillows were of a distinctively 1970's style, but they were new and inviting. Omitted either culturally or by design, there were no family photos in the room, in their place hung bright paintings of horses and exotic eastern temples. They were the type of paintings expected at an American flea market but here seemed less ridiculous. The decor adhered to a tacky, retro, Persian vibe, and it worked.

The party filed into the room with their dinner and got comfortable. Jaleel, Ali, and Holt took the couch in the corner. Abbad and Ali's son sat next to Fitz on the other couch. Picasso strategically positioned himself in the middle within earshot of every conversation. The rest of the men took the remaining seats and sank into the plush couches.

Ali made a point of turning on the TV and all the lights in the room for his guests. Fitz couldn't tell if the electricity was on now or if he'd fired up his generator. He knew from his government stability reports that these houses got two to four hours a day of juice. Most of the time.

Ali's son flipped through the satellite channels on the TV. It was either Turkish sitcoms, American movies with subtitles, or Arab music videos. The music videos were either 20 men in man-dresses chanting and dancing in a circle or a ridiculously out of shape, goateed Arab singing to a gorgeous woman. The coveted woman poetically picked fruit or stared off longingly into the distance. Despite emulating Western culture, Arab singers had not made the leap to hunky boy bands or lead singer sex symbols. Maybe that was a good thing. Ali said the music videos were from Jordan or the Emirates. No matter what, it felt pleasant to watch a little TV for a while. It was a welcomed diversion from the brutal, daily routine.

Jaleel and Ali chummed pretty hard with Captain Holt. The three talked while eating, Ali translating and Jaleel understanding more than he let on. Fitz caught the middle of their conversation.

"I think Iraq should be Amerika's 51st state!" Ali declared. Jaleel nodded.

"Ali, we're not the British. We don't want to be here forever," Holt responded between bites.

"Why not? The Iranians want to be here forever. That's why they own that puppet in Baghdad!"

Holt finished chewing. "But you guys elected him. That's the democratic process."

"That's only because there's more Shia than Sunni. What about your new election between Obama and McCain? What if the one you don't want wins?"

Holt put his food down and chose his words carefully. "As an Army officer that doesn't matter. Whoever wins is the Commander in Chief, and I have to obey him."

"I don't like that," Ali replied skeptically. "Who do you want to win?"

"Well… as a private citizen and not an officer, I want McCain to win."

Ali grinned. "You make Iraq a state and we'll all vote McCain!"

The other soldiers were content to let Holt play diplomat and conduct international relations: this was his show. Fitzgerald and Abbad savored their food in satisfied silence. Abbad didn't speak much English and they were both fine with that.

Fitzgerald wrapped his chicken, greens, and rice with pieces of flatbread and dunked them in the yellow sauce. The greens, resembling sliced cucumbers, supplemented the chicken's flavor nicely and Fitzgerald munched away happily. He only paused to wash it down with sweet, chilled Pepsi.

Once finished, Abbad and Ali's sons collected their dishes and then brought out hot chai. The boys carried them out on trays and handed one to every dinner guest. The scalding brown drink came in a clear thin teacup resembling a double shot glass. Each cup had been filled a third to half with white granulated sugar, because that was the way Iraqis drank chai. The little tea glasses tinkled as everyone stirred their sugar in with metal spoons.

Fitzgerald sipped his chai and leaned back into the couch. He half-relaxed. His belly was full and these cushions were comfy, but he couldn't let down all of his guard.

Then almost on cue, Ali pulled out some dominoes. Breyer jumped into be the fourth in the game. Shortly, Ali, Jaleel, Breyer, and Holt were all smacking dominoes loudly onto the tabletop and grinning.

Cigarettes were passed around, and most everyone enjoyed an after-dinner smoke. Ali's son came over to Fitz and sat down next to him. What was his name again?

"Want to play a game?" the child asked.

"Sure, why not?" Fitz said.

Ali's kid produced a deck of cards and half-assedly shuffled them. He started dealing piles of cards in front of each of them. As clearly as an eight year with spotty English could, Ali junior described the rules. Fitzgerald reasoned he'd start to play and figure it out.

The child dealt each of them four cards. He laid them out in front of each of them. Fitz couldn't reason if the higher or lower cards were better.

"I win!" the kid exclaimed.

"How?" Fitz asked.

Ali junior pointed to his cards and said because they were his, he'd won. It didn't matter. Fitz let him deal again.

"I win!" Ali junior proclaimed a second time.

"How? Show me." Fitz was skeptical. This time he had higher cards.

The kid re-arranged the cards in a seemingly random manner. "If your cards had been this way you would have won."

"Mmmhmmm, OK."

Fitzgerald let the kid deal another hand and surprisingly he lost. This time Fitz was dealt face cards that Ali junior had received last time. The kid kept enthusiastically dealing more cards until Fitz stopped him.

"Why do you stop?"

"Because I see what game you're playing. It's called 'I Win.'"

"No….no it isn't."

Fitz brushed the pushy child away. He finished the rest of his chai and turned back to the others.

"Ah — Ha! We Win!!" Jaleel snorted with a shit-eating smile. He slammed down his last domino with a loud "SMACK!" His grin was wide underneath his wispy mustache.

The evening ended uneventfully and the patrol made it back to Murray without incident. The men, except for the ones with upcoming guard shifts, bedded down for the night and prepared for the next day of patrols. They would dream of anything other than Iraq.

Fitz helped Captain Holt carry one of his bags back to the CO's sleeping quarters in the rear of the big Iraqi blockhouse that served as the TOC. Captain Holt bunked there with the XO, FSO, and First Sergeant Tapwell in a small room that faced out to the Euphrates. It had been a sauna room for whichever rich man this house had been liberated from. It was rumored to have been Uday Hussein's.

Holt creaked the door open and they were greeted by Nitmer snoring loudly. Nitmer and Peppel's bunkbed stood immediately inside, while Top and Captain Holt's separate bunks were off to the right and left. Nitmer and Peppel were the tripwire if some infiltrator busted in on them. From Nitmer's snores, Fitz could tell he was a useless sentry. Captain Holt said goodnight and veered left to his bed, momentarily pushing aside a hanging Ohio State flag that acted as a divider. Fitz laid Captain Holt's bag down by the door and noticed the light still coming from the first sergeant's side. Top also had a blanket hanging from the wall to give himself some separation.

Fitz took a few steps over to the first sergeant's section and knocked on the wall. "Hey, Top. Whatcha doing?" Fitzgerald definitely didn't want to barge in unannounced. Solitude could be a precious commodity here.

"Nothin'. Come on in, LT"

Fitzgerald slid back the camouflaged blanket and saw Top sitting and watching a glowing screen on his laptop. Tapwell was less foreboding now in his brown shirt, ACU pants, and shower shoes. He'd shed his scowl and stared lustily at the screen.

"What are you watching?" Fitzgerald wanted to know what warranted Top's intense gaze. He assumed it was porn.

Tapwell swiveled the computer around where Fitzgerald could see the screen. It turned out to be a bow hunter in Mossy Oak camouflage, walking through a forest.

"Hunting videos. It'll be deer season, when we get back. I *can't wait* to get back out there."

Fitzgerald hadn't been expecting that, but they all needed something to look forward to. Top turned his screen back to himself.

"Okay, Top. Have a good night," Fitz said.

"Good night, LT," Tapwell's eyes didn't move from the screen as Fitz pulled back the blanket to leave.

Fitzgerald made his way back to the CONEX that he and Corefelt shared. He hit up the pisstube and brushed his teeth outside. He rinsed his mouth out with one of his half-filled water bottles and spit in some bushes by the door. He paused and looked up at the blazing stars in the Arabian night. How could it still be so hot at 0100 in the morning?

He went back inside and curled up in his sleeping bag in the bottom bunk. Corefelt was already blissfully unconscious. Humming alone, the AC unit dutifully chugged away, pouring cool air into their shipping container home. The last thing he did was wedge his loaded M4 next to the wall by his leg before he drifted off to sleep.

CHAPTER FIFTEEN

SUMMER WORE ON and Captain Holt alternated patrol tasks to keep the men interested. Blue Platoon rotated over to the local, Iraqi Army camp each day and was tasked to train the IA to not suck at soldiering.

For whatever reason, Saddam-era methods of holding power, the lack of accountability of Arab culture, or attrition from the beginning of the war in 2003, the IA functioned as essentially offi cers and enlisted. Not that sergeants didn't exist, it was just that they were noticeably absent. So in practice, the IA had offi cers disseminating larger policy and missions to working-class soldiers who primarily wanted a paycheck. That vital link of sergeants in the middle translating organizational goals into action, checking details, and giving that necessary kick in the ass was sorely missing. And that was the nice way of saying it.

So, the IA needed some help. Having a pro-American, Iraqi Army would help keep a friendly democratic government in power and assist in rooting out Al Qaeda and other subversives. It would also be a source of jobs for all the hungry, unemployed, military-age males. It was a principle tenent of successful counterinsurgency.

To accomplish this mission, while alternating times between morning and afternoon to be unpredictable, Fitz would take his platoon over to the IA camp, PB Hawks, to train them. His sergeants would teach their

Jundi in soldier skills like rifle marksmanship, maintenance, unarmed combat, communications, and patrolling techniques. It looked all well and good, but if his *sergeants* weren't teaching any Iraqi *sergeants* how to do or control these things then there was no point.

From Fitz's vantage point, it didn't seem like misdirected effort. It briefed well up his chain of command, and it kept his men busy. Ultimately, keeping his men busy was all he cared about. This work detail wasn't that bad, once they'd arrived at the IA camp they could take off their body armor and helmets. They could reasonably assume that the IA protecting their own base could provide them some degree of security.

For the garrison's security, the IA base had been situated deliberately away from the town. Unlike PB Murray's intimate spot, PB Hawks stood removed, out alone in the farmland. Its perimeter was a tall stockade fence interspaced with gates and guard towers. Constructed out of black, lacquered wood, it contrasted starkly against the terrain. Inside lay ample open ground for training and parking vehicles, in addition to barracks, sheds, and the CO's office.

Fitz had already met the Iraqi commanding officer, Captain Mohammed, and his XO, Lieutenant Mohammed. The joke of them having the same name waned once a person realized that 50% of all Muslims were named Mohammed. Captain Holt had made great pomp and circumstance of coming out and doing formal introductions to Captain Mohammed a couple of weeks ago. Holt had secured assurances from his counterpart that the IA would participate in the training. Holt had been careful to personally pitch the training's value to Captain Mohammed and had known better than to send a lieutenant to negotiate in his stead. Even though Fitzgerald had more combat power under his control than this whole IA company, a gesture of mutual respect for rank mattered.

Captain Mohammed seemed unexceptionable, a portly Shia Arab bearing a bristly handlebar mustache. He was a Saddam-era regular who, like most Iraqi military men, spoke admiringly of those decades' strong order and coherence. However, being Shia, he obviously wasn't a Baathist, yet his genial, compliant face betrayed why he'd survived

Saddam's purges. Lieutenant Mohammed appeared skinnier and younger, but also sported a fine Tom Selleck mustache. He of course was Shia too.

Being Shia was why Captain Mohammed and his cadre still had jobs. Shia and Sunni are the two major factions of Islam in the way that Catholics and Protestants split Christianity. Saddam and his Baathists had been Sunni Muslims and the dictator had deliberately put Sunnis into all of the controlling mechanisms of his regime. So now with Saddam gone, the Shia majority government ensured their denomination held power, which in-turn disenfranchised the Sunni.

Like any Iraqi officer, once the scheduled visits by Captain Holt ended, Captain Mohammed wasn't consistently around. Sometimes Fitz would see him pulling in during the late morning, parking his car by his office, and going inside in civilian clothes to change into his uniform. It came across as merely a job to him. He appeared content that the Americans had full access to his base and trained his men without his supervision. He obviously didn't care about his troops' progress either, as usually Fitz's men had to wake up the Jundi for training when Blue Platoon arrived. Lieutenant Mohammed turned out to be equally on his own schedule. However, Fitz noted that whenever Captain Mohammed was present, so was the LT.

On yet another one of these sweltering summer days, Blue Platoon arrived to teach unarmed combatives to the Jundi. Fitz had the usual gang along with him: Corefelt, Breyer, Gonzalez, Brooks, Serrano, Northland, DeVaughn, Stenracker, Jordon, and Tom the interpreter. About a dozen IA had assembled to train.

Before they started, SSG Corefelt addressed the NCOs Breyer, Gonzalez, and Brooks: "Alright, sergeants! Find your IA counterparts and start instructing them on Combatives Level One. Let's not get too rough and remember task, condition, standards for each move at all times!"

The sergeants had no questions, and the men stripped down to their uniforms to roll around. Fitz and Corefelt took their gear off too, but hung back with the Humvees and weapons. They both leaned up against Fitz's Humvee and prepared to supervise the training.

"Oh man, sir! Just you wait until you see the NCOs in action!" Corefelt jovially began.

"Ours or theirs?"

"Well of course *OURS*, but a little *theirs* once we get them started."

"Yea, we'll see," Fitz said distractedly, watching the training begin.

About 100 meters away, SGT Breyer had circled the IA around him in a teaching formation. While Tom translated his instruction, Breyer slowly went through some grips and holds with Brooks.

Corefelt shot Fitz a mischievous look and spoke again, "I don't see any IA ossifers showing up this early for the training…"

Here we go again, Fitz thought.

"Sure… They must know they can trust their NCOs, unlike ours," Fitz shot back with a smirk.

"Oooh that hurts, sir!" Corefelt retorted feigning wounded feelings. "Why it seems like almost yesterday, when a brand new 2-L-T showed up on my doorstep without a clue!" He laughed and jabbed his finger at Fitz, taunting him.

"Ok, ok. I admit it was rough going for a bit. But I got through it, *despite your help!*" Now it was Fitz's turn to laugh.

Before Corefelt could find a comeback, SGT Breyer came walking back with a concerned look. Everyone had stopped training and was standing with their hands in their pockets.

"Hey sir — sergeant, there's no IA sergeants here."

That report stopped their jest.

"Really?" Both were puzzled for a second.

"Hey Tom!" Fitz yelled over to the terp. "Where's all the IA sergeants? Where's their 'Arefs' at?"

"Okay. Yessir. I ask." Tom answered back. He turned around and started talking with some of the IA soldiers. After an excited conversation, he yelled back.

"Lootenant!"

"Yea, Tom?"

"The Jundi say their sergeants come one day a week. Or when the officers come."

"Seriously?"

"Yes," Tom answered unnecessarily.

"*What the hell?!*" Fitz muttered under his breath.

"He also says they've already been taught this."

"Combatives?"

"Yes."

"By who?"

Tom took a moment to ask the IA more questions. "They say the American unit before you and the one before that."

Corefelt and Fitz looked at each other. Breyer stared back at them, only moving to spit tobacco juice onto the dirt.

"What do you want me to do?" Breyer finally asked.

Fitz thought for another moment and sighed. "Train them anyway, sergeant," he said resignedly.

Breyer went back over and restarted the training. Fitz and Corefelt gazed on.

"What are we going to do with these guys?"

Corefelt rolled his eyes in response.

"Sir! SIR!" It was Tom. The training had stopped again.

"What now?" Fitz yelled.

"The Jundi are wondering if they get 10 or 15 minute breaks every hour and if food and water will be provided?"

Corefelt and Fitz looked at each other in disbelief.

"Sir — I think these guys are better trained than we thought."

Despite reporting that no NCOs or officers were present, CPT Holt directed Blue to continue the training. They were supposed to keep it going and engage the IA officers about it when they finally showed up.

They had to wait until next Monday for Captain Mohammed to arrive. SSG Corefelt told the Blue Platoon NCOs to start the training and Fitz figured he'd give Mohammed an hour before he had a talk with him. The Sons of Iraq were supposed to join them as well, but hadn't arrived yet. It was supposed to be combined training to get the two groups to cooperate better. At least maybe that part hadn't happened before.

Fitzgerald tucked a dip of Skoal behind his lip and leaned back against his Humvee. He exhaled deeply and rubbed his temples. Another day in this country. The sky was a deep, aqua blue with wispy white cloud trails that traced along for miles. Just for a second, he had his thoughts to himself. Then, slowly, off in the distance, he started to register faint noises. It sounded like yelling and then a sharp, frantic, popping gunfire came from the front gate. Warning shots?

"Is that? ...What the hell?!" said SSG Corefelt.

More gunshots erupted from the front gate.

Fitz jerked out of his daze. "Get your gear on!" he ordered.

"GET YOUR SHIT ON! NOWWWWW!!" Corefelt hollered.

Blue Platoon scrambled over to the parked Humvees and hastily started strapping their vests back on. The Iraqis, still in their training formation, stood confused. Fitzgerald swung open the front passenger door on his vehicle, grabbed his own vest, and ripped the Velcro fasteners loose to open it. He flung it over his head, pulled his cranium through the top gap, and folded the sides down to cover his torso. The heft of the four Kevlar plates now came as a comfort instead of a burden. He Velcroed his sides up and looked around. The Iraqis scattered like a flock of spooked birds.

"SERRANO! Get on the radio and call troop X-Ray. Tell them the IA are firing at somebody and we might need back up!"

Specialist Serrano was already fully kitted up and holding the radio hand-mic. He always reacted faster than the rest of them.

"Roger, sir," he whispered.

Corefelt grabbed half the guys and started running over to the front gate. Fitzgerald spat out his dip and swallowed the rest of the tobacco juice. It tasted foul but he didn't have time to care. Fitzgerald grabbed his helmet and M4 and sprinted after Corefelt.

"TOM! Hurry the FUCK up!" Fitzgerald yelled after their interpreter. Tom begrudgingly started to jog after them.

They ran up the dirt lane inside the compound that led to the front gate. Fitz looked ahead, the gate doors that normally were wide open were now alarmingly closed. A couple of Jundi ran up alongside them in their ill-fitting desert camo helmets and vests. The Iraqis carried old M16s with wooden stocks.

As they approached the closed gate they heard chants of "ALLAH AKBAR! ALLAH AKBAR!!" from outside. That was about the worst phrase an American could hear.

The IA guard on the inside swung the door ajar a few feet, and Jaleel, Abbad, Lieutenant Mohammed, and some IA Jundi and SOIs pushed their way inside. An SOI shoved another SOI hard in front of him and two IA Jundi escorted a third soldier in the same rough manner.

"What the hell is going on?" Fitz asked. The IA guard closed the gate and put up the blocking bar to secure it.

Jaleel, LT Mohammed, and Tom started talking in a flurry of Arabic. Jaleel gestured emphatically, and Tom returned his hand motions in kind.

Tom turned to Fitz and spoke, "These two got into a fight outside. Jaleel says it's the IA's fault."

This statement caused LT Mohammed to bitterly start yelling in Arabic at Tom and gesturing at Jaleel's captive SOI. The detained SOI and IA both looked sullen and defiant.

"Mulazim Mohammed says the other man started the fight," Tom translated.

Fitzgerald was fed up with this stupidity. He erupted at all the Arabs. "IT DOESN'T MATTER WHO STARTED IT!" he roared. "EACH OF YOU — GET YOUR MAN OVER TO CAPTAIN MOHAMMED's OFFICE!! NOW!!"

This unexpected outburst immediately quieted the SOIs and IA. Even Jaleel, who would normally quibble, obliged. They paused for a second in silence, and then started quickly moving towards the CO's office. They encouraged their prisoners to move too with a couple shoves and kicks.

Fitzgerald fumed and strode after them. The Blue Platoon soldiers seemed confused without orders, and SSG Corefelt pulled them back from the gate. They loosely followed the procession, wary of danger all around them, holding their weapons at the low ready.

The shouts of "Allah Akbar" had abated but there were still alarming sounds of commotion and yelling from outside the perimeter.

The group marched up to Captain Mohammed's, and the IA and SOI guards pushed their captives down onto their knees by the entrance.

Fitz glared at the entourage and growled, "Keep these two outside and the rest of us will discuss this inside!" He was so sick of this shit.

He banged twice on Captain Mohammed's door and burst in. He didn't care if he now appeared as the imperious American telling these Iraqis how to run their country. Captain Mohammed was sitting behind his desk in his uniform quietly doing paperwork. Fitzgerald unclipped his chinstrap, took off his helmet, and walked up to Mohammed's desk. Fitzgerald took a long-aggrieved breath and said "Salaam, Nakeeb." He did some sort of half salute wave. He then turned to the rest of the men behind him. "Tom! Explain what's going on!"

Tom hesitantly edged up next to Fitz and started rattling off the Arabic explanation, gesturing at LT Mohammed and Jaleel constantly. Captain Mohammed interrupted briefly a couple of times and Jaleel and LT Mohammed responded in quick one-word affirmations. Fitz stewed angrily and wasn't about to lose control of this conversation. After letting Tom talk for a couple of minutes, he jumped in.

"TOM! Translate this — It doesn't matter who started it. Now the IA and the SOIs need to come together and fix this!" Tom paused, translated what Fitzgerald had said, and then looked back at him expectantly.

Captain Mohammed nodded his head in agreement. Fitzgerald gave him an intense stare and then looked around the room. "LOOK AT ALL WE'VE ACCOMPLISHED!" he shouted. "We've cleared Al Qaeda out of Zambraynia and here! We've started to rebuild Busayefi and are working together! And now two Jundi start fighting and you're both at each other's throats? ARE YOU SERIOUSLY GOING TO LET ALL OF THIS GO TO WASTE OVER THIS STUPID FIGHT?!"

He paused to let Tom translate. He started again, lowering his voice. "It doesn't matter who started this fight anymore. What needs to happen is Jaleel and Captain Mohammed need to bring their men in here and punish them EQUALLY TOGETHER!"

Fitzgerald continued his angry rant. "We have a saying from our American Revolution that applies here. Benjamin Franklin said 'We can all hang together or hang separately'. Which means we can all work together or we'll all be punished separately IF WE FIGHT AMONGST OURSELVES!" He didn't care if that made sense or not, he was on a roll.

With that, Fitzgerald let out a hissing, angry breath and stopped. The Arabs nodded in agreement and spoke for a bit. Captain Mohammed turned and spoke to Fitzgerald. Tom translated.

"I agree, lieutenant. We will bring in the men and punish them equally."

"Thank you," Fitzgerald acknowledged. He stepped away to the side to let the Arabs do their thing. He and SSG Corefelt sat down in chairs along the wall. Corefelt looked at him and nodded his head. He felt his anger converting into a massive headache.

After a moment, they brought in the offenders. The two men were still defiant but now their eyes betrayed fear. The IA perpetrator did an English stomp to attention and saluted, and the SOI braced and stood up straight. Captain Mohammed waited for the door to be shut and then began his adjudication. He sat up impressively in his chair and started chastising the two men in sharp Arabic. From behind his seat of authority, the IA commander gave a scathing ass-chewing that Fitz could recognize in any language. Jaleel, Abbad, and LT Mohammed displayed a unified, disappointed front to the perpetrators. It went on for some time.

Serrano surreptitiously opened the door and sneaked over to Fitz and Corefelt. "Sir, White Platoon is on its way if we need them."

"Thanks, Serrano. Advise them to check the perimeter, but I think we've de-escalated this."

"Yes, sir," the specialist whispered. He re-traced his steps and was out the door before anyone could ask him more.

Captain Mohammed's dressing down continued. Like many Arabic interactions it seemed there was a required time limit or else it wasn't effective. Fitz wondered if the commander had set a timer for twenty minutes.

The two men were now noticeably cowed by Captain Mohammed's ass-chewing. With a flourish and a wave of the hand, he finally dismissed them. The door was flung open and the wrongdoers were hustled outside.

A Jundi closed the door, and the standing men arranged chairs by Captain Mohammed's desk. Great, now they had to discuss this as well. The IA commander called for his attendant to get them chai, Lieutenant Mohammed opened the door and echoed his order. An orderly acknowledged and ran off.

Corefelt saw his opportunity to escape. "Sir. I'm gonna get the platoon ready to go and make sure White is fine."

"Fine," Fitzgerald acquiesced, his headache brewing, stronger than before. "Come get me if anything more happens."

"You have fun with….this," Corefelt said with a crooked smirk. He backed out of the room just as warily as Serrano and was gone before Fitzgerald could reconsider.

The Arabs started to discuss the events ad nauseam, and Fitzgerald pulled up his chair closer to Tom so he could understand. Tom commenced translating the conversation quietly for him as it began anew. Fitzgerald would stay for one glass of chai and then he could leave. It would be impolite to go any earlier.

Blue Platoon finally returned to Murray at sunset. The drivers lined their trucks up by the fueler outside the perimeter, and Fitz dismounted to walk back as they gassed up. He strode through the barrier gap at the Patrol Base's main gate and headed towards the TOC. He popped off his helmet, but there was no breeze tonight to comfort him.

Fitzgerald approached the TOC and walked in. He saw SSG Stalls manning the radio and Captain Holt on the couch watching the Armed Forces Network. Holt had an open can of Vienna sausages and was contentedly eating them. Fitzgerald made his way over to Holt and tiredly reported the course of events at PB Hawks. Captain Holt listened distractedly, nodding occasionally to convey understanding. His sole comment was, "Sounds like you got into an interesting situation today, LT" with a smile. Fitzgerald finished his report and then sunk down into the couch next to the captain. They sat there in silence. An episode of *Family Guy* played on the television and Holt merrily ate his last cold sausage from the tin.

Holt finished and stood up to leave. "Good job today, LT," he said and patted Fitz on the knee. He put on his boonie cap and eyepro and exited the TOC. Fitz could only lie there, numb in the TOC's cool AC. That was it. What else had he expected?

Fitz's head ached and his spirit was drained from the near riot. He needed to go to bed. But before he could pull himself up from the couch, the TOC phone urgently rang from the far wall. SSG Stalls pretended not to hear it, as he stared at his radios. Damn, Fitz sat closest. He weakly pulled himself up and strode over to the phone. He grabbed the receiver.

"Bushmaster CP...Lieutenant Fitzgerald speaking... how may I help you sir or ma'am," he flatly muttered into the mouthpiece. He waited for the delay.

"FITZ! IT'S MAJOR CAUSRAHAVEK!" the earpiece boomed.

"Wait one sir, I'll get Captain——"

"No no NOOO I'll talk to you. I don't want to bother Captain Holt." His usual bluster was now meek.

"Ok, sir. What's....what's going on?" Fitz's head throbbed, and he just wanted this conversation to end, but Major Causrahavek's voice sounded strange.

"The sergeant major has been trying to get class four, some wood and paint, to make parking signs at the Squadron TOC. I need to know, does Bushmaster have any white or red paint?"

"I don't know, sir. Why don't you ask your supply sergeant or the S-4?" Why did this even matter? Who needed a parking space in a war? His head hurt more.

"No.... I already asked the Four and he was too busy with other things. I just… really need to know, so I can help out the sergeant major and the commander. Can you look around Bushmaster for me?"

Fitz paused for a second, held his temple, and sighed deeply. The pain burrowed deeper and deeper into his cranium.

"Sure, sir. I'll look around." Anything to make this conversation stop. He had no intention of wasting time on this fool's useless errand.

"GREAT FITZ! I knew I could count on you! Get back to me with your results immediately!" the major's voiced boomed with its usual boisterousness.

"Roger that, sir. Out here."

Fitz wandered off to go find his bed, the absurd request already forgotten.

CHAPTER SIXTEEN

A NIGHT'S SLEEP DIDN'T CURE FITZ. He awoke the following day for the follow on operation, but this time he couldn't shake the weariness out of his head. His mind felt overcooked by the heat.

Blue Platoon's next task would be to take LT Peppel out to Busayefi and pay the Sons of Iraq their past three months' wages. The U.S. Army had started payrolling the SOIs and they were legitimately grumbling for their back pay. Bankrolling them had turned the tide for the counterinsurgency.

The root cause of the insurgency was that the Americans had disbanded the Iraqi Army after their 2003 victory. Immediately after, hundreds of thousands of former Iraqi soldiers became jobless and had no means to support their families. With no source of livelihood, no stake in the new government, and nothing to do, they were prime to be recruited by Al Qaeda.

And recruit they did. Insurgents made tantalizing offers to these aimless, unwanted men. 50,000 dinar or $50 for them to rig a bomb or report a U.S. patrol. It wasn't hard to convince an Iraqi to do this against the infidel invader who'd killed thousands of his countrymen. It was a no brainer. Especially if they had wives and kids to feed.

But luckily Al Qaeda and other insurgent groups overplayed their hands. Filled with foreign fighters, Al Qaeda extremists mistreated the Iraqis in their own country. They raped, maimed, and murdered conservative Muslims for not being pious enough. Al Qaeda revealed themselves to be self-righteous shitheads. And eventually the Iraqi government pulled itself together and rebuilt its military, although it filled its ranks with mostly Shia.

This caused tribes of Sunni Arabs, like Jaleel, Ali, and Abbad, to organize themselves as Sons of Iraq and approach the Americans. The Sunnis would police their own neighborhoods and root out these insurgents. They'd support the Iraqi government, stop bombings and attacks on the U.S. military, and establish stability and rule of law, all for a decent wage.

So each SOI fighter would get $1 a day to patrol his neighborhood. $5 a day for supervisors, $20 a day for tribal leaders like Jaleel. With 200 to 400 men per village this added up. These men didn't have bank accounts or debit cards, so a designated U.S. Army paymaster would have to draw the cash, go out, and periodically pay them. The American Army, despite its size, didn't have enough finance specialists to do this, so they had to deputize trusted agents at the lowest level to dole out the dough.

The job of Bushmaster's trusted agent fell to Lieutenant Peppel, the Troop Fire Support Officer. He was tagged, because, as an officer, he wouldn't be tempted to steal U.S. taxpayer's money and, as an artilleryman, he could probably do math. Fitz could tell that Peppel wasn't thrilled with this admin duty. Who would want to be personally liable for hundreds of thousands of dollars to the U.S. Government? It only took an accounting error or a misplaced pay slip for Peppel to go to jail. But that was Iraq, everything sucked — get over it.

That early morning, Blue Platoon organized itself, put Peppel and his bulging bags of dinar in the back of a truck, and rolled out to Busayefi. Ali had called the terp, Picasso, on his cellphone and coordinated a minor sheik's house to be used as the pay center. The house lay half a mile down a side road off the main street, advantageously away from normal traffic, but not too far removed. Set up on the house's front lawn was a white tent with two side flaps rolled up for access. Ali and Jaleel were there promptly to greet the American soldiers. Ali wore a fresh red running suit that read "Sport" in English on the front and Jaleel donned a crisp, white, man-dress. The sheik homeowner also came out and greeted them graciously. Like Jaleel, he wore a man-dress but with the head scarf keffiyeh tied tight with a circlet of black rope. The man had a bristly mustache and looked like a Saddam clone.

"Saalom Mal-akum, Mulazim Feetz-gharald."

"Saalom," Fitz said half-heartedly.

The Arabs were overly amenable because it would increase their clout or "Wasta" to be associated with the U.S. soldiers handing out currency. And they wanted to collect their cut.

The early morning heat remained a welcomed few-degrees cooler, but the sun was rising and Fitz knew it wouldn't last long. Their Arab hosts found a card table and some plastic green chairs for LT Peppel and Picasso to set up on, under the tent's shade. Fitz assigned a couple guards to him and positioned the rest of his guys outside for crowd control. He watched the first transaction to pay the SOI leaders, it would serve as the routine for the rest of the day. Jaleel and Ali presented themselves to the Americans, Picasso translated and recorded their names, Peppel confirmed their pay tier and calculated three months' pay, each one signed their mark, and then Peppel would hand over the purple and green Iraqi bank notes to them. Peppel wasn't dumb, he kept as many notes as he could in the bags, while only keeping out his working pile, but the Arabs' hungry gaze at the extra bills was noticeable.

After about 30 minutes, Sons of Iraq of all shapes and sizes started to filter up to the house, and Fitz's men checked them for weapons. The SOIs must have consisted of every man in the area: average men in their dusty tracksuits and t-shirts, teenagers looking too young, and older men too decrepit to carry a rifle. Ali and the soldiers formed them into a line down the road. Picasso reveled in his role as gatekeeper, while Jaleel and the sheik hovered near Peppel the bagman. Both Arabs beamed as each man stepped forward to sign for his wages, deferentially nodding to them.

After the first few had gone through, a bow-legged older man limped forward from the line, obviously scarred from an explosion or war calamity. His hands shook and his skin hung loosely on his face. He hobbled up to the table and gave Peppel an eager, keen look.

"Ali!" LT Peppel said indignantly, looking the old man up and down. "How can *this* guy be an SOI? C'mon, this isn't just a hand out! This money is for able-bodied fighters."

Ali feigned outrage, "Mulazim, this man is a lookout! He watch the roads for us!"

Peppel grumbled and paused for a second. The old man kept looking at them expectantly. "What about that kid over there?" he gestured down the line. "He can't be older than 12!"

"He carries the ammo!"

"Yes, LT. He's an ammo bearer," Picasso chirped in. Jaleel and the sheik nodded vigorously.

Peppel rolled his eyes but handed the old man the Iraqi bills. It didn't really matter. Money was an American weapon system. As long as they were giving money out to individuals and not a lump sum to their friendly gang leaders, they were influencing these men. It would keep the Americans' Wasta going for another few months.

After supervising the first twenty or so transactions, Fitzgerald grew bored. He walked away from the table over to Corefelt, Stenracker, and DeVaughn, who were under a nearby date tree, enjoying its cover. Fitz guzzled some water and entered their circle. He popped in a lump of Skoal Wintergreen behind his lip and joined their easy conversation.

Stenracker leaned against the tree, oblivious and presently rambling on about his new girlfriend, while Corefelt and DeVaughn looked on with indifference. Sten was good kid, but he never shut up. He stood tall like a mischievous ferret, playful, wiry, and athletic, although his RayBan sunglasses made him resemble Cyclops from the X-Men. When he grinned, he revealed crooked teeth and a few stray hairs that he'd missed while shaving. Sten kept going on and on, while occasionally puffing a cigarette he held in his right hand. He'd taken his Mechanix gloves off and had his shirt cuffs rolled up to let some air in. Fitz eased back on the balls of his feet and merrily spat some brown tobacco sludge onto the ground. He kicked dust over the spit pool and was pleased to see it vanish. Fitzgerald enjoyed the banter with soldiers and tuned into Stenracker's stream of consciousness.

"…Jen just gets me instead of Haley! Jen and I talk every day and she had a bad breakup before too unlike Haley who would only call me to complain about something and her family was *always* in the picture asking for money or trying to interfere I think her father didn't think I was good enough for her even though we are both from Appleton which really is unfair because I at least left Wisconsin to go off and make something of myself unlike her no good brother—"

"Maybe she wuz cheating on you," interjected DeVaughn brusquely.

DeVaughn was a shorter, heavyset guy with broad, squat features. He had a ubiquitous five o'clock shadow, because like most African Americans, shaving without running water wrecked his skin. In the field, the Army granted these temporary exceptions and called them shaving profiles. He usually held a look of unenthused, contempt on his face, but underneath could be counted on as a reliable scout. He'd been busted down to PFC for telling off SSG Stalls before the deployment.

"What?" Sten asked quizzically.

"That Haley chick wuz prolly cheating on you," DeVaughn said, trying to poke the bear.

Sten didn't see what DeVaughn was doing and puffed from his cigarette.

"Nah, like Haley often had guys over before we were dating but once we were together that stopped and last spring when I was on leave back home she'd even stopped hanging out with her high school male friends because we discussed how it caused too many complications with the distance between us and since her dad is a union worker—"

Fitzgerald saw his opportunity and took it. "Sergeant," he said deviously, "do you think the Illuminati control all the unions in America?"

For SSG Corefelt that bait was irresistible. His eyes got wide and he took it.

"Aw sir, you don't even know! I don't think the Illuminati have infiltrated down to that level, but I *know* that the Masons are controlling half of the unions. The Illuminati are mostly at the upper levels like in DC and at the Vatican."

"I thought the unions were controlled by the Mafia not the Masons," Stenracker said.

"Sten — that's just a misconception. Since the 1970's when the FBI, which is controlled by the Illuminati, took down the Mafia, there was a power vacuum in the unions and then the Masons moved in. Sometimes the Masons and the Illuminati work together."

There was a pause to let that compute and then Stenracker took over again with his narrative. Corefelt returned to reality and grew silent again. These conversations were part of the comradery that made their situation tolerable. DeVaughn would pop in with a crass joke, or Corefelt would continue on about the Illuminati if somebody egged him on. Stenracker would entrust every detail of his relationship to three men who by chance happened to be in his platoon. And the logic didn't matter, as long as it helped pass the time.

Fitzgerald stood there comfortable in the circle for some time and was satisfied to see the line of SOIs gradually shorten and then end. Peppel looked like he was wrapping up, Stenracker was not. Fitz checked his watch — it had been an hour.

Fitz shot his gaze at Corefelt. Corefelt returned it.

"Alright sergeant, let's get out of here."

"Roger that, sir."

The two men walked away from Sten to usher the platoon back to their vehicles. Stenracker didn't miss a beat and focused his monologue directly at DeVaughn, until someone yanked him away. The Blue Platoon men withdrew to their trucks and Fitzgerald waved goodbye to Jaleel and Ali. They slammed their Humvee doors shut and drove back to Murray.

Every night around 1900 hours each troop would report in to squadron via the BUB, the Battle Update Brief. This combined meeting amounted to a radio net call in which the troop commanders would give a quick brief, detailing their current and next day's operations for their units. The squadron commander would acknowledge and disseminate any guidance he had for the troops' activities. In garrison back home, when the tempo was less demanding, these meetings would be weekly.

Fitz avoided the BUBs when he could. If he could be anywhere else than the Bushmaster CP at 1900, he would be. However, Captain Holt and LT Nitmer had started corralling the platoon leaders there for their "Professional Development." Nitmer justified that the PL's should have situational awareness of what the other troops were doing. That was true, but it was also a sly way to get the PL's ready to brief if the CO or XO didn't want to.

Each night, Captain Holt, LT Nitmer, and whichever unlucky PLs had been caught that day would congregate around the radio in the CP, like an FDR fireside chat. The speaker would be turned up to max volume, and they'd all grab chairs to sit around in a semi-circle. Each would have a mug or a spit bottle, either enjoying coffee or their post-dinner tobacco.

The BUBs were predictably tedious but necessary affairs to keep the whole unit connected and controlled. At best they were long, with LTC Gute, MAJ Causrahavek, or the sergeant major emphasizing the latest directive by higher headquarters or an infraction they had witnessed. Last week the sergeant major had found a solider not wearing his gear in a guard tower, so he decided to remind everyone about the importance of Kevlar helmets. That lesson took about twenty minutes of airtime. Fitz was scared to brief and hoped that his time wouldn't come soon. Captain Holt always briefed with confidence and an easy-going finesse that Fitz couldn't help but admire. He reasoned that it just came with practice.

That night it was Holt, the XO, Fitz, and Lee who got roped into the BUB. Maloney and Peppel had somehow weaseled out of this one. They all settled in whichever chair they could find, taking off their ACU tops and draping them over the chair backs. Captain Holt had secured a comfy, rolly chair and had his green leader's book open with notes.

First Sergeant Tapwell came into the CP in his tan t-shirt and ACU pants. He went over to the coffee pot and poured himself a fresh cup.

"Top! You going to join us?" CPT Holt said with a smile.

"Ha! That's a good one, sir," Tapwell said with a devilish grin and darted out of the CP.

All the troops and the logistics company had come up on the net and Captain Christopher, the Angry Troop CO, was beginning his brief.

"*Mustangs, sir.*" Christopher had a nasally voice that the radio exaggerated. His shrill tone came across as whiny and made listening even more excruciating. He also didn't sound very angry.

"*Last twenty-four hours, Angry Troop conducted unit level maintenance and PMCS of all vehicles. First line supervisors ensured all 2404's were completed with platoon sergeants and myself ensuring them for accuracy. Mechanics cross-trained vehicle crews and gave instruction on operator level maintenance. BREAK.*"

He didn't need to say BREAK when interrupting a long transmission, but Christopher felt the need to.

"*Next twenty-four hours, Angry will continue to do monthly inventories of all unit and TPE equipment in order to submit to squadron. Platoons will ensure serial number accuracy and record all corresponding BII. This month, Angry will focus on grenade launchers, ASIP radios, and DAGRs. BREAK...*"

"*Angry Six — your inventories aren't done??*" LTC Gute cut in before Christopher could start another long transmission.

"*Mustang Six, ...we have until the 18th and there is that issue that I communicated last month,*" Christopher sniveled.

They all collectively grimaced. Despite not having much love for Angry Troop, they could see this was about to go south.

"*Angry Six,*" LTC Gute paused for effect. "*You have until the 18th for the Army but in 8-6 CAV we do things better. We have the internal suspense of the 7th of the month in order to exceed the standard.*"

"XO, we're good for the month, right?" Holt asked Nitmer.

"Yes, sir," Nitmer said, eyes popping open, looking like he'd dodged a bullet. "Sergeant Nixon submitted them yesterday."

"Okay," Captain Holt said easily. "Good work, XO!"

"Ha…ok. Geez," Nitmer said with relief. He spat into a paper cup he was holding.

Their attention went back to the radio.

"… and that's why we do property accountability before the larger Army suspense date. Angry Six, what exactly is the hold up?"

A long pause ensued before the net chirped again with Christopher's answer.

"Mustang Six…. There was a discrepancy on the number of night vision goggles… on two different hand receipts. I communicated the issue to squadron last month."

"Who did you communicate the issue to?? The XO?! He's on leave!"

"Neg..negative six. With the XO being on leave I informed the Three."

By Three, he meant S-3, MAJ Causrahavek, Fitzgerald could already tell that wasn't a bright move.

"I'm not tracking this! Why wasn't I informed?! This is unacccccceptable. Every Mustang Trooper KNOWS that communication is one of our bedrock values."

No response. An awkward silence hung in the air. Fitz glanced at the transmitter to confirm that it was still on.

"Captain Christopher — call me right now on SVOIP. Right NOW, CAPTAIN, and explain this." LTC Gute's tone sounded menacing.

"That's not good," Captain Holt said. He leaned back in his chair. "Losing a pair of NODs is a quick way to get relieved."

They listened intently to empty air for a hesitant moment. Was this BUB still happening? Nobody knew or wanted to be the first to ask.

Major Causrahavek came onto the net. *"The commander just left the meeting to take this offline with Angry Six. …Should we continue? I don't know, I think we should continue…"*

Please don't continue, Fitzgerald thought

"This is Mmmmustang Seven…" came the slow drawl of the sergeant major.

Dammit. Fitzgerald shook his head.

"Mustangsss….. this is un-accept-able. Like the commander said, un-accept-able. We're going to stop right here and redo this tomorrow night

in person… At Dolby. Just like a regular CUB in garrison… the RIGHT WAY. And you commanders better come pre-pared to brief or else we'll do it again… I'm em-bar-assed for the commander… the XO's em-bar-assed, we're ALL em-bar-assed. You're better than this Mustangsss… we will … we will see you tomorrow night. Mustang Seven out."

Dammit. Well at least that was over.

"Well that's just great," CPT Holt said sarcastically. "Looks like I'm going to Dolby tomorrow. Which platoon is going to take me?" He eyed Lee and Fitz.

"Black Platoon," said Lee immediately.

"Yea — Headquarters Platoon," Fitzgerald said, a little slower.

"Nope. They've got to take the FSO back to Talon for his SOI money thing."

"White Platoon. Maloney didn't even come to the BUB tonight."

"Nah, he's prepping for a midnight OP tomorrow night," the XO said.

Lee and Fitzgerald eyed each other. Dammit.

"Looks like its rock, paper, scissors," Holt said with a smirk. His eyes betrayed that he relished these moments.

Dammit. Fitzgerald sighed.

"Wait a sec, sir." Lee was up to something. "I've been to CUBs before but Eddie here hasn't. I *really believe* that for his professional development he should experience one."

DAMMIT. Fitzgerald shot a death look at Lee. Lee could barely keep a straight face.

"That's a great idea, LT. Blue Platoon it is," Captain Holt declared gleefully. He'd really enjoyed that entire exchange. "XO! Get on one of those computers and see if you can dig up the last CUB slides. Let's get to work on them." He got up and moved out to the other room of the CP.

"I hate you," Fitzgerald said to Lee.

"Have fun at squadron…" Lee said merrily as he got up. He was still suppressing a laugh as he slipped out the front door.

Nuts. Well, Fitzgerald figured he might as well go tell Corefelt the bad news. At least he wouldn't have to brief tomorrow.

CHAPTER SEVENTEEN

THE NEXT EVENING, they'd arrived at Dolby after SP-ing a few hours before dusk. Fitzgerald ensured they'd travel on cleared roads, hours before the darkness would allow any jihadists to potentially re-seed them. They'd have to wait until morning tomorrow to head back to Murray in the daylight. It was all a terrible waste of time.

Once they arrived and had gone through the clearing barrels, SSG Corefelt started ground-guiding the platoon vehicles towards squadron. Captain Holt and LT Fitzgerald didn't bother getting back in their trucks; instead, they marched on their own towards the tall headquarters farmhouse across the shifting gravel. Despite misery loving company, the officers could handle this one. There was no reason to include the men in this goat rope.

"Goodbye, sergeant. Have fun watching the trucks!" Fitz joked as he waved at them.

"No, sir! *You* have fun being mentored by the sergeant major," Corefelt bantered back. "We'll be right over there by the transient tents when you're done," the staff sergeant assured him.

Fitzgerald trailed Captain Holt as they approached the imposing squadron building. It appeared that there had been structural improvements since he last saw it — more sandbags, antennas, and camo nets. It loomed larger than he remembered. He wondered what type of ordnance it would take to bend its reinforced walls. He hustled to catch up, as Holt reached the front door. They breached the entrance together, left their rifles and kit neatly in the maw of the hallway, and climbed the staircase to the second floor. The cool, white, granite floor softened the heavy clod from their boots. Was that new too?

The Bushmaster men entered the squadron conference room, an expansive chamber overloaded with tables, chairs, and a display screen. Against the far wall, a tall stand peered judiciously down at the perpendicular line of meeting tables. This would be where the colonel would preside. Blood red tablecloths draped over the tops of the surfaces, disguising whatever unsightly furniture was underneath. Numerous chairs were nestled alongside the tables, while others stood excluded against the walls. Many were from the original dining set with worn, red cushions and cherry-stained wood, but a few gray aluminum folding chairs had been mustered to bolster their ranks. In the room's former life, it had been a pleasant dining room with welcoming windows on two sides and a balcony. Now the glass had been boarded up and sealed with sandbags. Red and Green CAT5 cable wormed through the walls and dangled from the ceiling.

The room was half-filled with other commanders, staff officers, and NCOs. Neat little placards were arranged at the table so that everyone knew his place. Captain Holt sat down behind his Bushmaster 6 sign, and Fitzgerald sat behind him against the wall. He leaned back comfortably in his chair, but a fresh spider web on the wall caught his eye. He thought better of it and scooted his chair forward a couple of inches.

His thoughts drifted to all of the battlefields he thought he'd be at right now, instead of a staff meeting. He sighed and tried to let it go. He needed to embrace whatever this was. Just represent Bushmaster well and get the commander back to Murray.

Fitzgerald observed Captain Holt mingle with the other commanders in the room. In order, there was CPT Strively for HHT (Headquarters and Headquarters Troop), CPT Christopher for Angry, CPT O'Henry for Courage, and CPT Robinson for FSC (Forward Support Company). Alpha, Bravo, and Charlie were the line units; HHT housed squadron command, staff, and support; and FSC was the logistical company. Captain Strively towered over the others with his large athletic build, flashy smile, and thick brown hair. He was a former Bushmaster alum who exuded smart confidence and spoke forcefully. Christopher came across as the opposite, an average-height, blonde man with the most punchable face. His manner revealed constant unease and he failed to instill confidence like he should have. O'Henry stood shorter, but owned it. He was a scrappy, black-haired veteran with a lot of teeth in his smile. He'd replaced the former Charlie Troop Commander, who'd lost a leg in Zambraynia. He held a reassuring, comradely look in his eyes and spoke with a Boston accent. Robinson completed the ensemble as a crotchety, balding man. He looked exhausted and complained constantly about cleaning up the other troops' messes.

The door creaked open and Lieutenant Colonel Gutierrez, flanked by Major Cauzrahavek and Command Sergeant Major DeCray, filed into the room. Everyone hurriedly stood up. The conversations died and everyone moved to their chairs. Cauzrahavek's short, boisterous laugh reverberated through the room, chuckling and agreeing with something the colonel had said. CSM DeCray resembled a half-asleep snapping turtle that should be left alone. He suspiciously eyed everyone from half-shuttered eyes, as he paced behind the colonel. Enjoying the room's deference, LTC Gute walked to the head of the command stand and grandly took his seat at center stage. He adjusted his chair and positioned himself, coiled for his meeting. His eyes had a pitiless gleam to them. The colonel pulled out his leader's book embossed with a new 8-6 CAV leather cover and laid it on the table. This signaled that everyone else could sit. A mustached sergeant first class and a nondescript 1st lieutenant claimed the chairs next to Fitz. With the squeak of chair legs dragging, everyone else sat. LTC Gute perked up in his chair and surveyed the room.

"Mustangs, I'm glad everyone could make it here," he said with a gleeful challenge in his eyes. After a moment, seeing no opposition, he continued.

"I've called you all together this evening so that we could communicate *properly*. These combat operations have disrupted our battle rhythm away from how they should be. How they function *smoothly* and *orderly* back in garrison. That's why the sergeant major and I, deemed it necessary to do this to get everyone back on track."

Sergeant Major DeCray smiled slyly when his name was mentioned. Cauzrahavek shook his head in approval.

LTC Gute turned towards LT Spinner in the corner, "Okay, S-1. Giddy up!"

The projector bolted to the ceiling flickered on and the "Mustangs 8-6 Cavalry" title slide appeared on the screen.

"Next!"

LT Spinner flipped to the next slide. Fitz pondered why a slide flipper was needed. Couldn't the colonel do that himself?

A peacock blue and imperial purple cartoony SmartArt graphic of a Greek temple with four pillars materialized onscreen. Written on the pillars were four vanilla words that could be applied to any situation: Competence, Communication, Credibility, and Care. Army values and other cliché platitudes were sprinkled in the temple's base, frieze, and roof. It was a shotgun blast of meaningless, corporate buzzwords.

"Here's our bedrock values slide," LTC Gute said, deadly seriously.

"I wanted to capture the principles that the sergeant major and I have been imprinting on soldiers, since we took command of 8-6. The Army values are fine, but they really don't capture the ethos that I want all Mustang Troopers to have. A lot of these younger soldiers are still developing and only now, after joining this great unit, can they truly be sharpened to excellence."

LTC Gute spoke with polish and confidence. He must have practiced and briefed this before.

He continued, "These core values should be intuitive for the leadership, but don't worry, I'll be your guide. Foremost, *Competence*. This is what makes us Mustangs and cavalrymen, we exude confid—"

"SCOUTS OUT!" "RECON!" Three or four officers and NCOs spontaneously shouted at hearing anyone mention cavalry.

The sergeant major shot them a lethal glance. LTC Gute paused, wiped away an annoyed look, and continued.

"Yes. That. The spark in our souls that make us good *Mustangs*. Getting the job done correctly the first time, flawlessly."

Fitz looked at his watch.

"Next, *Communication*. We clearly communicate to each other, especially to higher headquarters, so that no one is operating in a vacuum and that everyone can receive my guidance."

Lieutenant Colonel Gute took a breath and sipped from his water bottle. "If we don't communicate, we act selfishly and disrupt everyone, particularly our superiors." He shot a knowing look at Captain Holt.

"Next, *Credibility*. Every Mustang has to qualify on his 8-6 tasks and drills, so that the sergeant major and I can *trust* them. This stems from the new training task lists that the Three has disseminated, so that every sergeant and lieutenant knows how to act appropriately. I wish we'd gotten this done before deployment, but now as combat dies down, we can focus on this to get ourselves right."

"And finally, *Care*. This aligns with higher's value of Resiliency, but we've made it our own. I believe that makes it more genuine. We need every Mustang Trooper upright and rowing hard. Make sure you know your soldiers, their families, any issues they're going through, and build that resilient mindset for them. Whenever I hear that a Mustang is hurting and needs to be taken off the line, I point the finger at a leader that didn't *care* enough."

To emphasize his point, LTC Gute shot his trigger finger across the entire audience.

"I know with HHT and FSC being closer they've been soaking up these values that we've been pouring into them, but I want to ensure that this got disseminated to the line troops. Commanders, ensure that you sit down and discuss our values with all your soldiers. Confirm that the men adhere to your command philosophies, my command philosophy, and the brigade commander's 'Top 15 Focus Areas.' That's critical."

LTC Gute paused and then allowed himself a brief smile. "If you're really high speed, you'll align your command philosophies to the division commander's "Decisive 10." That's a hard lift though, I just crafted the squadron's to reflect his. It's very cerebral." He seemed to revel in that accomplishment.

Major Cauzrahavek was nodding along enthusiastically, until his face suddenly became vexed.

"Captains Holt and O'Henry, I don't think squadron's approved your command philosophies yet." MAJ Cauz looked very concerned by this.

Holt and O'Henry's eyes met. Fitz could tell that command philosophies were at the top of their lists.

"I'll make sure I get you that," Holt responded convincingly. "Roger, sir. Me too," O'Henry echoed.

"Good, good major. Make sure it's in the right matrix format." LTC Gute seemed satisfied with his preamble. "Alright Captain Strively, you may begin."

Spinner forwarded the slides to HHT's portion. Captain Strively grasped some printouts he had on the table and coolly started briefing. He set the pace for the meeting, detailing his command's stats for the next twenty minutes. He rolled through slide after slide of operations, training, weapons, equipment, medical, disciplinary, and soldier statuses without missing a beat. LTC Gute didn't pry too much on Strively's portion, assured that his troop closest to the flagpole was in good order. He only dove into certain particulars, like vehicle seating arrangements in case the entire squadron charged out into battle.

"This slide still doesn't reflect my new driver, Captain Strively," LTC Gute said with minor disapproval. "And doesn't show a driver at all for the S-3. Fix this!"

"Yes, sir," said Strively cheerfully, unfazed.

Fitz allowed his mind to wander. He was primarily concerned with the upcoming line troops' data. The cool air gushing out of a nearby AC unit wasn't helpful. It would be bad if he nodded off during this. He pinched the flesh underneath his thighs to wake himself up. His mind was starting to wind down, and he couldn't allow that.

"*Is that correct*, Lieutenant Fitzgerald??" LTC Gute said out of nowhere. His voice jarred Fitz back to the present.

The room had gone silent and everyone was staring at him. Fitz gulped and met the colonel's gaze. He hadn't dozed off, had he?

"Is what correct, sir?" Fitz asked uncomfortably.

"*Are...* you working with the Bushmaster supply sergeant to procure some red and white paint?" LTC Gute interrogated.

Major Cauzrahavek looked at Fitz, nodding vigorously, his eyes pleading for yes.

"Yes....sir. We're looking around for some."

That seemed to satisfy the colonel. "Excellent. Good work Three. Once we finish those parking spaces and improvements, Dolby can be upgraded from a COP to a Camp. That will show the brigade commander how much we've pacified and enriched the AO."

The relief on the major's face was noticeable. He nodded approval to Fitz and then leaned back in his chair. Fitzgerald canceled the alarm bells going off in his head.

Strively confidently concluded his final slides and smiled charmingly at the group.

"Excellent brief, commander. Captain Christopher, you're up!"

Captain Christopher started speaking with a nasally whine. This should be interesting, thought Fitz.

Fitzgerald watched CPT Christopher began briefing and conceded that not everyone could look the part of a commander. Strively naturally was tall, built, and unpretentious. Christopher couldn't help but be short, thin, and kind of resembled a fussy Gerber baby. Maybe he was very intelligent. There had to be some reason why he had been put in command.

He relaxed in his chair and observed Christopher's briefing style. It was more drawn out than Strively's. Christopher felt he needed to explain every bullet point in agonizing detail. He didn't summarize any issue or assume that the audience had also been in the Army for quite some time. Fitz followed the current slide that Christopher was on.

"…and here you'll see how Angry Troop conducted inventories in the past 48 hours. We focused on this month's line items which were: radios, PLGRs and DAGRs, night vision goggles, grenade launchers, and camo nets. We inventoried by serial number 56 radios, 23 GPSes, 84 NODs, 6 M203's, and 40 nets and poles…"

Fitz watched the colonel closely to see if he would question Christopher about those missing night vision goggles from yesterday — the original flashpoint for this meeting. But the moment came and went. LTC Gute said nothing. Captain Christopher finished his equipment slide and moved onto the next. Nobody said a word. Interesting — they must have resolved this themselves the other night.

"…on next to the manning slide. Angry Troop has 84 troopers, three currently on mid-tour leave, one on emergency leave. Our Black Platoon has 30 scouts total, Red Platoon has 18, White has 18, and Blue also has 18…" Christopher droned on in his underwhelming voice.

It was brutal.

Everyone in the room struggled for the next thirty some minutes. CSM DeCray looked like he was out cold. Fitz remained wide awake after that LTC Gute-near-miss; however, the LT next to him kept nodding off and jerking awake. The SFC next to him distractedly doodled elaborate letter S's in his open leader's book. Outside the windows, the sun had set without Fitzgerald noticing it.

Mercifully, Christopher finally concluded and it was Bushmaster's turn. Fitz straightened up in his chair, ready to assist and learn.

"Good, Captain Christopher. Captain Holt, you're next," LTC Gute directed.

"Evening, sir. Here's what Bushmaster's been doing," CPT Holt started.

"I think you mean what outcomes Bushmaster Troop has been shaping, *captain*," LTC Gute corrected sharply.

That was unexpected.

"Sure. Yes, sir. Here's the outcomes we've been shaping," Holt said calmly. He began anew. "Since Bushmaster Troop cleared Zambraynia, we've been focused on—"

"STOP! Bushmaster Troop did *not* clear Zambraynia! 8-6 CAV CLEARED ZAMBRAYNIA! This is not a squadron of troops doing their own thing! *GET IT RIGHT, BUSHMASTER!*" Colonel Gute was spitting fire at Captain Holt. Everyone reeled at this unexpected vehemence.

If this had been a meeting designed to have feedback and constructive discourse, it was no longer that. Everyone in the room clammed up. Where was this coming from?

Captain Holt seemed offset by LTC Gutierrez's attacks but kept on going. He calmly began reading Bushmaster's slides in a more formal manner. Holt briefed by task and purpose so that he wouldn't give the squadron commander any openings. He got through the first few slides until he got to Bushmaster statuses.

"Sir, here's our troop manning slide."

"*STOP!* Captain Holt, explain why there are blank spots on this roster?!" Colonel Gute nit-picked.

The slide had empty spots for some positions, exactly like all the other troops before.

Holt paused to craft his words carefully, "Sir, because those positions are empty MTOE slots."

"I KNOW that, *captain*." He scorned. "If there's a space on a slide that's blank it should say unassigned, or give details to when it will be filled!"

"Yes, sir," Captain Holt replied flatly.

Fitz started taking notes on all the corrections that the colonel wanted on their slides. That's how he could be helpful.

"And what's with the color scheme of your slides? They seem off compared to the squadron format. Spinner! Scroll back a few slides."

Oh god, now they were going backwards.

Lieutenant Colonel Gute started scrutinizing Bushmaster's slides up and down. He questioned columns, fonts, colors, wording, and alignment. Everything was suddenly wrong about them.

Captain Holt tried to cut through the criticism and move on. "Sir, whatever the corrections are, we'll fix them."

Fitz intervened to help. "Sir, I'm taking notes on all your edits." He couldn't tell what the colonel was having a cow over.

LTC Gute leveled his gaze at CPT Holt and frowned disapprovingly. "*Captain*, it's not so much about the slides as it is attention to detail. A sloppy slide shows that you don't care. What you're briefing and what your slides say are two *completely — different — things*. First you *said* you understood my guidance at Zambraynia when you obviously *did not* and now this."

"Sir, what do you mean about Zambraynia?" Captain Holt said guardedly.

"The way you rashly attacked early without any squadron or brigade support! You got lucky there, *captain*. You're lucky I defused the whole situation with the brigade commander."

Fitzgerald couldn't believe his ears. *Defused what with the brigade commander?*

"It's because of things like that and this today, I'm having trouble *trusting you*. That's now two times that you've said one thing and done another."

Fitzgerald didn't know what to think. This appeared petty, but a colonel would be above that. A *colonel* would only do this to make a grander point, not air personal grievances. This entire briefing now had become awkward and unpleasant to be in. Was this planned? What had set off the colonel? Was it that Captain Holt's Zambraynia plan had worked better?

Captain Holt responded as best as he could: "Yes, sir... I'm sorry to hear that. I'll work on rebuilding trust with you?" Holt wasn't rattled, but he was obviously confused as to what had triggered this.

"*Thanks, captain*," LTC Gute sneered. "*Many things need to be re-built.* This inattention to detail is indicative of a failure of one of our bedrock values, CREDIBILITY, and proof troops are doing their own thing!" The colonel now directed his ire at everyone at the table. "You, commanders, are disregarding my orders and are failing me! This CUB was sorely needed to re-calibrate you back to my guidance! There's no way you can see from your tactical perspective what needs to be done out there!"

Fitz sat rigid and uncomfortable in his chair. The air had been sucked out of the room. Nobody here was going to say anything or be a smartass back. LTC Gute could ruin anyone's career with a pen stroke.

This downward spiral of events had woken the sergeant major up. He jumped in, trying to salvage the situation.

"MUSTANGS! Mustangsss, the colonel has a point, but let's not forget all the great things that 8-6 CAV is doing! Think of all the results we've achieved! All the other units are talking about 8-6 and what we've accomplished. Look at all the Iraqis trained, combined patrols, SOIs paid, excess property and ammo turned in, sexual harassment training, and family readiness done! Those are actions that speak for themselves and show what 8-6 is really all about!"

The sergeant major's interruption helped. LTC Gute seemed placated for a moment. He looked at CSM DeCray, nodding his head. He unscrewed the cap from his water bottle and took a deep swig. The only sound Fitz could hear was the unsettling hiss from the AC units.

"Thank you, sergeant major," Colonel Gute said, his wrath abating.

"Let me put it this way," LTC Gute began slowly. "Often, you're not going to completely understand my guidance. The sergeant major and I have 46 years total time in service, we have the combined experience and strategic perspective that you lack. You wouldn't know what to do, nor should you be thinking at our level. Only he and I, *the most experienced men in the squadron*, have that higher perspective to comprehend what is necessary to lead."

Lieutenant Colonel Gutierrez kept speaking, growing bolder and more righteous with each proclamation.

"It's very similar to the *Book of Samuel*, when David would get directives from God. God would send orders to David and tell him to do things, and David would be like, 'I don't understand why,' but he'd do them anyway. THAT'S what I need you to be like! Be like David. You're often not going to understand what I'm saying, but I need you to *trust me* and execute my guidance!"

Fitz's mind was reeling. Did that just happen? He wanted to give LTC Gute the benefit of the doubt, but that felt pretty close to inappropriate religious sermonizing. Also, was the squadron commander comparing himself to God?

Everyone was quiet and desperate to be out of the colonel's crosshairs. The room had frozen silent except for the circulating air. LTC Gute inhaled sharply and then took another drink from his water bottle. The room braced for the next salvo, everyone eyeing each other anxiously.

"Alright Captain Holt, you may continue," LTC Gute finally permitted.

Captain Holt stayed silent. There was a moment while the Bushmaster deer considered running across the colonel's open meadow.

Cautiously, Holt started again slowly and got through his next slide unscathed. He picked up speed. Holt briefed the remainder in rapid fire and then O'Henry and Robinson followed suit. Everyone summarized as quickly and as tersely as they could. Lieutenant Colonel Gute didn't say another word. He merely acknowledged them with nods and took notes in red in his leader's book.

Once Robinson was done, LTC Gute surveyed the room for his closing comments. "Gentlemen, I hope you all internalize what we've communicated here today. As we finish our tour, let's ensure we do the right thing." He rose and everyone jumped to their feet, signifying the close of the meeting. They all saluted and yelled, "MUSTANGS!"

The meeting ended and it was safe to withdraw. Captain Holt and Fitzgerald warily backed out of squadron without looking like they were delighted to leave. The officers rejoined the Bushmaster men, who were uncomfortably lounging in their vehicles. The MRAPs were parked in neat line, all crew doors and ramps open, nighttime blue lights on, AC units and engines running full blast.

Fitz thought they'd have to wait until late morning to embark but Corefelt had done a drug deal with EOD. The Navy bomb defusers would escort them back to Murray for a case of Coca-Cola and Rip-Its. So instead of waiting another half-day they could SP at 0400.

Fitzgerald went back to his truck and positioned himself as best he could in the cramped driver's cab. The compartment seemed designed to maximize its pointy metal angles. On the passenger side, his seat didn't recline at all. He concluded that the Army probably made seats uncomfortable to keep drivers awake. He shoved his Kevlar and vest on the floor and put his boots up on the dash. Fitzgerald gazed out the windshield up to the bright stars, reflecting on the meeting and downplaying its ramifications. Internal politics wouldn't interfere with operations. He tried vigorously to nod off, but only succeeded in shifting positions a dozen times.

The men stirred in a couple hours and lined up their trucks behind EOD. They donned their gear and did their checks.

"Shake and Bake!" came over the platoon net.

The combined patrol rolled out, and they made their exodus from COP Dolby.

CHAPTER EIGHTEEN

THE CAVALRYMEN RETURNED SAFELY to Murray and it wasn't until the next evening that the trouble began. 1ˢᵗ Lieutenant Nitmer, more of a night owl than the CO, happened to be in the CP at midnight when the commotion reached X-RAY. He got on the net and figured out that one of the Busayefi SOI checkpoints had received small arms fire. Luckily, a White Platoon patrol was in the vicinity. They'd rushed to the SOI's aid and Dotson, a turret gunner, had fired a few bursts at shapes he saw in his night sight. He swore he'd hit somebody. Then the attack melted away.

Fitz and Corefelt were the first to be found, so they got volunteered to be the Quick Reaction Force. They resignedly put on their gear and ran to the TOC. Serrano and Stenracker were sent to assemble the platoon.

As they entered the CP, they saw the XO standing, talking into the radio mic. He was in his PTs and looked irritated.

"NO — you can't do a recon by fire. Request denied! BLACK FIVE OUT!"

Fitz and Corefelt approached and signaled that they were in receive mode.

"What's up, XO?"

"Lieutenant Fitzgerald and Sergeant Corefelt, I need you to take a QRF out to Checkpoint Six to ascertain what happened out there and assist as needed." Nitmer was acting more formal, since he was issuing orders as the XO.

He spun them up on the 5W's and asked for questions.

"Where's the rest of White Platoon?" Fitz inquired. Why had Blue been woken up for this?

"Maloney's with the other half of White over at Talon for a separate mission. They're too far away for this."

"Ah, roger," Fitz said.

"Good? OK — Good Luck!"

Fitz and Corefelt moved over to the TOC ice cooler and grabbed some energy drinks for the night. Fitz put two in his cargo pocket.

"Ready to see a dead body?" Corefelt said to him with glee.

Fitzgerald gave him an unenthusiastic expression back. He didn't really care about another dead Arab.

The platoon was outside ready to go. Generator-powered work lights illuminated the staging area. Four Humvees had been pulled up because they'd be quicker and nimbler on canal roads. Breyer looked amped, punching his fists together. Fitzgerald briefed the huddle of men quickly, exactly as Nitmer had given the mission order. He paused after his patrol brief.

"Sergeant Corefelt, I miss anything?"

"Yes, sir. TC's check your crew's NODs and night sights. I want them all on now, not when we get there. Dismounts, too."

"Roger that!" SGT Breyer said loudly.

As the platoon broke off to do their final checks, Captain Holt and First Sergeant Tapwell sauntered up in full kit.

"Mind if we come along, LT?" Tapwell snickered.

Fitz gave him a dour look. What choice did he have? "Jump on in, Top. The more the merrier."

Blue Platoon finished its prep, and everyone climbed in the vehicles. Holt took Fitz's TC seat and Tapwell took Corefelt's. Fitz and Corefelt took backseats to their own patrol.

They raced quickly through the town's deserted streets until they reached the farmland on the outskirts. The drivers used their night vision but the stars' natural illumination made the going easier. In twenty minutes, they were there.

They rolled up aggressively onto Checkpoint Six and White Platoon's trucks. If not for White's presence, it would have been impossible to find in the blackness. The checkpoint was nestled low in a well-traveled road, nothing more than a line of road cones and a ramshackle, wooden booth, all ornately decorated with plastic flowers and new Iraqi flags. The three MRAPs were positioned around it, two straddling it on the right side of the road and the other parked across the lane. The ground was uneven, so the tall trucks tilted at a precarious slant. Their turrets were pointed outward to give 360-degree security. Three SOIs in running suits and two White Platoon NCOs stood front and center at the booth.

Swiftly, Blue's four Humvees entered the perimeter and faced outwards. The dismounts leapt out at the first opportunity, slamming their doors and leaving behind the crews in the trucks. The farmland rose up steadily beyond the wide, sunken lane, forcing the drivers to make minor corrections to give their gunners the best vantage. The Bushmaster men spared no time in facing outward and spreading out. They were bored and missed combat's adrenaline.

Captain Holt dismounted and strode a beeline straight for the two White Platoon NCOs. Fitz popped out his door and raced after him, adjusting his night vision goggles and M4 as he went. He clicked on his NVG optics and his green eyesight flickered on. Fitzgerald immediately recognized one of the NCOs as Staff Sergeant Tremble, a large, lumpy looking man.

"Sergeant Tremble — what happened?" Holt quizzed him in a half-hushed voice.

"Sir... These guys here were taking fire when we rolled up. Two shooters from the south, they had tracers. I don't think they knew we were here or else they wouldn't have engaged. Dotson got PID on one of them and suppressed 'em."

"Distance? Direction?"

"Six or seven hundred meters that way. South. End of this field and into that gulley." He gestured off into the darkness.

Captain Holt stepped past the men to the lip of the raised earth. He lowered his NVGs from his helmet mount and scanned the open field. Tremble and Fitz flanked him reflexively for security. Fitzgerald leaned into the dirt bank and pointed his rifle muzzle outwards. He slowed his breathing, looked and listened, peering out ahead.

Stars twinkled in the expansive night sky, but nothing dared to stir on the earth. Fitzgerald examined the tilled ground stretching out ahead of him, its details growing fuzzier and blotchier the farther he scanned. His ears registered only the vehicles idling behind them. Their engines reverberated steadily. There was nothing, nothing there.

Then, Fitz heard two shots fired off east in the distance. *Pop! Pop!* An alarm, but for whom?

"Warning shots," he murmured.

"I heard them," Holt acknowledged. He didn't break his gaze from the fields.

First Sergeant Tapwell and Sergeant Corefelt crept up silently behind Captain Holt. "Whaddaya think, sir?" Tapwell whispered.

"They probably bugged out immediately, but maybe Dotson hit one of them." He looked at Top with a grin. "Let's check it out."

Happy to oblige, Tapwell turned around and motioned to Breyer and the other NCOs. He snapped his fingers to get their attention. "Hey! Numbnuts! Form up the men online over here."

In short order, Corefelt and Breyer arrayed the men in a thin line on the road's edge, facing out into the field. Some stood behind the earthen embankment and some knelt.

Captain Holt turned his head to Tapwell and Tremble. "Top — take a couple guys and hang back fifty meters from the line as we move forward, just in case we run into something. Tremble — keep comms with the vehicles and let us know if they spot anything."

Holt checked left then right and then ordered, "Let's go!" He gingerly stalked forward, the skirmishing line of men following. Fitz carefully lifted himself up over the rise and crept ahead.

"Watch where you step. Avoid natural lines of drift," Holt cautioned, barely audible.

Fitz skulked forward with his rifle up. The sediment shifted underneath his boots. He hunched forward, as he moved to be a smaller target. Fitz looked down more at where his feet were going than ahead to the horizon. He scanned to his left and saw the green shapes of four men walking parallel to him. One had turned on his helmet IR beacon to flag them all as friendlies.

After a few hundred meters, the level farmland became choppier. The symmetric lines of ploughed earth became uneven and deteriorated into deep trenches and gullies. The terrain broke up the screen of men, as they stopped to investigate pits and climb across the gaping gashes. Fitz peered warily into each depression he found, expecting to find a dangerous and wounded jihadist holed up somewhere. He flicked his M4 off Safe to Semi. He kept finding nothing.

Captain Holt on his right scuttled up another incline as Fitz crouched over a drainage ditch. He raised his rifle and scanned the horizon again, seeing nothing but more broken landscape.

"They're gone," Captain Holt said with finality.

Were they ever here? thought Fitz.

The soldiers searched the farm plots fruitlessly for another hour, before they wrapped up and drove home. They left the SOIs a case of water for their trouble.

Blue Platoon RP-ed back to Murray and got some rack time. In the early Sunday morning as they slept, three Iraqi Army Humvees arrived at Jaleel's house. Captain Mohammed knocked on the front door, while his men threw a rope over a streetlight.

"They what??" Nitmer was incredulous.

"The IA executed an SOI leader named Jaleel this morning. They hanged him from a light post," Staff Sergeant Stalls read dryly from his duty log. At least he'd had the brains to write something this important down, Fitz thought.

Everyone involved last night had slept late into the morning. Sundays already were a lazier day on the American battle rhythm, so SSG Stalls keeping quiet wasn't completely wrong here. It was going on nearly 1100 before Fitz, Nitmer, and Captain Holt had come into the TOC for coffee.

"That *has* to be inaccurate. Why would the IA execute Jaleel? Why didn't you wake us up when this came in?"

"I don't know who Jaleel is, sir," Stalls stared blankly at the XO.

"JALEEL, the SOI leader that comes over here with his brothers to play dominoes all the time! You don't know who that is??!!"

Fitz's mind was too groggy to comprehend, as he sipped his paper cup of joe. Captain Holt reclined, silently thinking in one of the corner office chairs.

This had to be a false report. More coffee and daylight would rectify this.

"I don't watch what you and the CO do with Iraqis, sir," Stalls said.

Nitmer seethed at the sergeant's deliberate ignorance. "Who sent you this report?!"

"Squadron said their Civil Affairs team heard it at a KLE this morning."

"Well now, I don't believe any of that. The same CA team whose truck breaks down everywhere because they don't do maintenance?!"

"No, that was the PSYOPs team."

"SAME DAMN THING!"

The XO stewed. SSG Stalls was just another messenger.

Captain Holt sipped his coffee and thought out loud. "If the IA are moving against the SOIs, they must not think AQI is a threat here anymore. They've been ordered to neutralize political rivals instead."

"Jaish al-Mahdi and the Sons of Iraq," Nitmer stated.

"Bingo. They moved against JAM in March, now it's the SOI's turn."

"And the SOIs are Sunni. That makes it easier."

Captain Holt spoke detachedly, "They all hate each other. Being Iraqi means nothing to them, it's all religious or tribal ties."

Fitz let his two seniors talk. Was he still asleep or numb? Jaleel being dead seemed abstract. He leaned on the table and observed Captain Holt. The CO wasn't emotional about this, he seemed accustomed to horrible things casually happening over here.

"We need to confirm this. XO — where am I going today at noon?"

Nitmer grabbed a metal clipboard from his desktop and referenced some pages. "You and Maloney are," he ran his finger down the schedule, speaking deliberately, "attending the Adwaniyah governance meeting. Jaleel and Ali are usually there."

"Alright. And if not, I'll swing by his house on the way back," he sighed. "Until then, keep requesting information from squadron. Call the S-2 or get someone credible on the phone."

"Yessir."

"Okay. I'm going to go get some breakfast." Captain Holt donned his boonie cap and exited the TOC.

Fitz took that as his opportunity to go with him. French toast sticks with syrup sounded amazing. Fitz walked with Holt silently down the wooden pallet gangplank through the graveled living area. Fitz paused briefly by his shipping container to rouse Corefelt and bring him along too. He lost the CO as he waited. Captain Holt strode on ahead alone past the last CONEX, vanishing from sight around the bend to the MKT.

CHAPTER NINETEEN

LATER IN THE DAY, Ali arrived inconsolable in the CP. It was too much drama for Fitz to handle.

"They murder him!" he kept repeating. Ali, in an agitated state, had arrived at Murray around 1500 and demanded to see Captain Holt. He couldn't stop burbling and wailing, tears and snot dripping from his face. If Ali's lamentations were proof of anything, then Jaleel was definitely dead.

The Sergeant of the Guard brought Ali to the TOC, and all the lieutenants were summoned to console him. At first they sat him down on the big couch in the TOC, but after a few minutes the XO kicked them all out. Ali was already a security liability, but now as a man having an emotional meltdown, he was too much. Nitmer directed Fitz, Lee, and Peppel to comfort him and figure out what had happened. The LTs escorted him outside and found a place away from the hum of generators and AC units.

They settled into green plastic chairs by a large wooden spool table underneath a camo tent. The outdoor furniture was coated in a fine, almond-colored dust. Fitz wiped the seats clean while Lee and Peppel produced some icy water bottles and a pack of Camels.

"Those dirty Shiites! Taking orders from that Iranian puppet in Baghdad," Ali bawled. "Iran, bara, bara!" He tossed away one smoke, then ignited another.

The lieutenants were noticeably impatient with the whole arrangement. Ali had been a stalwart ally, but none of them wanted to wet nurse this guy for the next three hours. They had better things to do. Only Captain Holt had the patience to entertain these Arabs for interminable periods.

Lee cut to the chase and tried to be analytical with their cordial interrogation. He pulled out a tan notepad and started asking him questions.

"How are you feeling?"

"When did they come for Jaleel?"

"Who came for Jaleel? Who saw them?"

"Where were you when this happened?"

"Did they arrest or execute anyone else?"

"I was coming back from Khamasiyah. They almost got Abbad, too! He was down the street and had to flee." He stopped crying to inhale a drag from his cigarette. "That puppet Maliki is after all of us!"

Fitz stared blankly past Ali, not hearing him. How much should he care about Jaleel dying? It remotely registered somewhere inside him as unfortunate. Did Iraqis sit around and contemplate Americans dying here? Not likely. What was he supposed to feel here?

Fitz wondered what would happen if he died? He hadn't thought about that before. His mom and dad would be devastated, but everyone else? Grieve for a day, and then back to work? What was life worth over here?

He jettisoned that thought and focused back on the conversation. The lieutenants sat with Ali for some time, both grilling and consoling him. Besides confirming Jaleel's death, the Sunni didn't produce much more info. In the absence of alcohol, nicotine became the substance to numb the pain. Fitz inhaled so many consecutive cigarettes that his throat burned.

About an hour later, Specialist Nulkey walked past them and then doubled back. Nulkey hadn't noticed the four until he'd caught a whiff of smoke emanating from the net. He peered in and recognized the three LTs.

"Sirs," he muttered deferentially, "River City just came across the squadron net. Top's shutting down the Spaware café and no messages are allowed back home."

River City was code for when a U.S. service member had been wounded or killed. It meant a communications blackout for 72 hours for the affected unit until families could be notified.

Shit. More of this.

"Nulkey, do you know what happened? Who got hurt?" Lee asked first.

"No, sir. Ten minutes ago, squadron reported a patrol got hit over by Hawr Rajab. No details."

Fitz felt some small relief. That wasn't Bushmaster's sector.

"Thanks, man."

"Yes sir," Nulkey started to walk away to tell others. He hesitated and then turned to say one more thing. "Oh and this also means cellphones and satphones, if you got them. Don't do what Stenracker did last time."

"Roger that."

Fitzgerald felt things unraveling. The squadron hadn't lost anyone since Courage Troop fouled up Zambraynia. Hopefully it was WIA not KIA. However, River City was only put out if someone had been hurt bad. And the bad possibilities were endless.

The four of them lit another round of cigarettes and smoked them in silence. That killed the pack.

They brooded for a while more, until Fitz had had enough. He stood up and said with finality, "Ali, you need to go home. Go see Jaleel's family and check that they're ok."

"But I need to see Captain Holt," Ali pleaded.

"There will be plenty of time to do that tomorrow. We'll come out to see you."

Lee and Peppel stood up as well. Ali slowly conceded. He glumly rose and collected himself.

"And don't say anything about River City to anyone," Peppel interjected sternly.

Great job Peppel. Fitz saw what he was doing, but it wasn't subtle.

Lee tried to cover it up. "Ali… don't talk to anyone about Jaleel's death that doesn't need to know."

"Yes. I understand. It has been a sad day, my friends."

"Sure has."

Fitzgerald could only nod.

Lee and Fitz herded Ali away from the TOC and down the path to the front gate. Peppel slinkered off at the first opportunity. Ali tried to hold hands with Fitz as Arabs do, but Fitzgerald was not having any of that. He brushed it off and kept moving him toward the exit.

Staff Sergeant Tremble and another soldier were standing watch warily in full kit by the front entrance. Ali halted a few feet short of it and gazed at the LTs with glossy sore eyes.

"It's been a terrible day, but we will get through it."

"You bet we will, buddy."

Ali nodded and forced a smile. "See you tomorrow sadeeki."

The Arab slipped between the gap in the barrier and walked down the gravel incline away from Murray.

"Bye Ali" They waved after him.

The rocks crunched as he strode away. The LTs watched him for a few hundred meters and then turned their attention back to the TOC. Now they had to see what was going on.

Fitz and Lee walked into the TOC and were taken aback by how full and noisy it was. The hair on the back of his neck curled up. LT Peppel and all the senior NCOs were sitting and standing in the main room, anxiously awaiting something. The XO and Top were on separate phones, intently listening. Tapwell's face grew angrier, and Nitmer's became ashen. Fitz spotted Corefelt and rushed over to talk to him.

"What's going on?" He whispered.

"It wasn't Hawr Rajab, it was Adwaniyah. Squadron didn't know what the hell they were talking about," Corefelt said grimly. It was the first time Fitzgerald had ever seen worry in Corefelt's face.

He continued, "The SCO and sergeant major called about ten minutes earlier and are still talking. It looks like White Platoon got hit over by Adwaniyah a few hours ago."

"Why didn't X-Ray hear a MEDEVAC request?"

"They must have been out of range. Over closer to Dolby."

The rising clamor of conversation had gotten out of hand in the CP. "HEY — SHUT UP!!! THE XO AND I ARE ON THE PHONE!" growled Top Tapwell. He silenced everyone.

Corefelt stayed mute for about 30 seconds, and then started whispering back to Fitz, "It's got to be someone of rank or multiple KIAs. They wouldn't have called, if it was just a driver."

Dread replaced the numbness that had been burdening Fitz. Now he felt something.

The hushed tones started once more, and then rose to a murmur. Everyone was talking again. Fitz leaned onto the couch arm to collect himself. Tapwell nodded his head, spoke into the phone, and hung up. The room froze and fell quiet except for Nitmer's conversation. Top scanned the room, looking in every man's face and then turned to look at the XO. Nitmer gave his last acknowledgment and then hung up his phone as well. Both their faces were grave. Their eyes met. And then Tapwell turned to face the group.

"Men. Captain Holt's dead. He was killed today by an IED."

Fitz inhaled sharply. He recoiled back into the couch.

Nitmer, relieved that Tapwell had broken the news, filled in the rest of the details.

"Today at 1400 hours on Route Bucks, White Platoon was hit by numerous EFPs. Captain Holt's truck was hit by several arrays on the passenger side. Sergeant Campbull attempted buddy aid, and they CASEVACed Holt to Dolby. He died enroute."

Everyone stopped their small movements. Their notebooks, coffee mugs, water bottles were ignored. Everything had become quiet except for the slight ringing in Fitz's ears. It was the first time it was silent enough for him to hear that knell sounding in his head.

Fitz tried to process this. He half expected Captain Holt to walk through the TOC door, in full kit, wearing his clear eyepro, jolly, dusty, and unstressed. He would look at the assembled crew and ask, "What the hell is happening in here?" That thought evoked a violent pang, releasing a sadness that tore into Fitz. They weren't winning anymore. Santa Claus wasn't real, saying your prayers didn't matter, and Mom and Dad were getting a divorce.

Someone hit pause. Fitz clutched his hair with his hands and stared straight down into the floorboards. His chest grew tight and constricted. The edges of his vision narrowed and he struggled to breathe.

They were all frozen and powerless in that dark moment. Only Tapwell stayed connected to their earthly requirements, timing grieving on his wristwatch. After an appropriate period, he spoke up. "Alright men. Get back to your jobs. Go tell your men, and remind them to not to call home about it."

No one stirred. A few forlorn sighs escaped. Corefelt palmed his face with his huge hands.

"Come on!" Yipped Tapwell, like he was getting a hog to run. "Captain Holt wouldn't want you all hanging out, feeling sorry for yourselves! He'd want you to finish the job." This shook the men out of their torpor. They begrudgingly stood up and started filing out. Fitz and Corefelt were the last to budge.

Nitmer sat motionless in his chair. He'd turned away so that the group could only see his back. Putting on a brave face, Top stood by the door alone, and parceled out encouragement to the men as they filed past. He nodded and locked eyes with each one. Fitz could barely meet Top's gaze.

Fitz and Corefelt walked outside and felt the night's warm embrace. Shadows had crept up on them while they were inside. The two of them didn't bother with their hats or eyewear. They tramped through the gravel for a few feet, and then stopped. Fitzgerald felt weak.

"We need to tell the platoon," Corefelt advised.

Fitz couldn't speak without beginning to cry. He struggled to nod his head.

Corefelt gazed at Fitz with unsteady eyes. "You want me to tell 'em?"

Fitzgerald considered it. Knew that was wrong. He shook his head and tried to compose himself.

"No," he forced out. "You round them up and I'll tell them… That's my job." His voice wavered with emotion.

"Where?"

Fitz choked back emotion and his eyes watered. He couldn't speak anymore.

Sergeant Corefelt's eyes betrayed his grief, but he was much more composed. He must have done this before.

"I gotcha sir," Corefelt said. "We'll assemble at the platoon area by our CONEX. We'll be there when you're ready."

Corefelt reassuringly patted his LT on the back and walked on ahead. Fitzgerald stood still, paralyzed, mired in his own pain.

Stop it! He could be sad later. His temper flared and he slapped himself hard on the cheek. He couldn't be some weak, weepy child. He had to be an officer and a role model to his platoon. Fitz looked down at himself and fixed his uniform. He fished his crumpled hat out of his pocket and put it and his clear eyepro on. Reflexively, he touched his holster to ensure that his pistol hadn't deserted him.

2nd Lieutenant Fitzgerald put a determined look on his face and marched towards the platoon area. He talked out loud to himself to get the emotion out of his voice. He only had a couple of minutes before his guys were assembled, and he had to put together an eloquent eulogy. How could he tell them that the CO had been KIA on some obscure farm road? How could he express to his guys everything that Captain Holt meant to them? He halted and leaned up next to a shipping container, frozen again.

He paused there for a lengthy moment and took a deep breath. Maybe he didn't have to. Maybe he just had to break the news and tell them that it'd be okay. He hoped that would be enough. Harnessing his last reserve of strength, he trudged on, donning his confident façade again.

As he entered the living area, he saw other sections stirring. The Bushmaster men knew something was up. He made his way down the wooden walkway, past Lee's container, down to his and Corefelt's. On the far side of it were two dusty black pleather couches, already filled up with Blue Platoon men. Half were in their PTs, the other half brown ACUs. The men were sprawled and leaning on every inch of the couches. The NCOs and the rest stood. Corefelt stood behind them all, taking attendance.

"Is this everyone?" Fitz asked.

Before Corefelt could say anything Northland and Stenracker sprinted in and joined the group. They stood to the side, huffing and catching their breath.

"It is now," SSG Corefelt growled, casting the two an angry look.

Fitz removed his hat and eye protection and walked in front, center stage to the men. He dropped it on a wooden table the platoon had leaned their weapons on. He scanned across all their faces, the gravity of the situation apparent to everyone. They were all quiet, expectant.

"Men," he crossed his arms and took a full breath. He had to do it. "The CO was killed today by an IED."

Gonzales scoffed loudly like he didn't believe it, but the look on his face betrayed that he did. They were all wide-eyed and silently looking at Fitz.

He continued, "White Platoon was hit this afternoon by an IED over by Adwaniyah. Sergeant Campbull tried to do buddy aid. Captain Holt died on the way back to Dolby for MEDEVAC."

They wouldn't stop looking at him. Fitz soldiered on.

"The SCO and the sergeant major called about an hour ago to confirm it. Captain Holt was the only casualty. That's why there's River City in effect."

As the men were comprehending this he knew he had to add his leadership touch to it. He had to tie together meaning for the guys and not leave them hanging. That's the job that he was supposed to do, he thought bitterly.

"I know this hurts all of us. Captain Holt was a good m—" Fitz croaked and trailed off for a second. He choked back emotion, "...good man." He finished with effort and then restarted.

"But that doesn't mean we can stop. Captain Holt was proud of all we've accomplished here. We rooted out AQI and allowed the Iraqis to rebuild their communities. We've given them all a chance at something better."

He paused. The men continued to eyeball him.

"We're close to going home. The CO would want all of us to finish strong, and keep together what we fought and died for. That's what Captain Holt would have expected Bushmasters to do."

The Blue Platoon men finally nodded and murmured agreement. A few were bleary eyed and looked away. Fitz let that hang and seep in for awhile. "Any questions?" he finally blurted out.

The group stayed mute for a long moment. Then Stenracker piped up, "When will there be a service for him?"

Stenracker's question blindsided him. *A funeral for Captain Holt.* A burial? A coffin? A body? That permanency shattered Fitz's fragile composure.

Fitz couldn't look at the men for a moment and stared at the ground. It took a minute for him to say anything. "I dunno," he eventually eked out. He felt his emotions creeping back into his voice. "But I'll find out. I'm sure we'll all be there."

He stood and stared at them for another long moment. He met Corefelt's eyes. Corefelt nodded approval at him.

"OK. That's it. You're dismissed."

He grabbed his cover and walked away from the platoon. He wanted to be alone for a long while.

CHAPTER TWENTY

C APTAIN HOLT'S BODY was shipped home immediately to his grieving family, but those he left behind in Iraq also needed closure. For them, a funeral was planned a week later. As the days led up to it, Bushmaster Troop halfheartedly tried to resume operations, but the men weren't themselves.

Captain Holt's absence felt temporary to Fitzgerald, like the CO had gone away on midtour leave, and would return, smiling, in a couple of weeks. It slowly started to register for Fitz when Bushmaster Troop was lingering outside the FOB Talon Chapel, everyone hesitating on going in. Each man kept lighting cigarette after cigarette, stalling for time. No one wanted to face Holt's death until forced to.

A whole troop shouldn't be pulled off the line at once, but there was no helping it. Until Bushmaster was given time to grieve it'd be a wounded animal, its actions timid, its spirit gone. A platoon from Courage had been sent over to Murray to watch the wall for a day. Nitmer and a few NCOs had stayed behind for continuity. The rest of Bushmaster donned clean uniforms and their best boots. They shaved and pinned on their combat and skills badges. The platoons had convoyed out in intervals on different routes to make it to Talon by noon. Thankfully there'd been zero complications getting there.

The chapel itself rested inconspicuously in the center of the FOB, a tan blocky building devoid of a spire or any religious identifier. It blended in with half the other nearby buildings, its architects hopeful that drab obscurity would be its best defense. The only way to derive the building's purpose was to read the small beige placards on its doors.

The funeral was set for 1400 so they had arrived early. To kill time before the service, they had all hit up the dining facility and savored the better cuisine and surroundings. Panini presses, ice cream, and the movie *Wedding Crashers* playing on large TVs made it harder to leave for the chapel. The NCOs forced everyone out by 1330, but now even they couldn't get the men to venture inside the church. Top Tapwell, one of the last to arrive, finally approached the rabble and was aghast to find his troop standing paralyzed outside.

"Why are all you men outside?! What if a round lands here in the middle of ya!?" he hollered.

The mob of men lamely returned blank looks. No one responded.

"Get inside! Get!" Tapwell pleaded.

Only Top Tapwell had the authority to make them move. Admonished, the Bushmaster men tossed their cigarettes, and started slowly shuffling inside. Corefelt and Fitz quietly merged into the line and joined the herd indoors. The discarded tobacco ashes smoldered behind them, refusing to die.

Within the chapel, the interior matched the Spartan exterior. Rigid rows of wooden benches crowded the floor in front of a small stage. A pulpit stood close to the wall, off-center. Displayed front and center was a helmet atop an inverted M16. Dangling from the rifle's stock, two silver dog tags hung suspended above a pair of desert khaki boots. Commanding the top of the pulpit was a framed picture of Holt grinning, a fresh Bronze Star and Purple Heart medal pinned to its edge. A thin, black, mourning ribbon lay draped across the photo's top left corner.

No one wanted to sit up front, as if proximity to the memorial would reap greater pain. The soldiers tried to claim the back seats like children on a school bus. The NCOs, normally assertive, lost their nerve and sat in the middle seats, also wary of the front pews. Fitz and Corefelt exchanged defeated glances and walked up to the front right bench. They took seats directly before the pulpit and CPT Holt's living image.

Being inside now, Fitzgerald felt his ribcage slowly tightening like he was in a vise. It seemed like the chapel ceiling was pressing down on him. He forcefully inhaled and exhaled a deep breath to calm himself and retreated into his thoughts.

He stared at the memorial, transfixed by the two medals on the framed picture. He admired CPT Holt a helluva lot, but he was baffled by why the Army appeared to be rewarding routine death. Holt hadn't perished heroically, he'd just died. Was dying inconsequentially a meritorious achievement? Would he posthumously make major? Would some S-1 clerk update Holt's personnel file to reflect his final awards?

It was such bullshit. The equivalent of military flowers. Fitz glared through the pulpit. Corefelt looked away, imprisoned in his own pain.

1400 arrived on time and the ceremony began. Other individuals from the FOB had filtered in and filled up the tiny chapel. The walls and pews were packed and it was standing room only. A kind looking Army chaplain stepped forward to the pulpit and officiated. The officer wore a black crucifix on his collar lapel. Fitzgerald didn't hear him, but responded to his commands. He rose when everyone else stood, he sat when the others sat. He bowed his head and tried to pray when told to.

After a Bible verse, the chaplain gestured to the far side. Fitz was dismayed to see Lieutenant Colonel Gutierrez mount the stage and approach the pulpit. The colonel posted up behind it and inspected the mourners. He wore a sincere and saddened face that looked appropriate for the occasion.

"Colonel James, Sergeant Major Keyhole, Assistant Deputy Sanford, Bushmaster Troop, and fellow Mustangs..." LTC Gute began his eulogy addressing the hierarchy of guests, "I'd like to tell you about my *guuuuud* friend, Captain Douglas Holt."

Fitzgerald's mouth went dry. He wished it wasn't the colonel's prerogative to speak at this.

"Douglas was a devout Christian man with deep convictions and great ability. I was *honored* to be his mentor and squadron commander. He was very proud of and grateful for the command of Bushmaster Troop that I granted him. And he was instrumental in all we, 8-6 CAV, have accomplished in Iraq."

The roomful of mourners dejectedly stared back.

"Captain Holt was part of a phalanx of aggressive counter-insurgency officers. He was a leader like General Petraeus, Colonel McMaster, myself, and other commanders with the *vision* of how to win here. We know that battalion-sized units need to act swiftly, and not be encumbered by the demands of higher headquarters. We must forge strong bonds with our Iraqi partners, train them, and conduct combined operations to harness their combat power. I communicated that strategy to him, and Douglas understood perfectly that only nimble, battalion-sized operations would work."

Most middle to upper management officers gave rambling speeches confirming policy at every opportunity, but this was more deliberate. LTC Gute continued to lead the crowd.

"That's how Douglas, myself, and my squadron staff planned 8-6 CAV's liberation of Zambraynia from Al Qaeda this summer. We coordinated effectively with higher Army and Air Force echelons and when conditions were right, I sent Doug in!" LTC Gute's face beamed, and he nodded seriously as he addressed the troop.

"He understood my guidance of lightning attacks without compromise, and when I saw the conditions on the ground I ordered Doug to attack immediately! Bushmaster's thrust synchronized with my other troops, controlled by my staff, drove AQI from the field! It was a masterful operation, and I was blessed to have a subordinate like Douglas on my team."

"Doug then understood my imperative of cooperation with our Iraqi partners, particularly the Iraqi Army and Police, and forged close relationships with them. Then, with our Iraqi allies in the lead, we could hold onto our gains like Zambraynia and consolidate our shared victory."

Then, right on cue, LTC Gutierrez paused and wiped away a tear. "Douglas Holt was a dear friend and I shall miss him every day... But I think he would have solace in the fact that our bold new strategy is revolutionizing how we conduct warfare. I am honored to be dedicating an academic paper that I am writing to Doug. It will showcase the many successful counterinsurgency tactics that we spearheaded here. Look for it this fall in *Armor* magazine and other journals. It's only fitting that he be a part of that."

'Only fitting' thought Fitzgerald. He felt bile surge up his throat. He gagged and swallowed it back down. Its acidic taste lingered in his mouth.

"TROOP — ATTTTENN — SHUUUUNNNN!!" First Sergeant Tapwell hollered.

They all sprang to their feet. Bodies braced, arms straight by their sides, fingers curled, eyes straight ahead. The pews complained loudly as an entire cavalry troop leapt up. An upset Bible thudded onto the floor. From Fitz's peripheral LTC Gute melted to the side and Top marched up onto the stage.

"BUSHMASTER, *Report!*" Top snapped. Fitz forced his windpipe clear. "LOOOOTENANT FITZGERALD!" Tapwell demanded.

"HERE FIRST SERGEANT!" Fitzgerald shot off as loudly as he could.

"CORPORAL GONZALEZ!"

"HERE FIRST SERGEANT!!!" Corporal Gonzalez bellowed behind him.

"CAPTAIN HOLT!"

.

Silence. Tapwell paused.

"CAPTAIN DOUGLAS HOLT!"

..

Fitz's chest caved in.

"Captain... Douglas... Gary... Holt," Tapwell said with slow finality.

...

Nothing stirred. The air in Fitz's lungs ran out. They stood suspended, directionless, until a recording of Taps started playing from the chapel entrance. The inhabitants of the front left pew faced the aisle and approached Holt's memorial in two's and three's. Each group paid their respects, saluted, and exited to the side. When it was their turn, SSG Corefelt quietly whispered "Left, face."

Fitz and Corefelt turned and marched into the aisle. They executed another right face. Captain Holt's smiling picture greeted them again.

"Present, arms," Corefelt quietly murmured. He and Fitzgerald saluted their commander together. They held their arms in it for an interminable wrenching moment until Corefelt gave the command to "Order, arms."

"Right, face."

Corefelt and Fitz marched straight to the side, along the wall, and then out the front door into the merciless daylight. It was too bright for them.

Blue Platoon took the uneventful drive back to Murray and, once home, its men slinked off to their shipping container homes. None of them worked out, played video games, or entertained the usual diversions. They sullenly retreated, wooden doors banging shut.

Fitzgerald led by example. He trudged back to his CONEX, pathetically removing his boots and throwing his gear in a corner. It was divine to close his eyes and make the world end for a while. Red, black, dull. He could finally give up in his bunk instead of faking composure before everyone else. Only there, could he give in and rest for a short while.

He stirred a few hours later for chow, feeling marginally better. SSG Stalls found him and relayed that the XO wanted to see him, after he'd eaten. Fitzgerald briskly ate half his soggy orange pasta and then walked up to the TOC.

Fitz found 1st Lieutenant Nitmer sitting alone, uncomfortably beside Captain Holt's old workstation. The XO's spot had been placed side by side with the CO's computer on a worn plywood workbench. Holt had taken up two thirds of the table and Nitmer had always been bunched on the edge. But now with Holt gone, Nitmer couldn't bring himself to claim more of the table.

"I'm here, sir." Fitz announced, even though junior lieutenants didn't address senior lieutenants as sir. It felt appropriate to give the acting CO that deference.

Speaking to him returned Nitmer back to the present. "Oh... hey, Fitz." His eyes were red and bleary. "How was Captain Holt's memorial?"

Fitzgerald met his gaze as best he could. "It was... good. Felt right to be there," he lied.

Nitmer responded like Fitz had said something profound. "I bet it was," he said longingly.

Nitmer nodded a couple of times, and then hunched forward in his chair, staring at his computer screen.

"Do you... have something for me, sir?" Fitzgerald proffered.

"Oh yea, roger." Nitmer discontinued his own thoughts and rubbed his eyes. "Blue has a mission tomorrow at 1000. Standard patrol across Busayefi." He stopped kneading his face, and handed Fitz a folded piece of notebook paper. "Here's the checkpoints and NAI's I want you to hit."

Fitzgerald unfolded it and read the six checkpoint grids.

"Yes, sir. Wilco. Anything else?"

"Nah."

With that, Nitmer numbly turned back to his screen and started scrolling down his email inbox. Fitzgerald turned to go and then corrected himself. Dutifully, he walked over to the map on the wall and started mentally charting tomorrow's route. It would be a typical few hour patrol, canvassing the town of Busayefi and nearby farmland. He just didn't know how he or his guys could do it. They were beat.

Maybe after some more sleep they'd rejuvenate, but deep down he was doubtful. He plodded back to his metal room and briefed SSG Corefelt about the mission. Maybe tomorrow they'd be fine. Maybe tomorrow he'd be fine. He took off his boots and rolled back into bed. He turned to face the corrugated wall and burrowed deeper into his sleeping bag. Fitzgerald closed his eyes, and reached out for a moment's peace.

CHAPTER
TWENTY-ONE

THE NEXT MORNING FELT like the day before. Fitzgerald roused to his wristwatch chirping, his dark CONEX clutching him close like a warm padded coffin. The soothing night's sleep lingered in his mind and wouldn't recede. With difficulty, he coerced himself to get up and go find breakfast. Unfortunately, the burnt hash brown flakes and instant eggs he discovered made him regret his life choices. Excessive ketchup and hot coffee kept him from throwing it all in the garbage.

Back in the troop living area, Blue Platoon was physically present and doing its mission prep. The soldiers were grabbing their gear and carrying the 240B machine guns up to the trucks. Fitzgerald kitted up and went to the Bushmaster CP to see if anything had changed or if there was any overnight intelligence. Only SSG Stalls was present, cluelessly manning the radio, as per usual. He stole a fresh cup of coffee from the CP pot and went back outside without a word.

The sweltering summer heat had tapered off to a manageable, arid fall outside. Double digit heat was downright cool compared to triple. Blue Platoon had lined up four Humvees by the TOC and were going through the pre-patrol motions. Fitz leaned against a wooden post, sipped his black coffee, and watched. He regarded the swaying palm trees inside the compound and looked over the HESCO walls at the bleak horizon. Corefelt and Breyer walked over from spot checking the soldiers and joined him. They were noticeably mute.

The jovial bullshitting wasn't there. Not even predictable shoptalk. It took all their effort to stand there like they were supposed to.

At 0945 Lieutenant Fitzgerald was required to give the patrol brief. The men intuitively congregated around him, and he said the obligatory words. He rattled off the checkpoints and stared into their vacant eyes. He didn't ask any questions and neither did the NCOs. The men stared back. He gave the order to mount up and they did so mechanically.

Fitz got in his Humvee's front seat, and Serrano swung their vehicle around. The gravel crunched underneath their tires as the column of trucks drove slowly to the gate. Absent mindedly, he remembered to grab the radio handset and inform X-Ray that they were SPing. He almost forgot to switch on his vehicle's electronic warfare jammer as they exited PB Murray.

No one said, "Shake and Bake," over the platoon net. No one said anything.

Blue Platoon drove a few kilometers down the dirt farm roads, skirting Busayefi. The trucks bounced on the potholes on the path. Fitz's attention wandered to the air vent on his Humvee's dash. He'd never realized before how he could swivel the vent, open and close the shutters. Fitzgerald played with it, felt the gust of air ebb and flow. He giggled. Just like a real car!

What the hell was he doing?

Fitz caught himself. He shook his head back and forth and pinched his thigh meat to wake up. He snapped his fingers in front of his face. *Snap! Snap! Snap!* He eyed Serrano and Northland, and realized they were on autopilot like himself a few minutes ago. Serrano's eyes were locked on the bumper of the truck ahead. Northland wasn't rotating the turret as they drove around corners, his legs dangled lamely. This was bad, they were combat ineffective.

"Northland. *Northland.* Face the turret outward to the terrain as we drive. Don't flag the vehicle in front of us."

"Roger, LT," he acknowledged weakly.

Northland swiveled the turret a few degrees and stopped. Nothing more.

They were approaching Checkpoint One quickly. It was becoming clear to Fitz that any enemy contact would be catastrophic for them. The road checkpoint loomed ahead, beside it sprawled a flat hillock overlooking the canals and farmland.

"Two this is One. Let's roll up on that hill and set up a perimeter."

"Roger, One." Breyer's response was deadpan.

The platoon drove up off the road and circled wagons on the patch of cleared land. The drivers maneuvered and jostled their trucks, until each faced outward. The gunners rotated their turrets out and a perimeter was set.

Fitz looked at his watch. 10:22. He grabbed the hand-mic.

"X-Ray this is Blue One. Checkpoint One reached, time now."

"Acknowledge, Blue One."

"Blue One out."

Fitz sat there and thought through what he'd do for the next five minutes. After some internal wrestling he grabbed the hand-mic again.

"Four, Two, Three, all TC's, let's talk outside."

"Moving One."

Fitz exited his truck and slammed the thick armored door shut. Sergeants Corefelt and Breyer joined him first. Corporal Gonzalez took a moment longer to get his huge frame out of his vehicle. Only Corefelt had brought his M4. Fitz looked at their faces and saw the same blank stare in their eyes.

Fitz waited another moment and drew a long breath through his nose. He eventually spat it out: "We're not doing this today... We can barely drive around. If we get contact we're going to be slow, somebody will die."

The NCOs stood there, grasping the front of their protective vests, not volunteering a word.

.

"Do you guys disagree?"

..

"Nah sir. You're right," SGT Breyer said. He turned his head and spat tobacco juice into a puddle.

They stood quietly for a little longer. CPL Gonzalez clicked off his MBITER radio in his vest webbing.

. . .

"What are we going to do then?" SSG Corefelt said. He knew, but he wanted the LT to say it.

. . . .

2nd Lieutenant Fitzgerald thought it through and deliberately chose his words. "We're going to sit here and I'll call up the checkpoints every 30 minutes. It's not right but I'm not losing someone a few weeks before we go home. Everyone is spent."

The three NCOs looked at each other and thought about it. Breyer and Gonzalez nodded.

"Yessir. We got your back," affirmed Corefelt.

"Alright, tell the guys not to talk about it. Let's get back in the trucks."

Fitzgerald popped back in his vehicle without giving the NCOs a second look. He didn't want them to change their minds. He settled into his seat and stared out across the Iraqi farmland.

After a couple of minutes, Serrano spoke up, "Sir, are we gonna start moving soon?"

"Negative. We're staying right here. All day."

"Yes, sir."

Fitz checked his watch. 10:55. Good enough. He grabbed the hand-mic and keyed it.

"*X-Ray this is Blue One. Checkpoint Two reached, time now.*"

He waited for skepticism. He waited for someone to call bullshit...

"*Acknowledge Blue at Checkpoint Two,*" SSG Stalls sounded bored and unaware as always.

"*Blue One out,*" he said quickly.

"Huh," he scoffed. He felt relief but also disappointment. His gut said this was the right choice, but the rules disagreed.

Every West Point leadership exercise had preached *The Hard Right over the Easy Wrong*. Standards would now drop, discipline would break down. Soldiers would see what they could get away with. Chaos would reign.

But that wasn't true. He had men who'd been here 14 months, who couldn't function anymore. They were done. Was choosing not to drive down some canal roads in Iraq a betrayal of everything? Could anything else they did here justify losing another man?

Bushmaster Troop was finished here. They'd soaked enough blood into Iraq's soil.

Fitz stewed in his existential crisis for a while. Serrano took off his helmet and scratched his head. Northland hummed to himself and merrily tapped his feet from his perch in the turret.

Fitz checked his watch. 11:28. He called up Checkpoint Three with the same response. Each one got easier. Then Four. He took his helmet off so his head could breathe. Serrano shared the blueberry muffins and packets of cinnamon shortbread cookies from breakfast with them. Fitzgerald washed them down with a bottle of water and stepped outside briefly to piss on the rear tire well.

Fitz called in Five and then finally Six. He'd committed to his decision, and there was no going back. He waited another twenty minutes after calling up the last checkpoint and ordered the platoon to head home. Blue Platoon RP-ed home safely without incident after conducting its patrol. The Bushmaster and squadron records corroborated that story completely.

They were saved by the bell. Orders arrived that Bushmaster and 8-6 CAV were slated to turn over their AO and leave Iraq at the end of the month. They were almost done with Murray, Dolby, Adwaniyah, Busayefi, Zambraynia, Talon, Iraq, and Southwest Asia in general.

Everyone was skeptical. The troop had been there 14 months and had shifted sectors numerous times already. This could be yet another operation. Going home at the end of this latest order seemed as real as winning the Powerball.

The XO's egress plan was straightforward. PB Murray's equipment would be gradually downsized until the remainder could be hauled out with the troop or turned over to the IA. They'd have a ceremony to hand over the Combat Outpost to the Iraqis and then get in their trucks and leave. There would be no relief in place with an incoming unit. Bushmaster would convoy to FOB Kalamazoo, turn in their trucks and equipment there, chopper to an airbase, and finally fly home. The rest of 8-6 CAV would travel down to FOB Scania and exit the country from there.

Active patrolling for most of the platoons ceased immediately, and Blue Platoon was markedly grateful for it. The men were refocused to loading shipping containers: unpacking, inventorying, and then cramming it back in like a game of Tetris. They would strip down to their tan undershirts and faded gray trousers and form human chains to manhandle equipment back and forth. Vehicle wheels, bench stock spare parts, road cones, cables, recovery tools, extra computers, cold weather gear, leaky cans of oil and joint lubricants, junk accessories still on the books. It was all duly checked, repackaged, and accounted for.

However mundane the task was, the men eagerly attacked a new container each morning. Sergeant Corefelt would make two copies of each packing list, leave one inside the CONEX, and take the other one for his records. Fitzgerald, quickly feeling useless supervising the loading, immediately discarded his tunic and joined the platoon each day. It felt more honest to heave boxes alongside them.

As the sun rose high every day, it bore down on the men and the soldiers slaving inside the metal boxes roasted.

Like clockwork, Fitzgerald getting dirty eventually irked Corefelt, getting the same reaction as always from him, "Ah shit, sir. Now you're gonna make me work!" Corefelt stripped off his uniform top and started tossing boxes. In no time, everyone was grimy with sweat and brown dust. At night the men would crowd the Spaware internet café sending messages to their spouses and kids. Hoping to see if anyone would meet them upon arrival, if this wasn't another false alarm. Fitzgerald sent emails to his mom and dad, trying to give them a timeline, while also being vague about specifics.

Eventually, after two weeks, the packing was done. Containers were locked tight and sealed with serial numbered thin metallic bands to prevent tampering. All that remained was the handover ceremony and their departure.

The momentous event got booked for noon the next day in the gravel motorpool. Iraqi Army colonels, Lieutenant Colonel Gute, Captain Mohammed and other "partners" had RSVPed for the transition of authority. The SOIs were not invited. Fitzgerald ensured that he and Blue Platoon would not be a part of it.

The affair concluded and the Brigade Newsletter published 400 words about it with the headline: "Victory in Iraq". After the colonels left, the IA started looting their new base. Bushmaster withdrew to its remaining areas and waited out their last night.

Fitz was restless and wanted to be useful that evening. The TOC needed to be emptied out, and it had five boxes of sensitive papers that needed to be burned. So, like a German retreating from Normandy, he took the confidential documents out back and set about incinerating them.

Fitzgerald unceremoniously dumped the CLASSIFIED stacks into a half-oil drum that had been revamped into a rustic fire pit. It was reams and reams of wasted paper. Some crumpled, others colored, a few with graphics and maps. Buried in some paragraph could have been something exculpatory, but largely it was mundane traffic about past operations. He teased the edges of a few pages with his lighter until the flame began to catch and spread.

The blaze grew and the pyre comforted him. He watched the fire's maw inhale the sheets, blacken, crunch, and consume the documents. The papers' immolation tamped down his darker thoughts. He lit a cigarette and watched secrets slip away. The smoke and warmth massaged the pain away from his forehead. The cinders flaked and flew disintegrating into the air.

As he regarded his ash heap a scraping racket ruined his zen. An Iraqi in civilian clothes, probably a Jundi, was dragging a two by twenty foot strip of aluminum sheeting across the yard. Fitz recognized the material as a shed roof from across their TOC. The metal screeched and the front of it coiled back like a toboggan as the man tried to sneak it past him.

"Hey! Ali Baba! What the hell are you doing?!" he yelled at the thieving Iraqi.

The Iraqi, surprised, muttered back in broken English, gesticulating spastically with his hands.

"Aref Campbeell said I could… have it," he pleaded.

Jesus. This Iraqi had seen Aladdin's treasures before him and had chosen a strip of roofing as his share. Fuck it.

Fitzgerald was at his boiling point. "Fine, dude. Whatever. It's your country."

If the Iraqis ratfucked everything the second they were gone, then that was their choice. America's help could only go so far. He was going home. Fitzgerald gazed back into the embers and tried to recapture his moment. He was going home. *He was going home.*

CHAPTER TWENTY-TWO

AT DAYBREAK THE BUSHMASTER MEN threw their neatly rolled sleeping bags into their trucks and prepared to roll out. They were groggy and irritable, but didn't dare stop moving. Everything that wasn't in the containers was shoved into the vehicle crew compartments, strapped to a buzzlerack, or hastily destroyed. It was a military, gypsy caravan. A well-ordered, neat, bristling with machine guns, gypsy caravan.

Without a kiss goodbye, the convoy left Patrol Base Murray and lumbered down the dirt road towards FOB Kalamazoo. Murray, the bustling outpost that had been a home for a summer, already appeared desolate. Its front gate and guard towers were unmanned, as the trucks passed through its entrance for the last time.

The thirty odd vehicles yo-yoed out of the surrounding village of Busayefi and onto the canal roads. Only stray dogs watched them go, as the orange sun crested above the horizon. The long, mechanized line snaked out over the early morning landscape, and the gunners poked their heads out of their turrets. Some of the slower vehicles struggled to keep the pace. Each truck's tires spun over oil and brown muck, a choking, dust tail forming after the last ten vehicles. They sped past palm trees, farmhouses, and intermittent SOI checkpoints, the lead drivers trying to achieve 40 MPH, and the trail drivers trying to keep up. The men were road warriors by now, accustomed to daylong stretches behind the wheel. For them, it was just another long patrol.

Sometime around 1030, one of the Headquarters Platoon Humvees, HQ7, sputtered and died. A short halt for the convoy was called and the men took the opportunity to piss or smoke outside their vehicles. A few emptied their piss bottles onto the side of the road, leaving momentary dark splotches. SGT Nixon, SSG Corefelt, and a few men hooked the lame truck up to another Humvee with a towbar. The convoy got back in motion in 20 minutes, before anyone could mess with them.

After seven hours of driving, Bushmaster Troop reached FOB Kalamazoo unscathed.

Despite safely reaching the sanctuary of the FOB, there was still plenty more to do. The troop wasn't merely parking their trucks at Kalamazoo, they were transferring that property off their books to another Army unit. Until they did that, no one was taking a helicopter to any airbase. Everything had to be cleaned, inventoried, laid out, turned in, or reorganized. Paperwork had to be corrected, in triplicate, and then some other unit had to sign for it. And no supply sergeant wanted thirty half broken trucks that had been banged up for 14 months. Bushmaster had to shine their turds, until they were reasonably acceptable to someone.

However, this transfer relied mostly on the XO and the supply sergeant's work. LT Nitmer and SGT Nixon spent 16 to 18 hour days rectifying and uploading paperwork or tasking out the platoons as necessary to manhandle, swap out, and clean equipment. For Fitzgerald, Corefelt, and Blue Platoon, it was mostly marking time: sleeping, eating, working out, and waiting to fly to Al Saad Airbase.

While they waited, Bushmaster Troop barracked in the FOB transient housing, a mammoth, khaki oval-shaped structure that resembled a big top circus tent. It and twenty other identical shelters had been erected in a grid to house the constant movement of troops through Iraq. Years ago, the canvas walls had been hosed down with foam polymers and the liquid coating had hardened to make it a permanent structure. A boxy, wooden alcove resembling an outhouse had been constructed at the front and back of the tent and a Quartermaster's number was painted on its door. Their tent was 10G. Inside were two rows of cots parallel to the long sides, a heap of broken cot poles and cloth, an AC unit, and overhead lights. The troop had moved inside its new home, and each man had claimed his own green Army cot, positioning his bags by the foot of his bed.

Fitz and Corefelt had seized two bunks next to other at the far end and let the platoon fill in the others. At first, Fitzgerald relished the extra rack time he'd been craving all deployment. But now, after a few days of being given his utmost wish, he was exhausted of sleep.

From then on, each day, Fitzgerald woke up, put on his uniform, shaved, and lay on his cot. No one knew how long it would take the XO to clear the books. Ten days? Two weeks? They were stuck here in limbo until then. Corefelt ran the platoon work details for what little labor they had to do, making the lieutenant effectively useless. Fitzgerald had all the time in the world to contemplate his tour's meaning.

Fitz was lying on his bunk one morning when Corefelt sauntered in with some plastic bags. He merrily sat down on his adjacent cot and started rummaging through them.

"Hey sir! Have you checked out the Haji shop here by the PX? The DVDs here are only a buck compared to three at Talon!"

Fitzgerald perked up from his cot. This was the most interesting thing in days. "Really? Show me what you got!"

Corefelt dumped the bags onto his cot and started organizing his haul. Each disc was a pirated movie in a thin plastic sleeve with a lifted image from the original film poster. Most included Arabic wording and misspelled English.

"Let's see… I've got the *Dark Knight*."

"Great, but I've seen it three times already."

"Okay — *Iron Man, Tropic Thunder, Quantum of Solace, Hulk, Twilight*…"

"*Twilight*?"

"Yea — I got it for my daughter. That and *Ku Fung Panda*."

"Nah, I've seen all these before."

"You've seen *Twilight* before?" Corefelt jested.

"No! I meant all the other ones! Got anything else?"

"How about this?" Corefelt held up a boxed set that looked fancier but was still clearly pirated. "I got every season of *South Park* for $20."

"Nice. Alright — let's watch some."

"Yea! I hope its good quality."

Corefelt pulled out his laptop from his ruck and fired it up. Fitzgerald sat up on his bed and they shared earpods to hear the audio. Watching that killed a few hours, until the next meal.

After lunch, Fitzgerald found himself where he had started again. To do something, anything, he started reading novels donated to soldiers on post. Novels so good that they were left behind forever in Iraq. He picked up one about the Gilded Age and learned how hard it must have been to be a Railroad Baron's daughter.

As he wallowed there, Fitzgerald sorted through his memories of what Iraq had been, and tried to make sense of it. He couldn't and it frustrated him. So he tried to think ahead to what home would offer: women, alcohol, family, friends, his own toilet. Those things would make this time away better. They had to. He'd stew on that until the next meal hour. Then, on cue, Corefelt would come gather him, and they'd walk over to the dining hall. They'd eat, talk, and then return to the big tent. He'd read for a bit and then fall asleep. Groundhog Day. Rinse and repeat.

The next morning, as if to break the monotony, a sandstorm rolled in and drove everyone indoors. The fierce outdoor heat normally confined the men to the tent for most of the day, but now they didn't have a choice. The storm could be seen approaching for hours before it hit the FOB, a monstrous dirty blob gradually consuming the blue horizon. As it advanced the last mile, the atmosphere darkened and the wind ratcheted up to cyclone speeds. The swirling mass assumed a blood orange hue and it became hard to breathe and see. Fine grit blasted every surface, each soldier had to cover his mouth or else taste the sediment in the air. Even the boldest soul donned goggles or sunglasses to protect his eyes from the onslaught.

After gawking at the storm as long as they could, Fitz and the men retreated inside their tent and secured the doors. The air outside bellowed and threw tantrums, flinging debris on the shelter walls. The loose dirt sounded like hundreds of beetles scampering over the exterior, their bodies clicking and scattering in every direction.

They sat in awe and listened to the maelstrom outside until SGT Breyer realized the walls had sprung leaks. Through every pinhole and crevice silently seeped wisps of brown sand, polluting their atmosphere.

"It's coming in! Everybody grab some 100 mile an hour tape and a flashlight and start patching holes!" he yelled.

Fitz and the men scrambled to seal shut all seams and cracks in the compromised tent walls. Only with their flashlight beams could they see the fine particles sneaking in. The dust kept creeping its way in through small holes and zippers, invigorating the men to examine every section of the wall with lights, frantically patching as they went. Outside the wind shrieked louder, distant horns of Jericho rising in pitch, threatening to topple the shelter and then dissipating away.

After ten minutes of concerted work, the shelter sealed as best they could, the men returned to their cots. Fitzgerald took off his watch and boots and burrowed deep into his sleeping bag. He wished he could hibernate until they were released to fly, and vowed he would try his best to. Outside the wails and Stuka sirens abated into hollow howls and gasping breath. The exterior commotion made his bedding cozier and lulled him back into sleep's arms once more.

The storm blew away and more meals came and went. Fitzgerald had lost track of the days, let alone what month it was. December? Definitely not Christmas yet or else there would have been a lavish meal in the dining hall. He hoped they could make it home before then. The

Bushmasters who had deployed at the beginning had already missed one Christmas with their families.

Mercifully, the XO and SGT Nixon came into the shelter one morning and announced that they were finished. Another unit had signed for their trucks and equipment. The paperwork had been approved and confirmed.

Everyone in the tent, moments ago bored and listless, suddenly was roused and elated. Fitz jumped up and slapped the two on the back. Sergeant Corefelt rushed Nixon and gave him a burly bear hug.

"It's about damn time, Nixon!" Corefelt grinned merrily as he squeezed him.

"Thanks Cory... ouch," Nixon grimaced. "Please put me down."

Even Top broke his usual restraint to congratulate them. "Good work men!"

"Took you long enough, LT," he said with a wink to the XO.

First Sergeant Tapwell and Lieutenant Nitmer conferred for a moment. While they talked, the platoon sergeants sent runners to recall everyone.

"Get everyone back here, NOW!"

While they waited for the whole troop to muster, the men hurriedly started packing up. Each man rolled up his sleeping bag, pulled out his gear, and compressed everything into his olive-green duffel. Whatever trash from candy or electronics they'd bought from the PX was policed up and thrown away. Hangers and other temporary fixtures were discarded or set somewhere neatly for the next transient.

Top and the XO waited until the platoon sergeants had accountability of everyone. After they got the thumbs up, Top pulled them all into a huddle around him.

"No need for a formation men, just hear what I have to put out. It's going on 1130, I want every man to take all weapons and NODs to the sensitive items container, and then grab chow. XO, Nixon, and the armorer will be there for you to turn in items."

"Then, the XO has gotten us cleared to leave, and we're set to fly at 1900 to Al Saad. We'll have a troop formation at the PAX terminal at

1600. All bags, all gear, Loddy Doddy Everybody. Platoon sergeants, make sure your soldiers eat now. We may have to miss dinner to fly."

"Any questions?"

"Everyone put on a clean uniform to fly home in!" interrupted Sergeant Corefelt.

"Any more questions.... or comments?" Top shot a look at Corefelt.

"No first sergeant!" they all shouted in merry unison.

"Alright. Let's get out of here."

Fitz felt strange without his weapon. Walking around without his rifle or pistol made him feel incomplete. All part of getting back home, he thought.

They'd already turned in most of their ammo and each man dumped his remaining rounds out of his force protection mag into a wooden amnesty box. The Bushmaster men sat expectantly on their bags outside the PAX terminal for hours only to be herded inside once it grew dark. Bored Army clerks checked them in and weighed them with their bags, directing them into a larger well-lit waiting room with uncomfortable wooden benches and the Armed Forces Network playing on TVs.

Fitzgerald waited anxiously for their 1900 departure, only to have his hopes dashed when the hour slipped by. After that, no one could give them a straight answer as to how much longer it would be. The men, accepting their purgatory, slumped down onto their bags and waited. Some of the joy wore off.

"Get up! It's time!"

Sometime after 2200, the gate doors were flung open and the men were hurried out into the rushing darkness. They tramped out onto the hardened LZ to two blacked out Chinook helicopters, their blades deafeningly loud, as the men approached. Fitz groped through his pockets to find his earplugs and jammed the hard plastic into his ear canals before he lost any more hearing.

Chinooks were the Army's transport mule, long, sleek, green, banana-shaped copters with two rotor blades. They boarded through lowered ramps in the rear, throwing their bags in the center, and buckling into benches on the sides of the craft. Anyone trying to yell commands was drowned out by the roaring rotors.

The Flight Crew Chief did a cursory check of them, ratchet strapped the cargo down, and then raised the mechanical ramp 45 degrees. He didn't close it but it did provide a little incline to prevent anyone or anything from sliding out. The Crew Chief walked to the end of the ramp, straddled a machine gun, and clamped himself in. The rotors' noise strained, and Fitzgerald could feel the craft lifting off quickly. His body braced against the G-forces, as brilliant blazing countermeasures fired automatically from the helicopter's tail feathers. The flares were beautiful amber will-o'-the-wisps in the night sky, both comforting and disconcerting. He hoped no one had them in their crosshairs.

Upon arrival at Al Saad Airbase, the elation of travel wore off, and the hurry-up-and-wait continued. They were shepherded into white buses from the LZ and shuttled to another cantonment area. The drive took thirty minutes, and then they disembarked. Cadre with reflective vests directed them through T-Walls into an open yard outside a khaki building. The ground inside the walls was topped with metal Air Force load palettes. It was still dark out, so tall, generator-powered lights were cranked on to illuminate the spot. Each man had to make a couple of trips to the buses to lug his bags, rucksack, and gear to the waiting area. The Bushmaster men instinctively made a loose formation and sat on their bags. And then, they waited there too.

Fitz had stopped checking his watch because time no longer mattered. He mentally checked that his platoon was settled and then plopped down on his own bags. He tried to rest his back on his rucksack but the angle felt all wrong, and he had to crane his neck forward. He dozed fitfully for a moment.

"On your feet!"

"Get up men!" came the more conciliatory command from Top.

They all grumbled and stood erect.

Top walked up to the front of the formation and peered at his troop under the electric light.

"Alright, men. Customs will be out here in five minutes to inspect your bags. So, open them up and dump them out. This shouldn't be a surprise. Any contraband that you have can still be put in the amnesty boxes. No questions asked! Once you get inside this building though, it's a different story."

Hooray, thought Fitz. He opened his bags and neatly laid out his belongings. The last thing he wanted was to fold it all again. His green socks, tan shirts, plastic baggies filled with uniform items, books, cold weather gear, warm weather gear, extra boots, camelback, PT belt, and camo tops and bottoms were all strewn about his little space.

More than five minutes later, Army customs agents and drug smelling German Shepherds walked out into the formation. The inspectors walked through each row quickly, occasionally stopping to flip over an item, open a sealed box, and to tell the soldiers to not pet the dogs.

"All done. Pack it up!"

The soldiers did as they were told. Then, they all dragged and hefted their bags to form a line into the customs building. Their entrance funneled them in cattle chutes to the airport X-Ray machines. They inched and pushed their bags forward. Their bags were run through machines and came out the other end. Each man was then directed to take his bags to a wooden cubicle with a large built-in tray and dump out his bags again.

Fitz complied and was relieved that the inspector didn't discover some contraband that he'd forgotten. Others were not so lucky. One soldier had mistakenly put a full magazine of ammo in his bags, a few others had lighters. Stenracker had a twelve-inch knife in his luggage for some reason.

"GET OVER HERE DUMBASS!" erupted Corefelt onto Stenracker.

Stenracker, terrified, sprinted over to Sergeant Corefelt, and stood at parade rest with his contraband blade.

"STENRACKER." Corefelt sounded exasperated. "WHY do you have a KNIFE in your bag? After we checked EVERYONE'S bag MULTIPLE TIMES!?"

"It's from my other deployment, sergeant. I forgot that I had it!" Stenracker pleaded.

"You forgot? YOU FORGOT?!?" Corefelt was apoplectic. "You forgot a GIANT KNIFE?! I'm giving you TEN seconds to get rid of it starting now…TEN…NINE…EIGHT…SEVEN…"

Panic-stricken, Stenracker frantically scanned the room for the nearest trash can and sprinted over to it. He flung the knife into it and darted back to SSG Corefelt.

"FOURTHREETWOONE!"

"It's gone sergeant!" Stenracker grimaced, ready for the next punishment.

"GOOD! Get the fuck outta here!"

The customs agents seemed satisfied with Corefelt's remedy. Stenracker hurriedly packed up his gear and retreated from sight as fast as he could.

Once each man was approved by Customs, he dragged his gear out the back of the building into yet another enclosed courtyard. It had grown light outside now. This was the final holding area before the plane. The area had latrines, a coffee shop, and three long recreation buildings filled with couches and TVs. Thankfully, each rec center's dayroom also included a table stocked with pop tarts, muffins, granola bars, and Gatorade drinks to hold them over. Each man claimed a new piece of real estate and bided his time.

So the Bushmaster men sat petulantly inside or paced the little courtyard. How many more hours? Coffee and pop tarts helped. Fitz finished his trashy novel and threw it away. He wouldn't subject anyone else to that rambling, pointless story.

Another six to eight hours later they were finally told to form up in the courtyard. They lined up alphabetically with their bags to manifest and did a last roll call.

"Here, first sergeant! *HERE, FIRST SERGEANT!!!*" they screamed at the top of their lungs.

The Air Force PAX handlers organized them into a single file line and led them out onto the tarmac. The line of men stretched out long and thin towards the idling airplane. A big beautiful 747 was there waiting for them.

As they walked towards it, they were approached by an identical line of debarking passengers in Army gray, an incoming unit. The fresh arrivals' uniforms were spotless and they looked younger. Both sides nodded silent greetings and filed past one another.

As they strode forward, every step filled them with excitement. A Bushmaster man behind Fitz spoke his thoughts out loud: "It's better to be in this line than the other one!"

CHAPTER TWENTY-THREE

THE FIRST LEG HOME was a ten-hour flight to Ramstein, Germany, another American waystation pinpointing the globe. When they landed to refuel, the men were let off the airplane to stretch their legs. The soldiers still couldn't drink alcohol or use their cellphones, but they could buy souvenirs. Chocolate, gummi bears, and beer steins fabricated a story that they had seen more of Germany than an airport.

Fitz separated himself from the mob of men in the terminal and wandered off on his own. His head throbbed mercilessly. He'd slept as much as he could on the flight only to awake to nausea and airsickness. Fitzgerald was fed up with enclosed spaces. He paced slowly along the cordoned area's walls, testing this new cage, trying to find its limits.

He discovered that the terminal had been walled off from the rest of the airport. Fitz rounded the perimeter of the sequestered wing, searching, until he found the entrance to the outdoor smoking section. He cracked open the door and was pleasantly surprised to see First Sergeant Tapwell, puffing away, alone. Cool, clean air gusted through the opening and beckoned to him. Freedom. Fitzgerald stepped outside to a patio protected by a small overhang. Above him, the dark, Teutonic sky rumbled. Beyond the patio's cover, single drops of cold rain began falling and wetting the tarmac.

"Can I get a smoke, Top?" he asked.

"Sure, LT," Tapwell said, offering an open pack of Camels. "I love it when people take a few of these away from me."

Fitzgerald took one and pawed the unlit cigarette for a moment in his hands. He then sparked it aflame with his lighter. The nicotine rush and relative solitude immediately soothed his aching head. He closed his eyes to revel in the reprieve. He devoured the first cigarette and then bummed another. He started chain smoking with Top, puffing faster, he couldn't stop. The sweet tobacco smoke spread through his respiratory cavities and wafted over his clothes. The casual nicotine buzz was welcomed and loosened his speech. It compelled him to reveal the demons that were tormenting him.

"How you doing, LT?" First Sergeant Tapwell said poignantly. He eyed Fitz with a perceptive look, the older man knew what he was doing.

Even though Fitzgerald didn't consciously know it, he'd been waiting for this opportunity away from the men. He gladly let down his guard to Tapwell.

"Top... I'm...I'm lost," he sighed deeply.

The next words took time to form from his churning emotions.

"We've all... lost. None of this... *is right,*" he said, "It's not fair." He slowly unraveled his mental tourniquet and the words began to gush out.

"We fought so hard for these Iraqis, hand it over to 'em, and then they FUCK IT UP!" His anger flashed abruptly. "They squabble and fight each other like children. It's a personal power grab over actually building a real country! IT'S ALL BEEN A WASTE!"

Fitzgerald's face got flushed and agitated. Somebody had to hear this. He went on.

"And despite all our brave words, we're no better than the Iraqis! You have men like Captain Holt, who are brilliant and care, and he's POINTLESSLY KILLED! And Lieutenant Colonel Gute, who's nit-picked and undercut him the entire deployment, says he was his mentor at his funeral?! Says Holt was following his brilliant vision the whole time! IT'S SUCH LYING BULLSHIT! How does he get away with it?? How do these terrible people exist?!"

Fitzgerald peered wildly around their little smoker's enclosure, confirming no one else had heard his heresy. His head and shoulders twitched and he flung his lit smoke out into the rain. He gazed away at the overcast Ramstein airfield and briefly contemplated darting out into the shadowy German fields. Instead he clutched his mouth, and muffled a frustrated howl.

He paced back and forth fruitlessly and then took a seat rigidly on the metal bench there. Fitzgerald sat unnaturally and stared at Tapwell, unnerved and spent, resentful, demanding answers.

Top regarded him and let a long moment pass in silence. He kept eyeing the lieutenant for another round of antics.

"You done, LT?" Tapwell finally asked flatly. He lifted his cigarette up beneath his bristly, cavalry mustache and sucked in more smoke.

"Sure," Fitz said, defeated. He threw out his hands angrily, demonstrating his surrender.

Tapwell stared back at Fitzgerald for another protracted moment. The quiet made Fitz even more uneasy. At last, deliberately, Top spoke.

"First off LT... A-Rabs are gonna be A-Rabs. Don't you fret none about them," Tapwell spoke in a fatherly tone now to Fitzgerald, homespun but wise.

"We gave 'em a chance at democracy and maybe we'll give 'em another chance ten years from now. Those rights mean somethin' even if they throw 'em away."

Top took another drag and paused. The smoke escaped out of his nose.

"Captain Holt knew that. He knew it better than all of us." Tapwell's eyes momentarily betrayed hurt when he said Holt's name. With effort he shoved that emotion aside.

He stroked his mustache and delicately continued, "Just because the A-Rabs couldn't handle it don't mean it ruins what that gift was worth." He stopped for a second. The rain grew louder, trying to hush their voices.

"And as for the SCO... that guy... there'll always be Bright-boy colonels that use the Captain Holts of the world to build their stupid little empires. They'll brag about empty formations they built, but all they did was get promoted and suck others dry. Don't waste another thought on them. Do your time, get out, and go do anything else."

"Wait. What?" Fitzgerald broke back in. "Get outta the Army?" He wasn't a quitter.

"Yep. I didn't stutter," Top said straight at him. "The Army needs good men that care, but it screwed the pooch on us here. I can tell that you no longer believe in it. I doubt you'll ever get it back."

"Sure LT, you'll never find half the meaning anywhere else as you did in Bushmaster, but you won't have to obey these idiots' orders anymore. There'll be a bunch of jobs back home with missions that sound important, that are there to help somebody, or solve whatever, fix the world or whatever highfalutin purpose, but it'll be bullshit and you'll know it's bullshit. Go have a family, start a business, make something real. Know that you loved America so much that you volunteered for this and that you've earned the right to never come back to it."

Fitzgerald scoffed and gulped in a breath. All this was a lot to process.

The crosswinds shrugged the showers sideways, and the raindrops scrubbed the asphalt before them.

"Well shit Top, then why do you stay in?" was all he could say back.

"I ain't got the education you got LT… And I enjoy making these field grades trip up from time to time."

Fitzgerald sat there, puzzled.

"So you stay in, and I should get out and build something?"

"Yep," Tapwell nodded. "Just don't be selfish like these A-Rabs or colonels or average Americans. Whatever you do, whatever you build, share it with others."

Fitzgerald chewed on that for a moment. He tucked it away carefully in his mind and then made a joke of it. "Like buy you a new pack of smokes?"

"Like buy yourself one, and then share it with me."

Fitzgerald chuckled for the first time in weeks.

"Don't worry LT. You'll be all right," Top said.

Fitzgerald didn't think so, but the laugh reminded him that there were better things still out there.

As the flight descended towards America, Fitz's spirits lifted. Tapwell was right about a lot of things. He needed to leave those worn out pieces of himself behind in Iraq, Germany, and this airplane. He sighed and released a little more of his despair. He felt relieved to soon escape the plane's cramped cabin after another twelve hours of flight. Fitzgerald closed his eyes and massaged his face with his palm. His mind drifted as he felt gravity pull the aircraft closer to the earth.

The flight hydraulics whined with the descent, but he swore he heard something else. Singing? Soft yet proud. A tone of unapologetic, defiant, survivor's joy. Fitzgerald couldn't tell what song it was. He tried to catch the cadence.

"I wouldn't give a bean to be a fancy pants Marine.
I'd rather be a Dog-Faced Soldier like I am."

Fitz craned his neck up and looked around the airplane cabin. He saw two grizzled specialists chirping away, daring someone to correct them. Smartasses. They were singing the Division's Dog Faced Soldier Song.

"I wouldn't trade my old OD's, for all the Navy's dungarees,
For I'm the walking pride of Uncle Sam."

More men joined it. They grew bolder.

"On Army posters that I read it says Be all that you can
So they're tearing me down to build me over again."

Fitz started singing the disgruntled melody. His voice was taunting, full-throated, bitter, and prideful.

"I'm just a Dog-Faced Soldier!
With a rifle on my shoulder!
I eat raw meat for breakfast every day!!
So feed me ammunition. Keep me in the Third Division.
Your Dog-Faced Soldier's A-OK!"

As soon as they ended, they started again. Now the whole cabin of soldiers was crooning along.

> *"I wouldn't give a BEAN to be a fancy pants MARINE.*
> *I'D RATHER BE A DOG-FACED SOLDIER LIKE I AM."*

They started kicking the backs of seats and some men stood. Like a boisterous bar chorus, they grew louder and fiercer. If they had beer bottles they would have thrown them. They proudly sang a round and then another. Again and again. Waves of elation and relief cascaded down Fitzgerald's spine. He was done! He was free of that place! He felt delirious with joy.

> *"...I'M JUST A DOG-FACED SOLDIER!*
> *WITH A RIFLE ON MY SHOULDER!*
> *I EAT RAW MEAT FOR BREAKFAST EVERYDAY!!"*

They'd taken the worst and endured it. No one could stop them.

> *"SO FEED ME AMMUNITION.*
> *KEEP ME IN THE THIRD DIVISION!*
> *YOUR DOG FACED SOLDIER'S A-OK!"*

The plane touched down onto the runway and the men cheered. The tires whooshed like a runner sliding into home plate. The Bushmaster men smiled and clapped each other on the back.

"Welcome to Savannah, Georgia," the pilot announced over the intercom. "You're home!"

The plane taxied and pulled close to the terminal. They stopped and a stair ramp was wheeled up to the cabin door. As the door opened, Fitz caught a glimpse outside of America, still there, waiting for him.

THE END

U.S Army Rank Structure

Enlisted

PVT – Private Soldier

PV2 – Private Second Class

PFC – Private First Class

SPC – Specialist

Non-Commissioned Officers

CPL – Corporal

SGT – Sergeant

SSG – Staff Sergeant

SFC – Sergeant First Class

1SG / MSG – First Sergeant / Master Sergeant

CSM / SGM – Command Sergeant Major / Sergeant Major

Officers

2LT – 2nd Lieutenant

1LT – 1st Lieutenant

CPT – Captain

MAJ – Major

LTC – Lieutenant Colonel

COL – Colonel

General

Iraqi Army Company Level Rank Structure

Jundi – Enlisted

Aref – Non-Commissioned Officers

Mulazim – Lieutenant

Naqeeb – Captain

Army Unit Structure

Team – 3 or 4 soldiers led by a specialist or corporal

Squad – 6 to 11 soldiers led by a sergeant

Platoon – 18 to 30 soldiers led by a lieutenant and a sergeant. Often designated by color (Red, White, Blue, Black)

Troop / Company – 80 to 100 soldiers led by a captain and a first sergeant. Designated by letter with corresponding names (A, B, C; Angry, Bushmaster, Courage)

Squadron / Battalion – 400 to 1000 soldiers led by a lieutenant colonel and a sergeant major. Designated by numbers and specialty (8-6 Cavalry)

Brigade – 1000 to 3000 soldiers led by a colonel and a sergeant major. Designated by number (4th Brigade)

Division – 5000+ soldiers led by a general and a sergeant major. Designated by number and specialty (3rd Infantry Division)

Common Terms and Acronyms

Abrams Tank – U.S. Main Battle Tank

ACU – Army Combat Uniform

AK-47 – Russian Assault Rifle

Apache – Army Attack Helicopter

AQI – Al Qaeda in Iraq

AO – Area of Operations

Black Hawk – Midsize Army Transport Helicopter

Bradley – Infantry Fighting Vehicle

BUB – Battle Update Brief

Charlie Mike – Continue Mission

Chinook – Large Army Transport Helicopter

CO – Commanding Officer

COP – Combat Outpost (same as PB)

CONEX – Storage Container

CP – Command Post (same as TOC)

CVC – Combat Vehicle Crewman Helmet

DAGR – Handheld Global Positioning System

DShK / Dushka – Russian Heavy Machine Gun

EFP – Explosively Formed Projectile

EOD – Explosive Ordnance Disposal

FO – Forward Observer

FOB – Forward Operating Base

FSO – Fire Support Officer

GPS – Global Positioning Systems (same as PLGR/DAGR)

HESCO – Barrier Material

HOOAH – Army Battle Cry

HMMWV – High Mobility Multipurpose Wheeled Vehicle or "Humvee"

HQ - Headquarters

IA – Iraqi Army

IED – Improvised Explosive Device

KIA – Killed In Action

KLE – Key Leader Engagement

Little Bird – Small Army Attack Helicopter

LZ – Landing Zone

MBITER – Handheld Radio

MEDEVAC – Medical Evacuation

Mid-Tour Leave – Leave granted soldiers halfway through a deployment

MKT – Mobile Kitchen Trailer

MRAP – Armored Personnel Carrier with wheels. Mine Resistant Ambush Protected

MRE – Meal Ready to Eat

Mu Zayn – Arabic for bad or not good

M16 / M4 – U.S. Assault Rifle or Carbine

M203 – U.S. Grenade Launcher

M240 – U.S. Heavy Machine Gun

M249 – U.S. Light Machine Gun

M9 – U.S. Army Pistol

NAI – Named Area of Interest

NCO – Non-Commissioned Officer

NODs / NVG – Night Vision Goggles

OP – Observation Post

PAX – Air Passenger or Personnel

PB – Patrol Base (same as COP)

PID – Positive Identification

PL – Platoon Leader

PLGR – Handheld Global Positioning System

PMCS – Preventative Maintenance Checks and Services

PSD – Personal Security Detachment

PT's – Physical Training Uniform

PX – Post Exchange. Military Market and Supply Store.

RIP-IT – Energy Drink

SAW – Squad Automatic Weapon (same as M249)

SCO – Squadron Commanding Officer

Sergeant of the Guard – Senior NCO in charge of a guard detail

SITREP – Situation Report

SOI – Sons of Iraq. Sunni Militia

SP/RP – Start Point/Release Point

SP-ing/RP-ing – Beginning or ending movement

TC – Track or Vehicle Commander

Terp - Interpreter

TOC – Tactical Operations Center (same as CP)

T-Wall – Sectional Concrete Wall

QRF – Quick Reaction Force

Walking Wounded – Wounded soldier who can walk unassisted

Wasta – Arabic word meaning influence or clout

WIA – Wounded In Action

XO – Executive Officer

2404 – Maintenance Paperwork

100 Mile An Hour Tape – Military Duct Tape